THE LAST RITE OF
HUGO T

THE LAST RITE OF HUGO T

J. N. CATANACH

ST. MARTIN'S PRESS NEW YORK

Design by Glen M. Edelstein

Library of Congress Cataloging-in-Publication Data

Catanach, J. N.
      The last rite of Hugo T. / J. N. Catanach.
         p. cm.
      "A Thomas Dunne book."
      ISBN 0-312-07014-4
      I. Title.
  PS3553.A8193L37   1992
  813'.54—dc20   91-41802
                                             CIP

First edition: April 1992

10 9 8 7 6 5 4 3 2 1

The text of this book was set in Meridian.

For Nick

who tried to teach me
the Polish National Anthem

.

CHAPTER

1

MARCHING feet. The dream was always the same. Day and night past the window. Marching to war. As Hugo T watched, an old farm cart loomed up in the yard and slowly tilted towards him, and a young body in a soldier's uniform slid out boots first. If his brother was dead, why did the vein on the boy's temple, visible through his fair hair, pulse on like a lizard's crop? Always the unanswerable question. He was dead yet he wouldn't die.

Hugo shivered. He felt an icy draught pass over him and took it at first for part of the dream. Conscious of a weight on his chest, he opened his eyes and saw by the bedside lamplight that it was his book. Beyond the book he saw his body stretched out on the blanket, naked and wrinkled as the day he was born. It was dark out. He wondered how long he'd slept. Again the cold air passed over him and he sat up.

Something was wrong, something awry in his familiar surroundings. Hugo donned his bathrobe and slippers and shuffled off to investigate. He didn't have to go far: instead of being on the windowsill, his potted geranium was on the floor, and the bedroom window was open—the bottom half—about a foot. Hugo reached under the mattress for the switchblade he kept there for emergencies and trotted around the apartment turning on lights. First in the front room, then back through the bedroom and down the passage to the kitchen and bathroom, checking all the closets.

The chain lock, he noticed, was off the front door, dangling, even though he always kept it set. Going out into the hall, he looked down the stairwell. A door banging somewhere. Nothing else. It wasn't fear he felt so much as anger.

Later that same evening Hugo had a visitor. "You're lucky to find me alive," he said.

Father Vince was too short of breath from the climb to respond immediately. He removed his fur hat glistening with droplets of moisture, uncoiled his scarf, slipped off his coat still cold from the outside, and handed the pile to his friend who continued all the while with his tale.

Bent over, his head a blur of heat and pain, Father Vince struggled with his galoshes. What good a switchblade would be against a .22 or a Saturday Night Special he didn't care to imagine. New York City burglars were not known for their gentlemanly instincts. "What did he take?"

"Sixteen dollars and forty-one cents from my pants pocket, hanging right beside the bed, this far from my feet." Hugo spread his hands an impressively short span. "Change from a twenty."

"That all?"

"Pretty sure."

"The police found no prints, nothing?"

"Send for the police? Forget it. There was kind of a smell, though. Aftershave, I think. Bay Rum."

Father Vince moved over to the kitchen window. It was set in a slight bay with a view clear across some rooftops to the backs of much taller buildings fronting on Third Avenue. By looking sideways he could see the bedroom window of Hugo's railroad flat. The roof of the neighboring tenement reached to the fourth floor of Hugo's building and was separated from it by an airshaft about three feet across. "The only surprising thing is it didn't happen before. Anyone could shinny up the airshaft and practically step across from that parapet. I'd put in window gates if I were you."

"What's there to steal?"

"That's what I'm saying. They climb up all this way and find it's not Jackie O's place and get real peeved. Or it could be some crackhead needing ten bucks for a high. Supposing you're *in* those pants, they kill you soon as wait for you to hand it over."

Hugo tried to picture himself gunned down by a crackhead as he lay in bed. Crackheads probably couldn't be counted on to shoot straight. Slowly, he shook his head. "It's not that simple to die." Then, seeing that Father Vince was observing him with the light of suspicion in his Irish eyes, he trotted quickly away to hang up his friend's things.

The sign said, THANKYOU FOR COMING TO MY LAST PARTY. It was propped against a candlestick in the middle of the table, red magic marker on a large white paper doily. Father Vince, seated with his teacup, took silent note. The edgy, backward-leaning script—the *L* of Last, for instance, with its generous topknot, beer belly of a downstroke, and rear-projecting bustlelike loop—betrayed middle-European schooling of a bygone age. Indeed, it was the *L* word that disturbed Father Vince far more than the tale of the intruder (probably just an old man's forgetful fantasy) and set his brain cells jingling. And, since his host made no move to explain and the priest was too tactful to ask, it now hung between them like an awkward smell as Hugo returned to his seat. With the very old the word *last* must be used sparingly if at all. Or so Father Vince believed. Last call, last gasp, last exit, last post, *Last Tango in Paris*. Not a word to be bandied about.

He knew that Hugo had seen the other side of eighty. Though his eighty-plus was nimbler in many ways than Father Vince's sixty—a rotund, red-faced sixty, especially after dragging itself up five steep flights of stairs. It was those stairs, Father Vince mused as he climbed them on his weekly visits, that kept Hugo as limber and spry as he was.

As if to demonstrate his dexterity, Hugo jumped up, looked into Father Vince's empty cup, and skipped over to the stove. "I'm neglecting my duty!" He refilled the kettle and set a match to the gas ring.

In the ten or fifteen minutes since his arrival, Father Vince had surreptitiously cast around for clues to the disturbing finality of the adjective on the doily and had found none. A waiter of the old school, Hugo took pride in his table settings: the tall red candle, poinsettia-patterned napkins, gleaming silverware, saucer of neatly sliced lemon, platter of mixed cookies carefully arranged, bottle of scotch. Festive. Enduring. The apartment—at any rate the kitchen area—seemed to be its usual ordered self. The other rooms, through a bead curtain never penetrated by him, Father Vince couldn't vouch for.

Now, with Hugo busy at the stove, Father Vince tugged at the corner of a piece of paper barely protruding from under his friend's place mat, a hiding place that had, in the past, proved a treasure trove of an old man's state of mind. Hugo never went to confession, never went near the church, and a priest—if he was good—should never be surprised. So Father Vince had to scrounge what he could of available evidence. Notable things, he knew, found their way under that mat. More mundane stuff—Con Ed bills, social security receipts, money order stubs from the rent, the chaff of city living—accumulated between two paperweights back behind the table lamp until such time as it disappeared behind the glass bead curtain.

Father Vince found himself looking at what appeared to be a photo clipped from a newspaper, probably the *Daily News*, because that was the paper Hugo bought. It showed a vast room filled with beds, rows and rows of them. He'd got as far with the caption as, "A Parking Lot for the Homeless . . ." when the kettle screeched and he slid the clipping back under the mat. He had seen enough.

"How about we go Irish?" Hugo, a towel draped professionally over one arm, bustled up with mugs of fresh tea, managing to make a weekly ritual sound like a new and brilliant idea. Uncorking the scotch—Father Vince's brand reserved solely for his visits—Hugo began to pour.

"Whoa there, Hugo."

"It's cold out."

"Na zdrowie!" They toasted each other in Polish, though Vince had nothing but Irish in his veins. As they sipped, it seemed to the priest that he saw an unaccustomed moistening in his friend's eyes. Perhaps just the hot fumes from the tea, though wasn't there a slight shake to his usually steady hand?

"Can you believe what's going on over there? Poland, Hungary, Czechoslovakia, East Germany, and now Rumania for crying out loud. It's like a miracle. You know what, Hugo, if I were you I'd be tempted to go back and take a look, maybe try to dig up some relatives or something."

Hugo pursed his lips. He didn't believe in miracles. "You think they'll give up so easily, those Communists, after all these years? Just wait. In a couple of months they'll clamp down."

Father Vince excused himself to go to the john, which was off the kitchen. Returning, he noticed at once that the doily with its red-inked message was gone. He guessed where, but took pains not to lower his eyes. Hugo could be pretty shrewd. The old guy was up to something and, judging from one or two skirmishes in the past, the way not to find out was to ask. If Hugo had a besetting sin, Father Vince had long ago concluded it was Pride. He knew that Hugo would sooner die than ask for help. And yet hadn't those pathetic scratchings on the doily been exactly that: an SOS?

"I assume you know you have a mouse in your bathtub, Hugo, since there's a hunk of cheese in with it."

"I'm teaching it to swim. An old man gets lonely with only memories for company."

"So get a phone for chrissakes."

"Who am I going to call? The city morgue? 'Come and get me, I'm deceased.' "

Stupid to bring up the phone. They'd gone through it all before. Just like with the television. An old black and white was sitting around the rectory that no one wanted. In what seemed to him a simple act of Christian charity, Father Vince had lugged it up to the top floor of Hugo's tenement, his "penthouse" as he called it. The effort nearly finished him. There, under the kitchen table for a year, it sat. A mute reproach to Father Vince whose feet never failed to tangle with it on his weekly visit. If Hugo had stuck on a label, A REJECT FROM THE RECTORY DUMPED ON A DEFENSE-LESS OLD MAN TO MAKE SOME PRIESTS FEEL GOOD, the message could not have been clearer. Such openers as, "Hey, Hugo! Some game Saturday," died on his lips. One afternoon when not a word had passed between them, he grabbed the set and staggered out with it, and heaved it into a dumpster on his way home.

"Hey, Hugo, talking of morgues, that mouse is a prime candidate."

"A couple died already. I don't know what's the matter."

"How do they get in there in the first place?"

"Come, I show you." The two men stood by the tub. "See that hole by the tap? They fall right out of there."

"Maybe they get concussed."

"I thought of that. See, I put the sponge under."

"Hugo, you thought of everything." Father Vince, by far the bigger man, went down on his haunches for a closer look. "This mouse is in big trouble. Maybe he had a heart attack with all that cheese."

"Should I give him a tiny bit of one of my nitros?"

"Too late. He's on his way."

"Then what are you waiting for?" He shot a mischievous glance at the priest. "The last rites."

"Get out of here, you old pagan. Did you give him water?"

"Water." Hugo looked crestfallen. "I'll be forgetting my own name next."

Father Vince sprinkled drops around the little sufferer, and they left it in peace. The Irish tea had cooled. Hugo topped it up from the kettle.

"So what's with Our Friend?" Father Vince asked after some sips. Our Friend, more often known as Herself, occa-sionally as the Old Croat (a reference to her place of origin) was always spoken of in hushed tones in the penthouse—

6

often accompanied by furtive sideways glances—and never by her real name. Most of Hugo's woes could be attributed to her. "Up to her old tricks?"

"I heard the building is up for sale."

"Who says?"

Hugo splashed whiskey into their cups, causing an overflow. "Mrs. Foley downstairs. Frank the Handyman told her. He got it from her gigolo."

Father Vince waved a dismissive hand. "In other words, the usual suspects."

"She's asking a million and a half."

"Listen to me, Hugo. Even if she could get that, which I doubt, there's no way anyone can force you out. You're rent-controlled, you're here for twenty years, you're a senior citizen, you're set in concrete. Even for landlords there are rules. There's only one way you're going to leave here, and that's by the exercise of your own free will."

Hugo T gave his special skeptic's smile, a jutting out of the chin, eyebrows at the bristle, lips pulled in. It bestowed on its recipient vast reserves of genial sympathy.

"Look at you, frisky as a goat on Mount Parnassus. My mother—God rest her—was ninety-two when she went, not a day younger." He raised his cup. "Here's health and happiness."

Malarkey, thought Hugo, but drank anyway. He had sneaked away his sign, so he thought, before Father Vince noticed it. What on earth had possessed him to think that the man would understand? First and foremost he was a priest. Secondly he was a congenital optimist. Sure, his mother had lived to a ripe old age, but her last years were an agony. Hugo knew because she'd lived and died in the apartment across the hall. Vince had come every day and sat up many a night at her side. He and Hugo met frequently on the stairs, which is how they'd gotten friendly.

The two men sat for a while, contemplating a patch of wallpaper, a make-believe pastel panorama of hills, lakes, and butterflies. Father Vince had helped paste it up one particularly dreary winter.

"So what else is new and exciting? Win the lottery yet?" attempted the priest, who had also been thinking about his mother's last illness and how the Old Croat had come pounding on the door yelling about overdue rent or some such trumped up charge with every obscenity in the book and then some—like the bunch of blue jays in the park he'd recently seen pestering a lame pigeon to distraction.

Shortly thereafter, when Father Vince got up to leave, Hugo pressed the half bottle of scotch on him in an oft repeated ritual. "Save it for next week, Hugo. That way those boozers at the rectory won't get their mitts on it."

Hugo leaned over the banister listening to his friend's descending tread on the marble stairs, watching a gloved right hand appear and reappear on the railing. On the bottom step Father Vince paused as usual to peer up five floors at Hugo's little pinkish face with its well-trimmed mustache beneath a shock of white hair. He gave the thumbs up sign and was gone.

The bottle stayed on the kitchen table. When Hugo came back from locking the door and setting the chain, he sat down and stared into its shiny depths. How could he tell his friend that there wouldn't be a next week. On that score he'd made up his mind. He sat for a long time, then suddenly blew out the candle. Carefully filling a tablespoon with whiskey, he carried it into the bathroom.

The mouse hadn't moved. Hugo bent down and held the spoon under its little gray nose. It didn't stir. He set the spoon in the bottom of the tub and pulled on a rubber glove. Picking up the mouse, he examined it closely under the glare of the fluorescent light. He noted its tiny eyes and big ears, the backs of which were a hairless, almost translucent, pink. Perhaps it was a baby. Without a doubt, dead. He dropped it into the toilet and pushed the handle to flush. The mouse executed a couple of elegant pirouettes and was gone. How neat, thought Hugo a trifle enviously. No fuss, no bother. Gone.

It is not that simple to die.

CHAPTER

2

IT is not that simple to die.

Not when you are the slightest bit fussy. And Hugo T was fussy, though not in the squeamish sense of the word. He merely wanted to make an efficient job of it. No fuss, no muss. Perhaps because, after a lifetime of serving and clearing away after other people, he couldn't bear the thought of someone doing it for him. Too well could he envisage the scene. The police with their itchy fingers, the meat wagon men with their ribald jokes (*ribald* he'd looked up in the dictionary, and it fitted the bill precisely), their slapdash disrespect, and petty thievery. Not to mention Frank the Handyman. Hugo had paid sixty-five dollars for his Omega in 1957, the year his citizenship finally came through, a week's wages in those days. He didn't want just anyone to get it.

So much depended on Father Vince's next visit. The keys he would drop off at the rectory. The letter, explaining everything, he would leave on his kitchen table. That way Vince would have nearly the whole month of February to settle things before the next rent check was due. Above all, Hugo didn't want to give Herself an excuse to come storming in, disrupting everything. Which is why he couldn't do It in the penthouse. Suppose Father Vince missed a week—which he sometimes did when he went on retreat to Ronkonkoma—and the body began to smell. With all the heat

9

it mightn't take more than a day or two. If a poisoned mouse behind the stove could stench the place up in no time, think what a human corpse was capable of. He might waft under the door and stink up the hallway. Somebody would complain and Herself would be over, or Frank the Handyman would be over, and the game would be up.

Hugo T's heart palpitated at the thought, and he popped a nitroglycerine tablet under his tongue. He was being too free with the tablets, he knew, rattling the almost empty bottle. When they were gone they were gone. No time to go through all the business of the prescription again at the hospital. Going in there you played Russian roulette, never knowing which doctor you'd get, the one who'd kill you or the one who'd just give you a scare. "Hi, how are you? What seems to be the problem?" He tipped the pills out on the kitchen table and counted—seven—then hurriedly scooped them back up. In those seven little white lumps he saw the rest of his life.

He looked again at the whiskey bottle. A pity he couldn't tell Father Vince about the incident on the bridge, oh, two or three mornings ago. In normal times it was the sort of thing they'd have chuckled over. Now, if Vince guessed what was on his mind, he'd do his best to stop him. As it was, undreamed of by Hugo, forces were at work with just such an intention and more resources at their command than a simple parish priest could hope to muster.

Hugo had left his building at the usual hour and boarded a northbound bus on Madison Avenue intending to go to the end of the line, all the way to the Cloisters, almost to the tip of Manhattan. But it was a cheerful, sunny day as seen through the windows of the bus, and, on the spur of the moment, he got out near the George Washington Bridge. He had never walked on the bridge before and felt some misgiving when at last he found the pedestrian ramp leading up to it. Its inaccessibility, obscuring concrete walls, and the din of traffic on the adjacent parkway made it a mugger's paradise. As he picked his way around potholes and debris he clutched his ammonia squirter tightly in his overcoat pocket for all the world like a man keen to hang on to life, not end it. With frequent pauses to catch his breath, he gained the bridge proper and set his face toward New Jersey, a mile away across the Hudson.

It took all his willpower just to keep walking along this shuddering causeway. Through the mesh of steel girders he saw cars and trucks rushing beneath him on the lower level. A foot or two to his right they thundered alongside. Far below, the river glinted greenishly, while way above his head soared the first of the two suspension towers that held the span. The effect, as he looked up, was like some out-of-control pulsating Meccano cathedral. Though his brown corduroy cap was pulled down to his ears, he let go his grip on the ammonia to tug fiercely at its peak with both hands. On a really windy day, what would it be like on this bucking bronco of a bridge? The mere thought made his stomach turn.

For several minutes he rested in the steel-mesh cocoon formed by one of the towers and contemplated retreat. But he was wise now to this trick that he played on himself. At the approach of the moment of truth—even knowing it was not *the* moment, just a rehearsal—something at the core of him would rebel, a rush of revulsion brimming up to dilute his purpose, which suddenly seemed warped and repulsive. In relief, he would turn away, then, back at home, curse himself for his weakness. And sometimes, exhausted and frustrated, he would set forth again to prove himself, and again fail and lie all night in a sweat of self-disgust. The worst of it was that at these moments of doubt he would see the face of his mother, not as he'd last seen her after the war when he was sixteen, but when, as a child, her cheek close to his in the candlelight, she had whispered the stories of Poland. "What am I to do, *Mamooshka?*" But she would just go on telling the stories.

Yes, when the time really came, the half bottle of scotch would be just the ticket. It was a trick he had used in his sailor days. Up close, some of those port prostitutes were grotesque; you had to be blind and hold your nose just to

11

approach them. But which was worse? To go with them, or go back to the ship? In the long run, the latter. A flask of schnapps in the back pocket usually saw him through.

Hugo inched on toward the crest of the great span, concentrating in on himself lest the dynamics of the bridge conspire to part him from an all too slender reality. He felt like an elderly flea clinging to a boa constrictor. Aware of the vistas stretching away, he dared not stop and look about as he'd have liked to do, and so he was startled when, with no warning, something bright blue and big loomed at his right shoulder. And relieved when it became a man in a jogging suit.

The jogger was in good trim, because soon he was a blue blob amid the massive organism of the bridge glinting silver against a pale sky. When the blob began to grow again Hugo realized it was because the man had stopped; he was doing those stretching exercises dancers and athletes get up to around town, one leg propped up on the railing.

About ten yards shy of the man, almost at the apex of the bridge, Hugo halted. Turning his back on the traffic and gripping the railing, he gazed down the length of the widening river to where it disappeared behind the bulge of lower Manhattan. On the surface of the water nothing moved, or almost nothing, which suited his purpose. Little by little he dropped his gaze till it came to rest at a point far below him. Separating him from the river, in patches now a dark khaki, was air. He leaned over farther. The ripples seemed to beckon. Jump, they signaled, we will take care of you. Quickly, he straightened up.

Funny, the man in the blue jogging suit was standing quite still, seeming to stare at him. Not only that, he was now much closer than before, maybe only five yards off. A white man, thirtyish, clean shaven with a blue chin and a pockmarked, rubbery face, not pleasant-looking. He's afraid I'm going to jump, thought Hugo, giving a small, reassuring wave. "Nice view from here," he called out, noticing for the first time that the man held a walkie-talkie—or was it a Walkman?—in his left hand.

The jogger seemed momentarily taken aback. With a hasty smile and some quick nods, he went on with his exertions, strapping whatever it was to a belt at his waist. Hugo had seen this type before when he worked briefly as a guard at Bellevue and escorted discharged mental patients through the gates. They were harmless. Reaching into his pocket he pulled out his ammonia squirter and let it fall from an outstretched hand. He counted to ten before a tiny splash told him it had hit the water: no net or protrusion was in the way. Then, turning, he headed resolutely back the way he'd come.

A few minutes later the jogger again passed him. Beyond the suspension tower Hugo was surprised to see him vault the dividing barrier and climb into a waiting silver-gray stretch limousine that carried him off toward Manhattan. These gangsters are so damn rich, he thought.

That was the first time Hugo noticed the silver-gray stretch.

The second sighting was the very next day. He'd been walking uptown, preoccupied as usual with his "last rite" (as he self-mockingly referred to his impending suicide), when he heard someone yelling from across the street. Third Avenue is no Champs-Élysées, but no cart track either. It is wide. And had widened since Hugo first saw it, when the elevated railway, called the El, ran up the middle and madams arranged their girls strategically in second-story windows. With the removal of the El and the avenue's lapse into gentility, the street had seemed to spread. Hugo T, diminutive and old world, could not imagine attracting anyone's attention across its six lanes. But, as the yelling persisted, so did the suspicion that someone—he could guess who—was trying exactly that, and to him.

"Hóla! Hombre! 'ugo!"

Hugo walked on, cane in hand, looking neither right nor left.

"Hey! Sonofabich! 'ugo!"

A slight tightening of hand on cane. Hugo was in no mood for banter with his friend Cassidy, the Mexican waiter, whose voice, with each step, sounded louder in his ears. Each day now for a week he had set out to cross a name off his list of likely places to do It. He needed all the time and energy he could muster for the task in hand.

"*Hóla, viejo!* Stop thief! Heh! He took my girlfriend!"

People were beginning to look. At last Hugo turned, his blue eyes burning dangerously. Cassidy, dodging traffic, was halfway across the avenue, arms waving. Hugo raised his cane, not altogether innocent of the impulse to bring its silver top down on his friend's head. At that exact moment he noticed the limousine.

A silver-gray stretch with smoked glass windows, rear end bristling with antennae, it was double parked on the avenue. Hardly a remarkable sight in Manhattan. Except that Cassidy, arms flailing, seemed to be recoiling from this one, almost as if he'd been hit, which clearly was not the case because the car was stationary.

The next thing Hugo knew, Cassidy had grabbed him by the front of his coat, turned him clean around, and dragged him, winded and confused, into a nearby bar. "What the Sam Hill is going on?" Hugo was quivering with rage and fright. In the excitement he dropped his cane.

Cassidy wasn't listening. He was peering out of one of the small, curtained windows of the dimly lit room, for all the world like a fugitive from the FBI in a Grade B gangster movie. In retrospect, Hugo had to smile. "Holy cheese. Holy cheese," Cassidy repeated over and over. "I'm telling you man. I'm telling you."

"My cane. Where's my cane, dammit?" Hugo yelled. It was special, that cane, more of a companion than a stick, and he'd cut it down to exactly the right height and glued the head back on. He'd once fought off two muggers with it in Central Park. Sentimental value, if you like.

"Cheese," Cassidy reiterated, "holy cheese." Gingerly, he moved the curtain aside and again peeped out. "They've gone, but they'll be back," he forecast grimly. When he did let Hugo venture out the cane was nowhere to be found. Along with the silver stretch, it had vanished.

A couple of patrons sat hunched over beers—regulars, by the looks of it, holing up in one of the last blue-collar bastions on Manhattan's silk-stocking Upper East Side. Beyond them, in the darkest corner, Cassidy leaned heavily on the bar as if it were the guardrail of a ship and he was about to throw up. "I'm telling you, 'ugo . . ." he shook his large and, at the best of times, mournful head. "You never been married, right? You promise me one thing: you ever *think* about getting married, you tell your old pal Cassidy first."

The guy was off his rocker, Hugo decided. Cassidy was known for the occasional bender. Or perhaps he was just in one of his weird moods. Whole days he would spend staring at his tropical fish. Just sitting by the tank, staring. "That was my special cane."

"Okay, okay." Cassidy pulled a money clip from his pocket. "How much? Fifty? One hundred?" He scattered greenbacks along the bar. Hugo barely glanced at them. "So, you lost a cane. So what? What is a cane? A bit of wood. A bit of metal. Some screws maybe. You lose it, you get a new one. Does it hire detectives to find you? Does it chase you with lawyers? Does it run to priests? No, my friend, it is content to remain lost. I tell you, man, I speak frank with you: your friend Cassidy, you know what he lost almost?" He was gesturing toward Third Avenue and thumping his chest. "His life. Okay, you don't believe me. I don't blame you, because—tell me if I'm right or if I'm right—you never bin married. Right?"

Hugo should have seen it coming. Ever since he'd known Cassidy—and it was getting on for ten years ago that they'd worked together at a downtown club—he'd heard about them: the Pursuers. They'd crossed the Rio Grande; they were in West Texas; they'd got as far as New Orleans; they'd been sighted definitely in St. Louis. It was simply a matter of time. His wife, her brother, the priest, the lawyer: the four demons of the Apocalypse, relentlessly riding him down. And now, at last—despite his name change to Herbert Cassidy III—they were here, in a stretch Cadillac on Third Avenue. Three men and a woman, one of them, according to Cassidy, taking careful aim through the lowered window, albeit, he did admit, with a camera. Evidence, no doubt collecting evidence.

Cassidy must have stayed in that bar drinking till closing time, because it was well after 2 A.M. that Hugo heard him yelling below in the street. He didn't catch the words, but the gist was clear enough: a pox on lawyers, priests, and wives. If they wanted him they'd have to take him by storm. But they better be quick about it because he was spending his wealth like water, and soon it would all be gone. Cassidy once had revealed to Hugo T the size of his bank account. To a man who'd crossed the Rio Grande unofficially—and especially to the woman he'd left behind—sixty-five thousand United States dollars surely seemed like a fortune.

Unlike his friend Cassidy, Hugo felt no ghost of a Past thundering after him. The double sighting of a silver-gray stretch limo with smoked windows on consecutive days, although under bizarre circumstances, caused him no alarm. He had other preoccupations. Had he been close enough to read the license plate, he might have played the number in the lottery. And that would have been the sum of it. Not to say that he didn't *have* a Past. Everybody has. But he'd left his behind so long ago, somewhere beyond the Carpathians, that, like old compost, it had surely rotted.

CHAPTER

3

HUGO returned the whiskey to its cupboard. He had a night's work ahead of him. Through the bead curtain were all the bits and pieces of his life that had stuck with him thus far on the journey. Tonight he was going to do something about them.

Already he'd jotted headings on a legal pad: (1) Garbage to be left as present for Herself. (2) Things for St. Vincent de Paul. (The Salvation Army, he discovered, did not do stairs, and anyway Father Vince might be happier with a Catholic charity.) (3) Things Father Vince might find a use for. (4) Stuff to throw out right away. This last category included personal letters and photos—bits of himself he didn't want to leave behind.

After pausing to register the solemnity of the moment, Hugo pushed through the swinging strands of beads. The bustle in his step as he moved through the tiny bedroom into the front room attested to his eagerness. A keen amateur historian, it amused him as he lay awake at night to see himself bobbing on the surface of his turbulent century like a cheeky rubber ball swept along on a swiftly flowing river. From his mid teens, thanks in large part to the timing and place of his birth, his life might have bounced any number of ways. For his childhood was rooted in a remote and unimportant corner of Franz Josef's Austro-Hungarian Empire: the so-called Crownland of Bucovina, on the

17

Rumanian border, where his father, an officer of the Imperial Customs, happened to be stationed.

On the off chance that his body was washed up someplace and identified, he would ask Vince, in his letter, to have it cremated. There was a place in New Jersey, or was it the Bronx, that did it for $275 inclusive. He'd saved the clipping since his heart scare in seventy-nine. Though come to think of it he better check that they were still in business and see how much the price had gone up.

Hugo riffled impatiently through papers scattered on his desk. Then he started pulling out drawers. When one stuck, he yanked at it, shoved it back, and yanked again. Suddenly, the only thing that mattered was opening the drawer. What he was searching for, why he was sitting at the desk, why he was in the room at all, everything fled from his mind. Finally, in rage and defeat, he laid his head down and would have wept had not the radiator chosen that exact moment to erupt with a hiss like an angry goose. As he struggled to his feet, his chair thudded to the linoleum. Groping his way to the adjoining room, he flopped down on the bed and closed his eyes.

Midnight by the dial of his digital clock found Hugo, refreshed after sleep, contemplating a pair of Don Quixote and Sancho Panza bookends that had come into his possession in the blizzardy winter of sixty-eight, when, as a fill-in doorman in the East Eighties, he shoveled snow for a Spanish diplomat who lived across the street. Hugo had a soft spot for the knight of the woeful countenance and his feisty sidekick and hesitated as he flicked at them with a feather duster: Father Vince or St. Vincent? Decisions, decisions. The top of his dresser was cluttered with knickknacks—presents from girlfriends, small souvenirs of his travels—all clamoring for decisions. Three china Bambis, two cuckoo clocks, a swizzle stick collection, a plastic pickle from the Flushing World's Fair . . . each had its story. An eight-ounce bottle of Sherman Billingsley's special formula men's cologne (filched in '53 when he waited tables at the Stork

Club) he set aside for Father Vince: there was still half an inch of brown liquid in the bottom.

At last, with everything dusted and replaced to his satisfaction, Hugo attacked the dresser drawers. St. Vincent swept the board here since Father Vince was several sizes too big in every direction. Shirts, underwear, handkerchiefs, socks, gloves, suspenders, even cravats, all neatly stashed amid the mothballs, the whoosh of camphor smarting his eyes with each new drawerful. Simple to stuff them into plastic garbage bags, which he must make a note to buy.

Back in the kitchen to jot this reminder to himself on his yellow pad, Hugo's eye fell on a package of clean laundry he'd picked up a day or two earlier. It was second nature for him to carry laundry through to the front room. Here was new evidence of his senility. He scooped up the parcel, only to find it had come loose and contained only three shirts as opposed to the five or six he always sent at a go. Oh boy, he was really losing it.

Later, stuffing Christmas cards and letters from vanished friends into shopping bags, he chanced to think of Father Vince's feet. Were they *that* much bigger than his own? A pair of black leather wing tips, worn but once at a funeral (because it took three pairs of socks for them to stay on), had reposed for years in his closet resisting the salesman's promise that, in time, they would shrink. He had a tin trunk already emptied out with Vince's name on it. The shoes could join his stamp collection there. He'd do it right away before he forgot.

Hugo kept his shoes in a row in the bottom of his bedroom closet. It was dark in there, so he opened the doors wide and reached in, shouldering aside coats and suits. No wing tips. He poked around some more. They weren't anywhere in the closet. And since the closet was the only place they'd ever been . . . Hugo sat down heavily on the bed, determined to keep his head and not repeat the fiasco of a few hours earlier. He was losing control and he knew it, as if bits of him were floating off to gloat just out of reach. The other day—case in point—he'd found a six-pack of Schaefer's in his refrigerator. Since when did he drink beer? And now the missing shirts, and this good-as-new pair of shoes.

Think, Hugo, think, he told himself. Only a few more days. Don't give in now. For a while he stared at the open closet, then, on an impulse, stood up and again reached in. This time it wasn't shoes he was after. He checked twice to be quite sure. His black gabardine raincoat with the zip-out fake fur lining was nowhere to be found, and what's more, the charcoal-gray suit he'd succumbed to at a Gimbels' President's Day sale, so uncomfortably tight around the shoulders, was also AWOL.

Hugo was flummoxed. Why would anyone go to so much trouble for some old clothes? Best of luck to him he thought, bemusedly. At least the thief had taste, perhaps even aspirations. If Hugo bothered to look, he'd no doubt find he was short a tie or two, perhaps a tie clip, cuff links, a belt or suspenders, a fancy silk handkerchief, a hat even. A proprietary interest crept into Hugo's feelings toward the man who'd robbed him. Yes, a creditable performance. He already looked forward to telling Father Vince. Except—how could it have slipped his mind—he wouldn't be seeing Father Vince again.

Hugo closed his front door behind him and carefully turned the key in the lock. For a moment he stood listening. As far as he could tell the building slept, which was as it should be at four o'clock on a weekday morning. Grasping the shopping bags, one in each hand, he proceeded to the top of the stairs and, pausing every couple of steps, furtively descended. Anyone chancing to observe him through one of the peepholes in the apartment doors would immediately have been suspicious.

One floor short of the bottom, Hugo heard voices. A man's and a woman's. They were coming from under the door of the rear apartment where a gap, engineered, it was said, by Herself to better accommodate eviction notices, made arguments hard to keep private. And it was an argument Hugo T thought he heard. Perhaps a lovers' tiff.

The woman, a new tenant, he had encountered quite recently in the hall. It seemed her mailbox key was giving trouble and she gratefully accepted Hugo's offer of help. Young, tall, with pale skin molded over high cheekbones, she had dark almost oriental eyes that betrayed a fine intelligence. His little act of gallantry quite set Hugo up for the day. Nor did it strike him as strange that such a keen young person was unable to accomplish a task that he, in his dotage, found so simple. The cherry on the cake was that they had something in common. A magazine she was holding had a Polish name, and he asked if she knew the language. "Of course," she declared, "I'm half Polish." "I, too, am a mongrel," he joked, "half Polish, half Czech." Now, at an hour when, to his mind, lovers should be locked in fond embrace, it saddened him to hear harsh words from under her door.

The last, and greatest, hazard facing Hugo was posed by a little twist of an Irishwoman who occupied one of the two street-level front apartments. Mrs. Foley's stock in trade was information. Early on, back in the bad old days when fire and brimstone stalked the halls in the person of Herself and no rent-controlled tenant could feel safe even behind a double-locked door, Mrs. Foley had been exposed as a spy. Not that Hugo had ever found it in his heart to blame her, defenseless, frightened widow that she was. He'd just stopped speaking to her, more than a nodding "good day." Fifteen years had passed. Meanwhile, without a doubt, every coming and going, every chance scrap of conversation in the hall or out on the stoop, every nuance of association had been faithfully relayed to Herself. It was rumored that Mrs. Foley kept a log book, and certainly her chickenlike countenance could usually be seen tensed in the window straining to see and hear. A marvellous deterrent to burglars, Father Vince, who bent over backwards to look on the bright side, had once observed.

So Hugo took special pains with the front door and was alert to the slightest stirring of the white muslin drapes as, muffled against the cold, he turned and scurried east along the quiet street. The glass of shattered car windows winked and sparkled under the streetlamps as he passed. He'd noticed a dumpster parked a block away beyond Second Avenue, and over its high metal sides he managed to heave his bags. A couple more of these night escapades and his papers would all be safely on their way to becoming landfill in New York Harbor. Comforting to reflect that his life had not been entirely without achievement and that the garbage he had faithfully—perhaps even patriotically—generated might, compacted, have increased the size of the Land of the Free by, say, a square foot.

New York Harbor, 1934. His first visit to these shores. He'd signed on in Marseilles as scullion on a French liner, jumped ship in New York, and was caught and locked up on Ellis Island till the next French vessel could remove him. Eager as ever to improve himself, and urged on by a well-meaning society matron, he'd taken up knitting. In the weeks before a ship came he completed one sleeve of a sweater.

Diverted by this memory, Hugo, to his horror, heard the front door of his building slam behind him, a trick it managed when the entrant was already halfway down the long, narrow hall. In sudden weariness he started up the stairs, tugging on the banister for support. No voices now from the second floor, but as his line of vision came level with the bottom of the door, a strip of light shone out, broken by a dark shadow. It seemed to Hugo that a pair of feet was planted firmly on the other side.

Lying in bed an hour or so later, chasing sleep, Hugo had an inspiration. His knickknacks: perfect for his new young friend downstairs. He'd concoct some story about moving in with a relative and have her swear not to breathe a word to Herself, and that very morning would slip a note under her door. "Dear M'selle," it would read, "Something of interest awaits you on the Fifth Floor. Please, when you have a chance . . ." No, too coy. She would never come. Perhaps, "Since, in the near future, I shall be moving from here to a smaller place, it would give me pleasure if you would make a 'home away from home' for some treasured knickknacks collected over the years. Perhaps, if you would care to call on me this evening . . .'' Composing note after note, each more flowery than the last, he drifted happily off to sleep.

CHAPTER

4

HUGO hefted his crossbow and deliberated. He couldn't very well consign such a lethal weapon to St. Vincent or even the trash, and surely Father Vince wouldn't want it. Years ago, for reasons now unclear, he had purchased it through a mail order catalogue, but the instructions defeated him. Was it even legal? He wasn't sure. With any luck, if he left it for Herself, she'd get into hot water with the police. In times past he'd fantasized about winding it up and taking aim at the penthouse across the street where, in her glassed-in terrace, basking amid the fruits of her ill-gotten gains, Herself sipped wine, cuddled her Yorkshire terrier and schemed against her tenants. In the end Hugo laid the crossbow on the bed alongside the rest of his arsenal: a sword stick, a hunting knife, a hunting slingshot, a knobkerrie and a switchblade. An oddly defensive collection for one intent on leaving this world sooner rather than later.

The knock at the door must be the girl from downstairs. Hugo started toward it, then doubled back to fling a blanket over his armory. He unhooked the chain, in his excitement forgetting to look through the peephole. But yes, she it was, and alone, thank goodness.

"Please come in, M'selle." He was unsure how to address her, but somehow it seemed inappropriate to use the name she had given him, Elie, or even Elizaveta, for which it stood. The American tendency to call strangers by their first names hadn't rubbed off on him, thanks probably to his years in service. Besides, his shrewd waiter's sense of a person's class told him that here was one of life's aristocrats. A judgment that was quickly bolstered when she handed him a magazine.

"For you, in case you are interested."

Hugo fetched his reading glasses from the kitchen table and flipped through the glossy publication, full of black-and-white photos of people in evening dress holding drinks. "The Voice of the Jagiello Society," proclaimed the cover, "The Association of the Sons and Daughters of Polish Nobility." He looked up at her over the tops of his glasses. "Are *you* in here?"

She shook her head, amused. "These are just the big shots." Smooth as her accent was, it left no doubt in Hugo's mind that English was not her first language.

He had set out cups and glasses and a bottle of Yugoslavian cabernet sauvignon hoping to prolong the visit, but she turned aside all offers, apparently not wishing to dally. The knickknacks, dusted and polished, he'd arranged on the sideboard along with an electric juicer (with a defective part), two large Christmassy centerpieces, and a toaster. As her gaze swept the display, it seemed to Hugo, watching intently for signs of approval, that the trace of a curl showed on her upper lip. Embarrassment seized him at the tawdry quality of his offering and anger at his presumption in thinking she could want anything of his. He grabbed a tea cloth from the drying rack to throw over everything and put an end to the farce. Too late. Bending over the table, Elie pounced on a booklet that had come with the juicer, *Tips for Tipplers—the Key to Healthy Drinking*.

"I have a friend who could use this."

"Take it," he gestured eagerly. "If you like books, I have many more, but in the other room. If you wouldn't mind waiting . . . only a minute."

Before she could respond he was parting the glass bead curtain. No doubt about it, this woman with her fine features was an intellectual, uninterested in trinkets and such nonsense. He should have guessed. Still, all was not lost. His books were in two places, a few—those he called his treasures—on shelves by the bed, the rest in the front room. He was hesitating between some paperbacks on health and a leather-bound set of Harrison Ainsworth retrieved from Mrs. Roosevelt's garbage when he worked in her building, when he heard the bead curtain jangling.

Was it his imagination, or was she blushing? "I hope you don't mind." Hard to tell in the dimness. "I really shouldn't put you to so much trouble."

Trouble was the last thing on his mind. As long as she was here in his bedroom—an occurrence for which, in normal times, he'd never have forgiven himself—his one idea was to load her up with books, the books that had become his closest companions and for which—as if sent by the gods—a worthy successor had, at the last minute, appeared.

From the shelves by his bed he pulled volume after volume, holding each one lovingly for a second before placing it in her outstretched arms. Michener's *Poland*, Hedrick Smith's *The Russians*, *Spadework* about Ur of the Chaldees, *Winning Chess Tactics Illustrated*, *The Sleepy Hollow Country Club* (where he'd once worked), *How to Retire without Money*, *Laughter Incorporated* by Bennett Cerf, *Don't Be No Hero*, "a novel of suspense," *Island of Hope, Island of Tears* about Ellis Island, *The Practical Handbook of Painting & Wallpapering* . . . Elie accepted them all without demur. A translation of Homer caught his eye: "Did you learn about him in school?" He added it to the pile. Then, "Something to shock you." He held up *Never Underestimate the Power of a Woman: A Man's Guide to Women*. "Perhaps your friend would be interested."

Her lips trembled slightly as she tried not to laugh. "You have no idea how funny that is."

A surge of happiness invigorated Hugo. Contact at last. He wished himself fifty years younger. As he placed the book on the pile he noticed how alive and open her eyes were, far more alert and interested than the rest of her would lead one to believe. She indicated a title, gesturing with her foot: *Habana, Cuba, Presente y Futuro.* "An admirer, perhaps, of Fidel?"

He took down the volume, somewhat bulkier than the rest. It was bound in imitation leather, its edges sumptuously gilded. With the aplomb of a practiced showman, he raised the front cover. Then he lifted the flyleaf to reveal a panel inset under it, which he also raised. "Have a cigar." He proffered the book to her with a waiter's little flourish.

"But where are they?" Her fingers probed the contents.

"All smoked, long ago. Before Fidel. Even the smell has left. Now it's just a hiding place."

"A very good one. It fooled me."

"Ah, but not for long. You found it because of your curiosity about Cuba. But burglars don't bother with books."

"How do you know I'm not a burglar?"

"You are the sort of burglar to whom I would give a key."

He shot her a quick look, afraid he had trespassed, and suddenly realized how tired she must be from the weight of all those books. "Set them here," he patted the bed, thanking his stars that he'd covered his weapons. "I'll get shopping bags from the kitchen."

He was back in less than a minute and found her squatting by the bookcase. She had pulled out a slim volume and was flipping through it. "So, a real bookworm." He bent to read the title, *Starting Right With Milk Goats.* "A farm girl at heart? That was one of my dreams too. A small homestead, maybe in the Ozarks or the Adirondacks, a few goats, a little woman to make the cheese."

She looked up, perhaps at the note of wistfulness. "Your American Dream? And . . . ?"

"The ponies. Always the ponies."

"The . . ." she frowned. "What is 'ponies?' "

He imitated a jockey on horseback. "Too slow, that's what."

"Ah, *ponies,*" she laughed, apologetically. "And now, what is your dream?"

One question he wasn't prepared for. "I've had my life."

27

She looked at the pile of books on the bed and the shopping bag he was starting to fill. "So, no more dreams?"

"Does that shock you? It's nothing to me. I've had good times. I don't mind."

She nodded, as if understanding, but he doubted she really did. "And your relatives, children perhaps?"

He was shaking his head, the old smile back. "Children? A sailor never stays long enough to find out. At any rate, they are better off without me. A few books, my memories, that's all I have left."

"Sisters and brothers, nephews, perhaps nieces?" she insisted.

A bit late in the day to launch into the story of his life. Besides, she was only being polite to an old man, trying to show concern. He shook his head. "I am alone."

She took another book from the shelf and handed it to him. It was *Dust of Our Brothers Blood: A Story of Poland*. It seemed to Hugo that her accompanying look—coaxing, that of a mother bent on extracting a confession from a naughty child—was almost too frank. Puzzling, even a little alarming, that this stranger had managed to put her finger on such a spot.

"You are looking at an old man," he began reluctantly, "almost as old as our century. My generation, you could say we lived several lives. Little people blown apart by big winds. Perhaps, also, your own grandparents?"

"Perhaps," she said, noncommittally, and stood up. Clearly the visit was over.

Hugo packed the remaining books into the shopping bag and presented it to her with a little bow. Elie added the volume on goats. Noting that his bushy white eyebrows rose in amusement, she said, "I also have dreams." And from the touch of defiance in the way she said it, he inferred that ponies were to play no part in her future.

In the kitchen she paused to admire the philodendron that Hugo had trained on a string from its hanging basket in the window almost to encircle the room at ceiling height. Its lush green leaves were within a foot or two of meeting, with the end of one strand flopping down.

"But you can't leave it like that," she laughed.

"I'm too lazy to tie up the last little bit." It wasn't laziness, superstition perhaps.

She set down the books and pulled out a chair. Kicking off her shoes, she climbed up. "Twine," she commanded, reaching down a hand. Hugo bustled about, cutting pieces to the right length. "I wish I were so tall," he said enviously.

The job finished, she stepped down from the chair and stood back admiringly. "Another six inches. Can't you wait that long?" Her smile of encouragment enveloped both Hugo and the plant, and he, at least, felt taller.

Come again, he wanted to say as he held open the door. Choose some more books. Watch the plant grow. The words caught in his throat. He knew that neither of them would ever see that six-inch gap bridged. So many little excuses for hanging on another week, another day, another hour, just to see what would happen next, what the human race would get up to. And now, out of the blue, this new neighbor and friend, someone he could talk to, someone young and sympathetic, drops into his lap: one last bad joke, like fate dealing him a royal flush while holding five of a kind. "Ve get too soon oldt undt too late schmart," read an old motto he'd tacked up by the door. Now, as he set the chain, it seemed to mock him.

After Elie left, Hugo sat at his kitchen table leafing through the magazine she'd left, not reading it. These people with their jewels and phony titles, Count this, Baroness that, they sickened him with their posing and their big smiles. All glitter, no substance. The same crowd that had sold the Polish people down the river time and time again. He'd waited on them at their clubs and banquets and scornfully accepted their paltry tips. Whereas people like his great-grandfather, who had put life and land on the line in an abortive uprising against the occupying Russians in 1863, were stripped of everything and buried alive in Siberia. The Jagiello Society, hiding behind a great name like that . . . With a dismissive snort, Hugo tossed the magazine into the trash.

A short time later, pattering through the apartment at his waiter's trot, he noticed the cigar box on the bed where he'd left it. He was about to put it back among the books on the shelves when, spurred by a remark of Elie's, he opened it and tipped the contents onto the blanket. Something was missing: his United States passport! So he'd been wrong about burglars and books. And yet—he picked up a little cloth bag heavy with coins—the thief had left these behind. Shirts, underwear, a tie, a suit, a raincoat, shoes, and now his passport. The complete disguise. Another Hugo was out there, masquerading. So in a way he would live on. The idea tickled his sense of the absurd. He liked it.

He spread the coins out: Eisenhower dollars, Kennedy half-dollars, Susan B. Anthony dollars, things he hoped might get valuable but hadn't. And in a small black plastic pouch, the item he was after: a gold one hundred crown piece struck in 1908 for the sixtieth anniversary of the reign of Emperor Franz Josef. It was the possession that had been with him longest, and perhaps the one he'd looked at least.

CHAPTER

5

GOLD. If you must put your faith in something, make that something gold. That's what Viktor had whispered to his brother the night before he slipped away as they lay side by side on their cots in the cold stable. And the next night, when at last, exhausted, he climbed into bed alone, Hugo had found the coin, his brother's prize possession, waiting for him under the sheet.

So Viktor hadn't taken his own advice. Advice which, looking back across the gulf of years, was pretty sage for a seventeen-year-old. Because if one lesson could be salvaged from the wreckage of the century, it was surely this: buying power has all the other powers licked. Yet Hugo hadn't taken the advice either. Witness: he still had the coin. Not that he'd hoarded it like the guy in the Bible. The thing had simply clung to him despite his indifference. Or *because* of it: like the battered umbrella one props in odd places to drain, hardly expecting, not particularly wanting, to see again. The most he had done for the coin was the black plastic pouch, and this—though he wouldn't admit it—more to cover its shame than afford it protection. Truth to tell, he couldn't bear to look at it. Even now, seven decades later, it possessed the power to hurt. The hurt that comes from self-reproach and when someone whose love you count on acts toward you in a way that baffles you.

First Viktor, then Hugo, a year and a bit apart. Yes, the

Inspector of Customs was a literate man, and perhaps the naming of his two boys after the poet novelist he most admired made up in some small measure for the isolation of his posting, where a highlight of the cultural calendar might be a wandering Gypsy with his dancing bear.

June 28, 1914, changed all that. Church bells sounding through the lush Bucovina countryside announced the news: the assassination of the heir to the throne, Archduke Franz Ferdinand, and his wife, at Sarajevo. Declarations of war came one after another. The first week of August, Austria-Hungary declared war on Russia, and because of his rank and the fact that the Russian border was less than a day's march across Rumania, Hugo's father was ordered to report to Budapest immediately.

Brother Viktor was away at the time, visiting an uncle who managed the estate of a Rumanian boyar near the border with Bessarabia, some fifty miles to the southeast. To the family's relief he arrived back the day before his father was to set out. Though luck might have been better served if he'd come too late.

The trouble began at the dinner table, the last meal—though no one could have predicted it—they were ever to sit down to all together. At some point, apropos of what Hugo could never remember, Viktor, in the casual manner he adopted when big things were afoot, produced the coin. As it made its way up the table toward the Inspector, who adjusted his pince-nez the better to scrutinize it, Hugo found himself in sole possession for all of three seconds. Not an object of beauty, he decided, glancing at the stern imperial profile he knew so well, but of an intriguing sheen and weight. He shot a glance of guarded admiration at Viktor, who smiled back enigmatically.

Meanwhile, their father examined the item with proprietorial thoroughness, polishing it up with his napkin and tilting it to catch the light. All waited attentively. No one spoke. After all, here was a piece of potential contraband that had crossed the border—his border—and landed up under his very nose at his dinner table from the pocket of his eldest son. A certain amount was at stake. It was Viktor's undoing that he had not thought things through in a logical way himself. Already, without a word being spoken, he was beginning to regret his move.

At length the Inspector set the coin down beside his plate in a gesture of finality, removed his pince-nez, and frowned down the length of the table at his son—a frown calculated to wither the protestations of the wiliest of smugglers had there existed any on that particularly dull stretch of the imperial border. "How did you come by this?"

"I found it." Viktor was now very much on his guard.

"Where?"

"Dobraveni." The estate where his uncle was employed.

"Under what circumstances?"

"It was in a drawer." Even to Viktor this sounded inadequate. "Uncle says that when the Russians come they'll take everything. Already they are . . ."

"Never mind the Russians. So your uncle"—here a glance at his wife whose brother this was—"permitted you to do some preliminary looting, eh?" The official voice dripped sarcasm.

"It wasn't him." Viktor shook his head. "He had nothing to do with it."

"So," the Inspector adjusted his spoon, his plate, his glass and ran a finger down a resplendent sideburn. Slowly he pulled the napkin out from under his chin as if he were tightening the noose around the neck of a criminal. "Here sits a customs inspector for the Empire whose son turns out to be not only a smuggler but a thief. Is that it?" He thumped the table. "Is that the state of affairs?" He lowered his gaze and his voice till it was barely audible. "Tomorrow morning, without fail, you will leave here to replace this piece of private property. When you have done so, you will obtain a receipt signed by your uncle."

"But be reasonable, Stephan, there's a war on." His wife could no longer restrain her anxiety.

"In which, as of this evening, Rumania is a noncombatant. He'd better hurry."

The Inspector's old deaf widowed mother had journeyed the few miles from Radautz to be with them as long as hostilities lasted. She picked up the coin and looked at it, wondering what all the fuss was about. Hugo, sitting next to her, leaned over for another look at the trophy exuding, as it now did, the aura of contraband. His grandmother passed it to him.

"Please," the Inspector held out his hand for the coin. By birth a Czech, he spoke, as usual, in German, the language of the Empire.

Hugo hardly wavered. Instead of returning the coin to his grandmother to pass to his father, he leaned in the other direction and placed it near his brother: an act of open defiance in a household where punishment was taken seriously. As Viktor's hand closed over his treasure, there came the scrape of wood on stone as chairs were pushed back. Father and brother stood facing each other across the table, the one bristling with parental indignation, the other watchful and sullen.

Viktor was the first to move. He made a dash across the wide expanse of the kitchen and disappeared through the door that led to the adjoining barn. Here fodder was stored and there were pens with sheep and pigs and stalls for the horses used on inspection trips along the border. The sweet warm smell of hay and dung filled the kitchen, and the air stirred with the sound of shifting beasts. The inspector made no attempt to follow. "He'll be back," he declared.

But Viktor did not reappear that night or the next day, not until the Budapest train had pulled out of Suceava station and was puffing into the forested foothills of the Carpathians. The inevitable beating fell on Hugo after his father pursued him through the house brandishing his sabre of office. It was an inauspicious beginning to the war.

Later Viktor told Hugo how he'd spent that warm August night tramping the lanes around the village, barked at by dogs, hissed at by geese, and had sought shelter, as first light streaked the sky over the valley of the Siret, in a disused barn where he'd slept the morning away. Injustice—as a thirteen-year-old is given to see it—was the main thing on his mind. And for the first time he seemed to regard his brother as a worthy recipient of his confidences. Neither boy had visited their uncle in the south before, and the tales Viktor brought back of life on a princely estate seemed, to Hugo, scarcely credible.

To begin with, its size: sixty thousand acres, including fourteen villages and three forests. The prince himself lived in Paris and came to Dobraveni for a few weeks in late summer and early fall with family, friends, and retainers. This year, what with the political situation, he hadn't come at all and had sent orders for the house to be closed up and the valuables locked away in the vault. Not, according to the uncle, that this would be much use. The Czar's army was massing along the border and the contents of a number of stately homes in the area were reputedly already on their way to grace the great houses of Moscow and St. Petersburg. The Russians were like locusts. It was only a matter of time, he told Viktor.

An elderly relative of the prince lived in a small villa in the grounds of the big house. The villa was supposed to be haunted by the ghost of the relative's mother, who, it was said, rushed about the place slamming doors, rattling locks, and doing the things ghosts do. Not to be outdone, the relative, an amateur scientist whose gray matter had curdled somewhat, devised a scheme to confound his unlamented parent. He turned darkness into light. A powerful generator kept every bulb in the place blazing all night, and during the day the household slept. Over the years the villa, with its reverse lifestyle, had attracted to itself enough cardsharps, mountebanks, and freeloaders to delight the heart of a Gogol. On occasion—Viktor's uncle told the wide-eyed boy—the servants were made to grease and powder their bodies and arrange themselves on pedestals about the garden holding lamps, as naked as the day they were born, while the guests partied under the stars.

But what intrigued the boy most was the description of the heads of stags, bears, and wild boars that glared from the walls with bright electric eyes that winked on and off. Late one night, in an attempt to see this phenomenon for himself, Viktor crept around the villa peering in at the windows. Caught red-eyed, so to speak, by a butler, he was dragged, kicking and struggling, into the dining room and laid out like a suckling pig on the table between vast silver candelabra, where some very expensive brandies were poured down his throat. Next day, coming to in his bed at his uncle's house with his aunt hovering over him, he made them swear on the Bible not to breathe a word to his father of what had happened.

A day or two later he sneaked back into the villa and stole the coin in revenge.

CHAPTER

6

IN the absence of its paterfamilias, the household prepared itself for the unexpected. The few valuables were buried, the livestock sold. As property of a government employee they'd have been confiscated by the advancing Russians. And advance they did, breaking through in Galicia and seizing the Austrian stronghold of Przemysl some hundred and fifty miles to the north. By mid-September troops were pouring through Hugo's village. Day and night they came, marching toward the Carpathian passes and a hoped-for breakthrough to the fertile plains of Hungary and the prize, Vienna.

Hugo watched from a window. Then, growing bolder, he crept up behind the neat new wooden fence shielding their large garden from the road, till his mother spotted him and called him in.

Perhaps dogged by a feeling of responsibility as the oldest male, or perhaps because of his uncle's sobering tales of the Russian army, Viktor, from the start, did not relate to the soldiers in quite the way that Hugo did. With troops bivouacking in the village every night, it wasn't long before the Customs Inspector's garden, so conveniently close to the road, became the field kitchen. And it wasn't long after that until the Customs Inspector's nice new fence turned into firewood. It was on the issue of the fence that Viktor decided to draw the line, a young teenager alone against the might

37

of the Czar's army. Well, not quite alone: he detailed Hugo to accompany him.

But Viktor chose the wrong approach. Understandably hazy about army hierarchy, he vented his wrath on one of the cooks—a commanding figure of a man, it's true, with even a bushy black beard, but, just the same, not an officer. Also, his timing was off. By waiting till the evening trumpet summoned the men to stand in line for their rations, he ensured the cook an audience. As is common knowledge among recruits, army cooks are seldom selected for the lightness of their soufflés. This particular one was, in civilian life, a lion tamer with the Minsk Circus. He was a showman, and he roared at Viktor as at a naughty lion.

It was all Hugo could do, half hiding behind his brother, not to turn tail and run. Viktor, to his credit, stood his ground. The cook, encouraged by guffaws from some of the men, grabbed a flaming brand from the nearest fire, beat it on the ground so that sparks flew, and tossed the smouldering remains down at Viktor's feet. "He wants his fence back, he can have it." Words to that effect. A little cheer went up.

Hugo saw his brother's face redden and the vein on his temple, visible through his fair hair, pulse like a lizard's crop. He knew that Viktor was on the verge of tears. Perhaps a couple of the men noticed too, for they spoke some kind-sounding words. Barely in control of himself, Viktor turned and walked away, breaking into a run as he approached the house. Hugo might have followed, except that by now it was all far too interesting. The copper cauldrons bubbling with soup, the ovens disgorging shoals of black loaves, the delicious smell of roasting meat, and the lines of shuffling, uniformed men, shouting to one another, smoking and laughing and holding their pails out to be filled. It seemed to Hugo that he'd stepped into one of the tales of Sienkiewicz that his mother read aloud at night, of fierce knights and battles and the comradeship of heroes. He stood there, absorbing it all, hardly knowing where to look. And then, spoiling everything, came his mother's voice shrilling insistently from the house.

"Hey, *malchik*." The lion tamer grabbed three loaves and was juggling with them. One by one he lobbed them over the heads of the line of men to where Hugo stood. The first Hugo missed, the second glanced off his arm, and the third he caught. With cheers ringing in his ears he trotted back to the house.

After that it was always Hugo who was dispatched for a pail—sometimes even two pails—of the leftover soup. His grandmother would skim off the fat, mix it with wood ashes from the stove, and make soap, otherwise unobtainable. At first Viktor refused to touch anything from the Russians, but soon, as supplies dwindled, he became less scrupulous. And so the weeks passed and the troops kept on coming, each unit staying four or five days and moving on. Sometimes an artillery regiment would park its vehicles across the road from the house; sometimes a detachment of cavalry rode by, the tall fur caps of the Cossacks bobbing up and down. Hugo investigated them all. After a year he'd picked up enough Russian to join in the songs. By the end of the second year he was fluent and was teaching Viktor.

Because theirs was the only building in the village, besides the post office, which was made of stone, high officers were sometimes billeted on them. Two of the five rooms were set aside for this, and the boys often ended up sleeping in the barn. This did not sit well with Viktor, and he would drag his bedding into the kitchen and doss down outside the room where his mother and sister slept, an iron poker on the floor beside him.

The highest rank ever to stay over was the general commanding a division that was quartered in the surrounding villages. He had a white pony, a beauty, taken—so Hugo was told—in the north from the Germans. In the morning when his grooms exercised the horses, they let Hugo ride the pony. This same general also had six Russian wolfhounds, or Borzois, with long, silky hair and aristocratic expressions. One of the dogs, Myshka, used to follow Hugo on the pony as if Hugo were his master. A friendship grew up, and Myshka became the first love that Hugo fought over. The circumstances of the fight—had he perceived them for what they were—might have spared him much anguish in the years to come. But in those days Hugo had a very trusting nature.

He'd been out after lunch on the white pony and, as usual, Myshka followed him back to the kitchen for a grooming in front of the stove. It was early spring and still the odd frost hung about the hedgerows and the shady back lanes. Hunched up under the window, Viktor was reading. He'd read every book in his father's library, some twice, school having been suspended for the duration. For a while he watched the movement of the comb through the lank, creamy hair, till Hugo, aware of the scrutiny, looked up and caught his eye. "It's a pity," Viktor said in a pleasant, neutral tone, "that Myshka will have to die."

Hugo's arm stopped in mid-stroke. Surely he'd misheard his brother. The dog, sensing something, gave him a couple of quick, encouraging licks.

"Remember the stork," Viktor pointed to the roof.

Of course Hugo remembered the stork. In the fall of the previous year the storks, as always, left their summer nests on the chimneys and belfries of the Bucovina and headed south out of warring Europe. In the spring, as every spring, they returned. It was an honor, and lucky to have a stork build its nest on your roof. Only this spring the nest on the roof of the Customs Inspector's barn remained empty. A Russian soldier had seen to that. Target practice.

The spoiled dog and the dead stork: all that Viktor hated about the invaders. Their haughty privilege, their destructive insolence. For some time he'd been trying to work out a way of getting back at them without exposing the family to reprisals. The dog was the way. To get at the dog he had to enlist Hugo. But from Hugo's point of view the dog was just that, a dog. Something to love and have fun with. It wasn't the dog's fault that it was owned by a Russian general, that it had an aristocratic nose and silken hair. Hugo was too young, or too dumb, to make connections. So Hugo must be manipulated.

"An eye for an eye," Viktor added.

He'd already worked out a plan. In all the fuss and frustration of the departure, the Inspector had forgotten about his service revolver tucked away in its hiding place. In Budapest, or perhaps on the train, he'd cursed himself for this oversight, knowing that the discovery of a hidden weapon would put the household in grave danger. But he might also have comforted himself with the thought that it was so *well* hidden that not even his wife knew where it was. Doubtless it would be waiting for him, safe and sound, on his return.

In this, of course, he was mistaken. Like many pompous people, he underestimated the powers of observation of those closest to him. Not only did his wife know that the gun was under a flagstone beneath the bed in the very room occupied by the general, but so did his eldest son. In fact Viktor had already inspected it to make sure it was loaded and removed it to the barn. Discharged through some old sacking at point blank range, he hoped it wouldn't raise an alarm. All Hugo had to do was hold the dog still. Then they would bundle it into a sack (to be burned later in the stove) and under cover of night dump the wretched animal in a ditch by the main road to look like the work of some disaffected soldier. Of these, Viktor had begun to observe, there were not a few as regiments, pulled from the defeated northern front, were sent south.

Luckily for everyone, not least the dog Myshka, none of the above took place. After a moment's fierce silence, Hugo threw himself on his brother—despite the year between them they were physically almost of a size—and began hammering his fists against Viktor's head. Never before had he attacked Viktor with intent to harm him. Myshka, sensing perhaps this dark aspect, set up such a howl that their mother, working some way off in the fields, hurried in to investigate. The game was up.

The years were passing: 1915, 1916. By 1917 the demoralized Russian Army was slowly retreating, and by July all they had in mind was getting back to Mother Russia as quickly as possible. Roads from the front were awash with deserters, their plunder piled on anything they could steal that moved. The more resourceful had unhitched the surviving horses from artillery pieces and commandeered farm wagons on top of which might be perched some Austrian harlot released from jail in the confusion. The Russian locusts were living up to their name. Hugo's uncle was later to report that they'd ripped the very covers off the books in the prince's library and carried them off for the gold in their tooling. Discarded rifles and military equipment were abandoned to become anyone's fair game.

Meanwhile, in the Kremlin, Kerensky made a truce with Austria, and soldiers' soviets, fomented by the Bolsheviks, vied with commissioned officers for control of the troops. Rival deputations came by train from Moscow to tour the front. Viktor began to spend more and more time away from home. He wouldn't say where he went or with whom, and, to his mother's anguish, rumors spread. Then one thundery afternoon Father Jaroslaw walked from the far end of the village, the skirts of his cassock trailing in the mud, to utter words of wisdom, if not consolation.

The Frau Customs Inspector received him politely in her kitchen, as politely as possible without open reproach. It was his first visit since the invasion. He'd made himself so scarce that people began to wonder whether he hadn't left, and it was even hinted (by his housekeeper, as it turned out) that something akin to blessed martyrdom might have transpired. But Father Jaroslaw was a pragmatic old bird with an instinct for self-preservation honed over the years. His little flock—Catholic, Slavic—was just a patch in a quilt of predominantly Orthodox hue. The lower the profile, he figured, the better off they would be by the time it all blew over. Hadn't he prepared them year after year from the pulpit for times like these? Render unto Caesar whatever you must and keep your heads down. . . . So while blue smoke wafted nonstop from the thuribles of the Orthodox in the villages around, the incense burners in his own church remained cold.

Now Father Jaroslaw was worried. A new and less tangible threat was emerging, one that he had not foreseen. He blamed the Jews. All along the front it was happening, Jewish storekeepers were giving easy credit to the soldier soviets, unearthing goods no one *had* anymore: vodka, smoked goose, delicacies not even available at Mother Gewolb's in Suceava. Some soldiers! From all he heard: unwashed bullyboys, the scum of the earth. And his teenagers were getting sucked in, the ones who'd grown up without fathers or older brothers. This was his worry.

The Frau Customs Inspector heard him out. As did Hugo in the barn, as the door to the kitchen was open. She didn't say much. Perhaps it crossed her mind to ask, Where were you, Father, with all the other fathers away? Perhaps she thought of the liquor she fancied she smelled on her son's breath once or twice on looking in to say good night; or perhaps it was just that soon her husband would be back to take care of everything, and then she'd sleep. How tired she was and worn out.

As the priest sermoned on, events were in train far away to the north that would shake every place on earth, the Bucovina being no exception. The summer of 1917 wore on. As always, on the birthday of the Emperor, she placed lighted candles in half-potatoes in all the windows, even though Franz Josef had died the year before. Coming home after dark, Viktor openly ridiculed his mother for this, calling it senseless, insulting, old-fashioned, so that even his grandmother heard and had to hold her ears. Hugo watched bewildered as his brother stormed around pinching the candles out, railing about starving people and the oppressor class. Once again the storks gathered to fly south.

Then, one October night, news reached the front that Lenin and his Bolsheviks had seized power. Senior officers who had remained at their posts had to jump fast. Within minutes many were shot in their beds, the same fate awaiting any junior officer who did not voluntarily strip himself of his insignia of rank. The canny had already taken to the mountains, hiding in remote villages with supplies seized at gunpoint from the peasants.

The officer billeted at the Customs Inspector's was either too blind or too foolhardy to have prepared. Or too preoccupied with making sure his orderly polished his riding boots to a mirror finish. It was the sight of those boots lying in muddy disarray exactly where he'd left them as he groped drunkenly to bed the night before that alerted him to danger. And when the orderly, shouted for and roundly cursed, failed to come running, and no one paid any attention, he knew things were bad. He peered from the window into a gray drizzle, listened intently, dressed himself fast without assistance, threw some essentials into a bag, and cautiously opened the door.

The kitchen was empty, though the stove had been lit for some time. A glance out to the yard revealed the broken-down cart in use since the farm wagon had been commandeered. The officer threw open cupboards frantically, not knowing where anything was. Splendid, a whole loaf of bread. Turning to toss it on the table, he saw he had company: the Frau Customs Inspector, her mother-in-law, her young daughter, and two sons, all silently watching. Typical peasants. He smiled. Then, unbuckling his revolver, which these days he kept loaded, he casually gestured with it.

"Hitch up the fastest thing on four legs you can find." His command embraced both lads, and somehow the cart in the yard as well. "At the double, and the women will have nothing to fear. And you," he turned on their mother, "put all the food you have on the table."

In case the roles of the girl and the old lady weren't clear, she told them, "Don't move. Do what he says."

The officer looked sharply at the brothers. It was their mother who spoke. "What are you waiting for? Fetch the mule." Even before they were out the door, she was tossing things onto the table. A cabbage, carrots, bags of turnips and potatoes, more loaves of bread, lard, some bacon.

"And don't forget," he added as he watched her scurrying around, "all that vodka you're hoarding."

Only then did she meet his gaze. "We have no vodka in this house."

When she'd stashed everything in baskets he ordered her to load up the cart. A glance through the window told him the boys had not yet returned. He stood in the doorway, toying with his gun, making her squeeze past him as she came and went. When the last bag was loaded and she was reentering the kitchen, brushing the dust off her skirt, he casually stretched out a spurred and booted leg and barred the way. She stayed still, not moving even her eyes. He pushed up against her roughly, jabbing the gun into her buttocks. She remained impassive. A strangled squawk from the direction of the stove for an instant diverted him. The old lady had pulled the girl's face to her shoulder and was holding her tight. It was enough. The moment passed. He dropped his leg.

"Maybe I'll take you along." His kick caught her so that she stumbled and clung to the table for support. "It'll be lonely up there in the mountains. And who's going to cook for me and clean my boots?"

Sounds of pushing, shoving, and cursing came from the yard. The boys were bringing in the mule. "Quiet, you fools," the officer hissed and watched as they backed the recalcitrant animal between the shafts. At last the mule seemed to resign itself to its fate. It stood meekly, Hugo holding its head and caressing its soft muzzle. The officer climbed into the cart and took the ropes that served as reins. Gesturing with his revolver, he told Viktor to rearrange the load so that he could sit on it and not have to stand. He had a long, hard journey ahead.

Hugo carried out the instructions his brother had given him to the letter, with predictable results. He jabbed the freshly whittled point of a small, hard stick into the flank of the mule. In the ensuing confusion, the shot that rang in his ears sounded more like a crack of thunder, the opening salvo of a storm, so that he glanced, in spite of himself, into the leaden sky. The women, all three, rushed to the kitchen door, fully expecting to see one or both of the boys sprawled dead on the cobbles. The boys were fine, Hugo trying to control the panicky mule, hanging on to its bridle. The officer, boots first, was sliding toward the ground, staring upward, as if he too had heard a thunderclap. He had a hole in his chest and was very dead.

Wordlessly, working fast, all five of the family set to and emptied the cart. Viktor removed the unfired pistol from the grip of the officer, now sprawled on the cobbles, and substituted his father's service revolver, one chamber fired. The mule was returned to a neighbor's shed, whence it had been "borrowed," the cart to a far corner of the yard. Viktor notified the local soviet of the apparent suicide.

Later soldiers came for the body. The head was cut off and fixed to a pole and took its place in a grisly procession alongside the hacked about features of other unfortunate officers. As for the boots, they were claimed by the long-suffering orderly in lieu of wages. Primed with liquor and in the mood for a celebratory orgy, the bloodthirsty band linked forces with others and headed for army headquarters at Botosani—in the name of the People and of Lenin, the liberator.

The next day Viktor was gone, and Hugo, when at last he dragged himself to bed, found the gold coin under the sheet.

CHAPTER

7

IF you live on the same block in Manhattan for twenty years and you walk out your front door, without even thinking you take a reading. On this particular February morning, Hugo sensed a difference, though as he paused on the stoop, nothing specific claimed his attention. The lines of parked cars glinting in the strong sun, a discarded Christmas tree, a movers' van blocking traffic, some kids hanging out who should have been in school—it was all very much as usual. He picked up his shopping bags and carefully negotiated the steps. No ice today to contend with, thank goodness. A kind winter, touch wood, so far. Turning east he set his course for the dumpster.

He now saw that something was up. People were peering in unexpected directions. One kid, who had a small audience chanting "Go, Tyrone," was trying to squeeze under a parked car. A man from the S.R.O. building was sifting through gutter garbage with a stick. Three Chinese kitchen hands from the restaurant on the corner who normally formed an oblivious knot, smoking and talking under a tree, glanced animatedly over their shoulders. As Hugo waited to cross Second Avenue, he had the distinct impression that people were turning into his block as if they were late for something. Finally, curiosity got the upper hand.

On the north side of the street, a woman who ran a small pottery was hanging wind chimes on a branch of a tree.

"What's all the commotion?" he asked. In warm weather he would sometimes stop to watch her shaping a bowl on her wheel out on the sidewalk, and pass the time of day.

"Some joker stuffed five-dollar bills under all the windshield wipers."

"New York. Always something." Jeez, Hugo thought, it had to be Cassidy. Who else would be that crazy?

He catapulted his trash into the dumpster then crossed to the sunny side of the street. Leaning his back against the railings of the Greek Orthodox Cathedral, he closed his eyes. He was tired. The sun felt good. His batteries needed recharging.

For a good five minutes he didn't move, letting the warmth find its way into him, caring not a whit who passed by or what intentions they harbored. He thought of Cassidy, of the tangled thickets people make of their lives, each blunder driving them willy-nilly into the next. Other people's lives! Yet who was he to talk? An old man alone and decaying, not enough friends left to lift his coffin. Was it, in the end, that much sweeter?

Chancing to open an eye, Hugo saw shuffling toward him up the street, bent and grizzled, a walking argument for euthanasia. Too late to run. He tried to melt into the railings, feigning invisibility, willing the shuffler to pass. But the man tottered to a halt right in front of him. "I've come twenty-five blocks already. If I don't find anywhere soon I'm going to piss in my pants."

Reluctantly, Hugo accepted that he was being addressed. He opened his eyes. From the carefully parted gray hair and the moist, quivering lips to the orthopedic shoes, the newcomer smacked of age, bottled and preserved like some fancy vinegar. "There's plenty of restaurants," Hugo said.

"Closed."

"Nonsense." Painstakingly, Hugo listed the fast-food places along Second Avenue that were wide open: the Angus Burger at 73rd, the McDonald's at 70th, the Burger King at 79th, and so on. "Take your pick." Finally, he said,

"There's a church right here that most likely has a rest room."

The man shaded dim eyes to look. "What denomination is it?"

"Orthodox."

"Oh no, I couldn't go there, I'm Reformed." Wheezing laughter, eyes watering, the ancient seemed well pleased with himself. And why not? Hugo had set him up like a pro: he'd delivered the punch line with panache. Foraging in a plastic shopping bag, he came up with a partially smoked cigar, examined it, and began to cough. "See, I only have to look at one."

"I thought you'd given them up, Sydney."

Sydney, vegetable man emeritus at a local supermarket and self-employed practical joker, did not skip a beat. "I did, but I had an offer I couldn't refuse."

Against his better judgment, Hugo said, "Oh?"

"A box of genuine Havanas and an all-expense-paid trip to Florida." In attempting a comradely punch on the arm, he almost toppled over.

Hugo steadied him. Sydney the joker, the man with the Jimmy Durante ears and the George Burns leer. The most tedious man in the world. Hugo couldn't think why they still talked, except that Sydney, whose wife had long since died—probably from a surfeit of his jokes—lived in the neighborhood and spent every waking hour on the street in search of an audience. It was hard to avoid him. He lay in wait. "You're a born liar. Since when could you get Havanas here?"

Sydney reached into his bag and thrust two fresh cigars under his friend's nose. Hugo examined the bands. Genuine-looking, he had to admit. He sniffed them. "Probably fakes."

"Fake, schmake. You can taste the difference. Believe me, I should know." Long before vegetables, Sydney had made a killing in bomb shelters. For a few years back in the fifties—before the bottom dropped out of that particular market—he'd tasted the good life.

Lest he be reminded of this in detail, Hugo asked about Florida. "So when are you off?"

"Off? I'm back already. I'm there one day, I start to croak. It's a graveyard. Like a holding pattern over Death Valley." He dropped his voice. "So what gives, smarty-pants? Tell Sydney. The wheel of fortune spun your way, eh?"

What now? Hugo wondered. A wave of tedium hit him. All he wanted was to get away. He looked at his watch. "Got a date with a dream."

"Playing it nice and cool, are we? Well, I'll tell you right now, wise guy, I sung for my supper. Made them very happy. So remember Syd in your will."

"And to my friend Sydney, who asked to be remembered in my will: Hello Sydney."

"That pick-me-up we came up with, recollect? Beet juice, celery juice, a touch of bitters. I told them all about that, how we coulda made a fortune. 'Drinka glassa our Beecella! You'll feel like a Rockefeller!'" He produced a ghost of a shuffle.

Hugo felt a headache coming on and closed his eyes so the sun would warm his pupils. The guy was hopeless. "Sydney, I don't know what you're talking about. What's more, I don't care. I gotta run."

"Guy and a dame. Questions, questions. Hugo this, Hugo that. Classy number she was, too. Guy more like your average bodyguard. Onion breath." Sydney aped his shoulders the better to segue into his bodyguard routine. (What did one bodyguard say to the other?)

Hugo cut him short. "What medication they got you on now, Sydney?"

"They seen us together and reckoned we were best buddies, she said. So they want the lowdown, 'This is Your Life' type of thing. I figured your horse came in. 'What's in it for me?' I said. The cigars plus they threw in Florida. I'd have settled for the cigars, but who's counting? You should be happy."

"Give me a break. There's Hugos all over New York."

Sydney gestured dismissively. "Believe me, you won

something, a Grand Prize, who knows? They have to do a thorough check. These guys don't futz around.''

"You're putting me on.''

"As God is my witness.'' Sydney glanced at the church.

"They just walked up to you in the street?''

"What can I tell you?''

"No ID. Nothing?''

"I told you, Florida.''

"You really went?''

"I said already. A week at the Eden Rock. The guy—Onion Breath—drives me out that same afternoon. United Air from La Guardia.''

"But you're not there, you're here.'' Hugo leaned against the railing. He felt weak and confused.

"There's this old woman sitting with her friends on the boardwalk at Coney Island, right. 'God,' she says, 'help me. I can't piss no more.' 'Lady,' the voice comes back from over the ocean, 'you pissed enough.' See what I'm saying? I didn't stay. I didn't piss enough. Believe me, pal, there'll be something in the mail for you. Did the mailman come yet?''

"I better go check.'' It was an exit line, no more. The sun had slipped behind a high-rise. Behind him, as he walked, Hugo heard Sydney's reedy voice raised in a shaky rendition of "My Coney Island Baby.''

Hugo arrived home in a daze. A feeling of dread had settled on him since his encounter with Sydney. With not so much as a glance at the muslin curtains, he let himself into his building. His mailbox was empty. Yet what was there to worry about, he asked himself as he coaxed his tired frame up the stairs. In a few days he'd be out of it, beyond their reach whoever they were, beyond anyone's reach. Which was precisely the point. He paused on the third floor landing to catch his breath. Something was going to go wrong. He knew it. Nameless people were out there, asking questions about him, gathering information. Then, his break-in. Not your run of the mill break-in. What were they after? What sort of a world was it where you couldn't even die without interference? The thought made him bristle.

He unlocked his door and pushed it open, but made no move to enter. A sheet of notepaper was lying on the floor by the sink. Someone must have flicked it under the door, or perhaps a breeze had caught it. Ignoring the paper, Hugo went into the bathroom. Coming out, he carefully stepped around it. Only when he'd checked the rooms beyond the bead curtain and found nothing amiss did he pick up the paper, carry it to the kitchen table, sit down, and put on his reading glasses.

"Dear Friend of Poland," he read. "I took the liberty of speaking of our recent meeting with an acquaintance who is concerned with the Polish émigré community here and active with the Jagiello Society (about which we spoke) and the Committee for a Free Poland, of which he is a past president. The Baron (as he is known) expressed a fervent wish to make your acquaintance, and would be honored if you would join us for lunch tomorrow at the restaurant Le Repas. Since you are not 'on the phone,' I will myself call for you in your apartment at midday, unless I hear otherwise. Looking forward to good food and good company. Please come, American dreamer, Your neighbor, Elie."

The handwriting was big and deliberate, as if unsure of its reception. As well it might have been. Hugo pushed the note away. He removed his glasses and rubbed his eyes. He felt exhausted. Too much was happening, all of a sudden, when all he wanted to do—all he had time for—was to tidy things up for Father Vince, and make as dignified an exit as possible. In days gone by, he'd have jumped at the chance to eat at Le Repas, where reservations, reputedly, were harder to come by than taxi medallions or seats on the Stock Exchange, and only secured with substantial down payments to the head waiter months in advance. Though perhaps for lunch it was easier. To go for a meal at Le Repas with his new friend and neighbor—in normal times what a memory to cherish. Now? How could he even think about it? Especially with one of those pseudo Polish barons, all cuffs and smirks and little bows, patronizing him over an expensive meal and flirting with Elie. Probably the whole affair was an excuse for an old goat to have a fling with a beautiful girl and put it on his credit card. Hugo would be part of the scenery, his glass topped up every five minutes by a well-tipped wine steward. He wouldn't fall for that sort of malarkey. No way.

He pulled Elie's note toward him, folded it neatly, and stuck it between the paperweights with his Con Ed bills. Out of sight, out of mind. Suddenly, he felt much better. And as for Sydney, more than likely he'd made the whole thing up: Florida, the bodyguard, the classy dame . . . And even if he hadn't, entirely, how many classy dames were there in the city of New York? A whole lot. Poor old Sydney. He was old. He had no life left in him, so he had to invent one. Sydney made Hugo feel like a young man again, a young buck entering a new city the way it used to be with him. Hamburg, Madrid, Paris, Marseilles, Chicago, Miami . . . at his feet, waiting to be explored. Jobs, girls, museums, restaurants, shops, the passing parade. That's why Hugo tolerated Sydney and listened to his jokes, however awful. That's why he forgave so much about him, like the way he claimed credit for Hugo's pick-me-up when all he'd done was sell him the beets and the celery—not even the angostura that was at a different counter—and come up with the stupid name and the jingle. Though the line about feeling like a Rockefeller wasn't bad, he had to admit. He hummed it over to himself reflectively.

Later that afternoon Hugo had a bit of a scare. Perhaps he'd gotten careless about his trips to the dumpster, over-confident because he'd not encountered Herself or her minions: he had not seen her in more than a week, in fact. At any rate, he made it safely down the stairs with two full shopping bags of papers, had walked the length of the hallway, and was grappling awkwardly with the inner of the two front doors when right behind him he heard the sharp clack of a bolt being released and the creak of a door opening. Then—and he couldn't be sure because in his panicky

53

effort to get them through the door, the papers crackled like a forest fire—the door behind him closed. Doubtless Mrs. Foley had seen not simply him, but what it was he was carrying. If she was on her way out, she'd follow him, or at least look to see where he went on these little excursions. Or perhaps she was already on the phone to Herself.

Thinking quickly, Hugo turned left instead of right. Without a backward look he strolled with elaborate nonchalance up the street, crossed it, and proceeded down Third Avenue. It was here he'd been accosted by Cassidy a few days before, and the memory triggered an idea. Crossing the avenue with the light, he went into the Mexican restaurant where his friend could sometimes be found behind the bar. Only when he was safely inside did he turn around. The street lamps had flicked on, also some car headlights, and streams of northbound commuters dominated the sidewalk, their breath making little steamy trails. No one appeared to be the least bit interested in him.

"Hey there, Hugo!" It was Mike, one of the bartenders. Early yet for patrons, just a busboy setting out little vases of flowers. "Looking for a job?"

"Cassidy around?"

Mike ducked behind the bar. Shaking his head, he poured a small sherry and pushed it across. Then he puffed out his cheeks and deflated them noisily, still shaking his head.

This was no simple negative, Hugo realized. He sipped the drink, grateful for it after his little scare. "What's the story?"

"My exact words to you: what's the story? What's with him lately, Hugo? What gives?—more than the usual I mean."

"Was that him last night?"

"The big cash giveaway? Don't tell me." He opened the till and took out a handful of fives. "I'm fool enough to try to pick up after him. He throws the stuff back in my face."

"He's not coming in today?"

"He's in the hospital."

"Ai yai yai."

"Picked a fight with a guy in a double stretch who was minding his own business. Guy turns out to be a bruiser."

"Is it bad?"

"Keep him off the street for a coupla days. Not long enough."

"It's something about his ex."

"That's a cross we all gotta bear. No pun intended. Between you and me, the guy's a paranoid schizo."

They brooded for a while as Hugo sipped his drink. "I guess I'll look in on him." The hospital was a couple of blocks away. It had an incinerator. He could dump his trash there.

CHAPTER

8

HUGO woke in a panic. For a few seconds he lay still, listening. Then it came, the noise that must have disturbed him: a battering with intent to smash, giving no quarter, like a jackhammer breaking up the street. It didn't come from the street. It came from the kitchen. *Herself.* In his kitchen. What in heck was she playing at now? He sat up, feeling under the pillow for his ammonia squirter, which, of course, wasn't there. Groping under the bed, his hand closed on the swordstick, but as he righted himself dizziness flooded his brain.

For a minute, maybe two, Hugo sat on his bed, mind numb, eyes closed, hands resting on the pommel of the swordstick, till a fresh blast of noise yanked him to his feet. Through the glass bead curtain the kitchen was as empty as when he'd left it. The windows were tightly closed. The chain was on the door. It was from the door that the din was coming. Someone was playing it like a steel drum. Tiptoeing over the tiles, Hugo stealthily raised the peephole cover and applied an eye to the glass. Immediately, he drew his head back. The face he saw was not the face of Herself or any of her minions. It was the face of Elie. Though not an Elie he'd ever seen before. Flushed and grim, she was brandishing something, on the verge of hurling it directly at him, or so it seemed.

Hugo reached for the chain and unhitched it just as a fresh

barrage landed. Flinching, he managed to get the door open. It took Elie maybe three seconds to rearrange her features. She looked at Hugo, looked at the shoe in her hand, looked back at Hugo and burst out laughing. Hugo blinked. "It's been a long time since a girl was that keen to visit me."

She took in the bathrobe and the bare legs sticking out from under it. "Perhaps you didn't get my note?"

He smiled ruefully, acknowledging the legs and all that they implied. "Please come in."

"But the Baron," she looked at her watch, "he's waiting. And the table's reserved, and . . ."

"Please." He pulled out a chair. She made no attempt to sit. "I'll get dressed." He'd put the note right out of his mind, and here she was.

"Be sure to wear a tie," she called out as the bead curtain swished behind him.

Why not? he thought, breaking the paper seal on a clean shirt. You pass this way but once.

She waited impatiently at the bottom of the stairs monitoring his descent. He'd taken his time dressing, too: he was not about to be hustled through the last few days he had, even by a good-looking woman. For the first time a taste of the power conferred on him as master of his own fate was making itself felt. After all, to feast at one of the preeminent restaurants in the city was an end not unbefitting an old waiter. To order the best wines, the most expensive entrées. He found himself quite looking forward to it.

He followed her down the long hallway. It would certainly give Mrs. Foley something to squawk about. Here he was, dressed to the nines, walking out with the new tenant from second floor rear. He coughed to alert the widow. What harm could it do? It might embellish his image, bestow a certain je ne sais quoi.

On the stoop Elie paused, looking this way and that. Hugo took in the scene. A short way down the block, an altercation was in progress. A man with a bandaged head stood in the street gesticulating and yelling at the driver of a large truck who sat impassively in the cab of his vehicle with his

57

hand on the horn. Other cars were backed up behind the truck, their drivers in various stages of apoplexy.

In a move that surprised Hugo—as well as the (doubt-lessly) watching Mrs. Foley—Elie slipped her arm through his. Arm in arm, like a couple from old Europe, they negotiated the steps and set off down the block. Hugo sensed a tension in his partner, an on-edgeness that the situation did not seem to warrant. Perhaps it was simply his age, and she was afraid he might fall. How old he must look to people compared to the way he saw himself!

The man with the bandaged head went on flinging incomprehensible insults up at the driver of the truck who leaned, imperviously, on his horn. It was David and Goliath. Two men stood in the road—a doorman and a passerby—trying to encourage the truck to squeeze on past the obstructing vehicle, alternately beckoning and estimating with their hands the clearance on either side. Goliath ignored them. Not till Hugo was alongside did he get a good view of the car causing the problem. Double-parked, half-hidden from the sidewalk, it was a silver stretch.

Clean forgetting he was attached to someone, Hugo stopped. Various images chased through his mind. Cassidy in the hospital the previous evening, bandaged up to his eyes. Mike the bartender waving a handful of five-dollar bills. His own lost cane. The jogger on the bridge. Elie's voice in his ear cut through the confusion. But it wasn't him she was speaking to—or yelling at, more like. The man with the bandaged head was coming towards them. He did not look happy. A second broadside from Elie deflected him. He moved toward the stretch and held open the rear door.

Given a choice, Hugo would have said good-bye and gone back to his room. But his arm was still in Elie's, and the door to the stretch yawned open. He had no choice. Elie's face, when he turned to her, wore the sweet smile of determination, and in her eyes—or was this just a fancy?—he saw the glint of victory. What was it she wanted so much?

They had the back seat to themselves. The driver was screened out by the same brown glass that shielded them from the gaze of the street. The space seemed as big as Hugo's bedroom. It was warm and cozy. He'd never ridden in a stretch before. Elie pointed out the TV, the cocktail cabinet, the plush of the red velvet upholstery, trying to make him feel at ease. She seemed at last relaxed. "The Baron sent his car for us."

Nice Baron. As if he were Santa Claus. He must be a real ogre, Hugo decided, wondering what she'd have done had he refused to get into the limo. Probably she was the Baron's mistress, his little thing on the side. It would account for the car being in the neighborhood at all hours. He could hardly wait to tell Cassidy. Paranoid was right, the Mexican thinking it was his wife and her merry crew. He peered through the partition for a better view of the driver. The bandage made him look like a Sikh. The jogger on the bridge? Who was paranoid now? And how many silver stretch limos cross the George Washington Bridge in a day?

"The Baron is very patriotic, I think you'll find." They were edging downtown in heavy traffic. It seemed to Hugo an odd sort of topic to bring up. Elie glanced sideways, expecting a response.

"We should be flying the Stars and Stripes, like some big politician. They'd have given us a police escort."

"I am speaking of Poland." No sign of amusement in those eyes. The Baron evidently was no joke.

The car slithered through the lunchtime traffic like a giant silverfish. "So he isn't an American citizen?"

For a moment the question hung between them. He wasn't sure she'd heard. "As a matter of fact, no. He has a West German passport. He comes here frequently, on business."

"At heart he's a Pole?"

"As Polish as you or me."

"Quite a mongrel, then."

From the rather prim set of her mouth, he realized he had trespassed. "His family is from Silesia. His father was, I believe, German. When the Communists took over after the war, they lost everything: their estates, their coal mines, their castle, the works. The father committed suicide. The mother died of a broken heart. The Baron was lucky to get out alive. He's very anticommunist. But please,'' she said, placing a hand on Hugo's on the seat, ''don't mention that I told you this. It's a painful subject.''

Hugo found the cool touch of her palm not painful at all. Her nails were painted red and matched the velvet. ''I don't understand why he wants to see *me*.''

''Perhaps that's my fault,'' she smiled coyly. ''I told him about you, American dreamer. The Baron is also a dreamer, as you will find out. His dream is one day to live again in his castle in a free Poland.''

''He must be crazy.''

''I guess you'll find out. Between you and me, I think he has a job for you.''

Hugo leaned back in the comfort of the seat and closed his eyes. A smile played around his lips and twitched his little mustache. Slowly, he shook his head. ''He's going to be disappointed.''

''Not if it's an offer you can't refuse. Oh, don't worry''— Hugo had sat up, startled—''he's not a bad boss. I work for him myself, in case you were wondering.'' She glanced at her watch and said something he didn't catch into an intercom. The bandage swiveled, nodding.

''Does *he* work for him?''

''Sure.''

''What happened to his head?''

''Some maniac tried to give him five dollars. He threw it back in his face, so the man came at him with a knife.'' Mistaking Hugo's gasp for empathy, she added, ''Keep your tears, he didn't have much up there to begin with.'' The car stopped in a side street. ''We're here.''

Le Repas, with its window tightly curtained with lace, presented an unpromising face to the general public, most of whom, as they passed, paid it scant heed. Which was fine with Le Repas, whose clientele came in chauffeured limousines and glanced neither left nor right as, clutching their jewels and briefcases and shepherded by Jacques the doorman, they scuttled inside under the narrow awning. Nor did Elie, as she sailed haughtily through the opened door as if for the millionth time, notice the wink that Jacques—known as Ricky in the Flatbush neighborhood where he grew up and still lived—bestowed on his friend Hugo.

Once inside, their coats and hats were taken by a motherly old person in black behind a little window not unlike a box office *guichet*. Indeed, entering Le Repas was a bit like stepping into a theater foyer. Not the functional space of today, but something exquisite from the previous century. A flunky ushered them through a double door into the dining room, where the first thing to confront the senses was a magnificent bank of flowers rising from an ancient sarcophagus. From behind this floral bunker, the headwaiter, a silver-haired potentate, maintained a sharp watch over his domain.

Hugo's finely tuned antennae sensed that their reception was not all that it might have been. First off, the headwaiter—a species he'd observed for sixty years—barely acknowledged that they stood before him. Once resigned to this fact, he led them on a circuitous tour to a distant outpost near the door to the kitchen. The message being, to any valued customer who might look up, that circumstances did exist—believe it or not—beyond his control, and that here was a perfect example.

Hugo felt like an imposter and saw no reason not to be treated like one. He only hoped, as busboys and waiters dodged between and around them and tantalizing smells floated by, that none of his former colleagues were present to witness his humiliation, though reaction from that quarter would more likely have been envy. Already several pairs of eyes had turned from sauté de veau and coquilles Saint-Jacques in the direction of Elie's retreating figure.

It was with a little start of surprise that Hugo found himself bowing deferentially across a table to a man who, had he encountered him in other circumstances, he might have taken for a butcher, albeit a distinguished one. Perhaps it was the pugnacious thrust of his shoulders and the droop of his jowls that placed him, in Hugo's mind, cleaver in hand behind a side of pork.

Elie made the introductions as a waiter jabbed the backs of their legs with chairs in his eagerness to get them seated. Leaning over, she untucked the Baron's napkin, which, dangling from under his chin, swished dangerously close to the glass of wine he'd been sipping. The gesture, potentially intrusive and personal, was achieved with such an air of impersonal efficiency that Hugo was forced to revise his earlier surmise. This was the action of a caretaking secretary, not a mistress.

As a waiter filled glasses from an opened bottle cooling in a silver ice bucket, Hugo felt the eyes of the Baron upon him. Eyes set so deep under bushy brows that, in the dim light of the place, they seemed like holes. He felt their power to probe, to char him at his core. At last his host lifted his glass and, with a shrewd sideways look at Elie and a single appreciative nod, said, "So far so good. *Na zdrowie!*"

"*Na zdrowie!*" they echoed.

Hugo was thankful to be able to immerse himself in the familiar language of the menu. The Baron did not come up to expectations, except possibly for a row of medals pinned to his chest. (And these, after all, could be rented by the yard.) Here was no vapid aristocrat with quavering voice and diamond pinned cravat. True, this man wore a nicely cut suit in an expensive material—new, by the looks of it—but it enclosed a fleshy dynamism that left Hugo more than ever perplexed. He had to remind himself that, whatever was going on, it didn't matter. He was here for one purpose: to enjoy a meal at Le Repas before he died. The last meal before the hanging, he thought with grim amusement.

The Baron seemed to read his mind. "Please, whatever you wish, order," he commanded expansively. "If it is not on the menu, no matter, they prepare. Even if it is *bigos* they prepare if I tell them. Here we are, three Poles in a fancy French restaurant speaking English. Damn crazy, you know what I mean. Monsieur!" He called for more wine.

Elie looked uncomfortable. "Is it necessary, another bottle?"

"Always so serious, this one," the Baron sat back, smiling at Elie. "Listen to me, woman. We eat, we drink, we enjoy the meal, okay? Then we talk business. Over coffee and perhaps a cigar, we talk business." He picked up the menu and glanced through it. "Ah yes, the sturgeon caviar. So appropriate. With the sturgeon we pat ourselves on the back. We deserve a little congratulation, no, Elie? You see," he held up a beckoning hand for a waiter, "you were not the easiest person to find, Monsieur. So inconsiderate to friends in need, first to alter the name so, then to be not on the telephone."

Hugo looked questioningly at Elie. It had been years since he'd knocked some syllables off his name for the convenience of headwaiters. As in the car, she laid her hand on his. He'd have liked to think she blushed. "I must be honest, American dreamer. We were searching for you. No one else quite fits the bill. Let's say you are tailor-made."

"And I must warn you," the Baron leaned toward Hugo as if to divulge a confidence, "this woman is the most excellent seamstress." Whereupon he erupted into not altogether pleasant laughter. Laughter that seemed to ring a distant bell in Hugo's memory.

CHAPTER

9

IN November of 1918, the Inspector of Customs returned from Budapest. Within the month, the border he had so assiduously patrolled dissolved. It ceased to exist.

News came that the former Crownland of Bucovina, under the general peace agreement, would be annexed by Rumania. For Hugo, aged sixteen, it was time to return to high school. This meant learning Rumanian, since they were living in what was now Rumania. Hugo balked. His father—taking his cue as usual from the powers that be—insisted. Hugo rebelled. He declared he did not feel like learning what he called a Gypsy language. If he felt any sense of belonging, of patriotism, it was to the Poland of his mother's dreams and stories, a country that did not exist on the map, although rumor had it that, out of the chaos of post-war Central Europe, a Polish nation would rise, reconstituted.

In later life Hugo maintained that this business of the language was why he ran away from home. The deeper reason, one he could not acknowledge even to himself, had to do with his brother.

It wasn't long before the Inspector of Customs pieced together fairly accurately the story behind Viktor's absence. His wife, convinced from day to day that her son would return, had made the family promise on no account to tell anyone what had happened, least of all the Inspector. And, because they feared the consequences as much as she did if he were to find out, they kept quiet. A bit too quiet perhaps. He grew suspicious.

All the years he was in Budapest, he had worried about his service revolver and cursed himself for leaving it behind in its hiding place under the flagstone. Not, of course, that he blamed himself entirely. If Viktor hadn't made trouble that day, he'd have been in a calmer frame of mind and remembered to pack it. And, incidentally, he hadn't forgotten the thrashing he owed that young man, to be administered with interest. He permitted himself a low grunt or two as the train carrying him home puffed on through the chilly November night.

Almost the first thing on his mind upon reaching his house was to check on the revolver. As it was, he had to restrain himself. His mother, who had not been well, was installed in the room in question, and he could hardly go scrabbling about under her bed while she lay in it. The secret must stay with him. Several days passed before, on hands and knees with much grunting and wheezing, he was able to prize up the flagstone. And he was stunned at what he found. A revolver to be sure, but certainly not his. So stunned that he didn't hear the door open and someone come up behind him.

"What's the matter, Stephan?"

It was Liliana, his wife, and she appeared to him to be equally amazed. Not unnaturally, for surely she hadn't known of the hiding place. Was he mistaken? Had he forgotten the make and shape of his own gun? He told her what had happened. They agreed not to say anything to Hugo, his sister Odilia, or the old lady. But the more the Inspector of Customs dwelt on the incident, the more convinced he was that Viktor was at the bottom of it.

At first he'd seen no reason to doubt the story that was put about: Viktor had gone to help his uncle repair the ravages the Russian army—supposedly Rumania's ally—had inflicted on the estate on the Bessarabian border. Now, his mind consumed with suspicion, he began to ask questions.

And one misty afternoon his questions led him to call on Father Jaroslaw at his cottage at the far end of the village. He returned through the dusk in time for supper, his face set and grim. Before he'd even wiped the droplets from his brow and mustache or the mud and leaves from his boots, in front of the whole family, he started to chastise his wife.

"So, our young hero pals around with anarchists, murderers, and rapists, *hein?* Our blameless one runs off with the enemy like a deserter to pillage and preach the gospel of Bolshevism, *hein?* This is what happens when my back is turned."

"Stephan, please, the children . . ."

"Children!" He glared at Odilia and Hugo as if they too might be contaminated. "Children! I have only one son now." He looked Hugo up and down, "Remember that, boy, in case you should take it into your head to catch any of these fashionable mental diseases that are going round."

Day after day he hammered at them, meal after meal. From hints from frightened neighbors, he was able to piece together more or less what had happened; but he must hear it from them and obtain a full confession. His own family had conspired against him in a manner no man could be expected to tolerate. He would show them who was master here. In the end it was Odilia, aged thirteen, who broke. "But he saved us, Papa!" she cried, through tears of indignation. "They were taking Mama off to the mountains . . ." It was enough.

Just before Christmas, Hugo was sent into Suceava on some errands, including seeing about a box of his father's effects that was due by rail freight from Budapest. While at the station, he heard an announcement that the train for Chernowitz was about to depart. He climbed aboard. It was one week after his sixteenth birthday. Oddly, as he jogged north in the crowded carriage, his chief regret was that he'd used the money given him for the errands to buy his ticket. It was six months before he was able to refund it.

What was on his mind? He wanted to find his brother, that was for sure. Perhaps to warn him what sort of recep-

66

tion awaited him at home. The Inspector had sworn—in a fit of temper, but one never knew—that he personally would turn Viktor in to the authorities on a murder charge if he ever came back. And perhaps the decision to leave home wasn't as last minute and spontaneous as it seemed. True, he'd brought no money and only the clothes he stood in; but for some reason he'd slipped Viktor's gold coin into his pocket that morning before leaving. Why?

The first few weeks were very hard on Hugo. Winter settled in. Chernowitz, the capital of the Bucovina, teemed with refugees displaced by the war. Whole families camped out on the streets, huddling around braziers that burned whatever sticks of furniture they had managed to salvage from their homes. Few found any sort of paid employment. For the first and almost the last time in his life, Hugo had to beg and steal to stay alive. It never occurred to him to hawk the coin. It was Viktor's. Eventually, he found menial work at the Polish-Peoples Home, scrubbing and cleaning. And always he kept an eye out for his brother, trying to second-guess his whereabouts. Once or twice Hugo asked some likely person—a soldier or a traveler—if they'd seen him, but astonished laughter was the inevitable response. The world was on the move. All was motion and fluidity as if some buried giant had turned over in his sleep and disturbed an ants nest. "He looks something like me," Hugo would insist, and the laughter would change to a sad shake of the head or a squeeze on the shoulder.

Meanwhile, in ornate conference rooms in the capitals of the victor powers, a new Poland was being patched together. And, inadvertently, the fate of one Hugo T was being sealed. One morning in spring, when the muddy roads of the Bucovina were beginning to dry out, an official commission arrived in Chernowitz and checked into the Polish-Peoples Home. They were recruiting Poles for the new army. Hugo was quick to register. He gave his age as eighteen, was passed fit and dispatched to the new Poland for training, to the city of Lwow.

Before long he was goose-stepping around the parade

ground in an ill-fitting French uniform with an enormously heavy German rifle at the slope. The next thing he knew his unit—the 4th Division of Sharp-shooters, 29th Regiment—was marching south, bound for the Black Sea. Civil war was raging in Russia, and a White army, squeezed by the Reds, was retreating toward the port of Ackerman where a flotilla of French and other warships lay at anchor waiting to whisk them to safety. The Poles, allied with the Rumanians, who had been awarded Bessarabia by the peacemakers, wanted to discourage any designs the Whites might have west of the River Dniester, the new border. As it was, they arrived too late; the Whites were safely embarked and on their way to the Crimea. The danger, had there been any, was over. The 29th turned around and trudged back.

It was on the journey back that Hugo's constant inquiries began to pay off. The regiment was ill-provisioned, which is to say it was not provisioned at all. And the countryside, off which they were forced to live, had been licked clean by its recent landlords: retreating Russian armies of various hues. So when Private Hugo discovered a farmer with a dozen eggs for sale, he gobbled them up, hard-boiled, on the spot. With predictable results. He was so sick that the regiment dropped him off at a hospital run by Russian doctors and nurses in a town called Bendere. The nurses were delighted to find he spoke Russian, fussing over him for the kid he still was. For the first time he felt homesick. Word went round about his search for Viktor, and one nurse was particularly helpful. She promised to keep an eye out, jotting down details about his regiment and how he could be reached. Hugo was never certain, but he always assumed that this was how Viktor eventually made contact.

As soon as he was fit to travel, he rejoined his regiment at Lwow and continued his training. He was now in a heavy machine gun company. Every day he went out to the fields with his crew and their Russian-made Maxim gun. The gun was water-cooled, and Hugo's job was to replace the water after it started to boil. For this he carried a funnel attached to his belt, which made marching even more difficult. He swapped his German rifle for a lighter French cavalry one despite a warning that it tended to explode when fired too much.

Fall turned to winter, winter to spring. The year was 1920. Armies were again on the prowl. War broke out between Russia and Poland over the new borders, and Hugo's regiment was ordered to the front. The Reds were chased back into the Ukraine with hardly a shot fired, the Poles in hot pursuit. But then came what Hugo was to call his ''baptism.'' Inside their borders, the enemy turned and fought. Actual bullets whizzed this way and that. Luckily, Hugo heard rather than felt them, and by the end of May both parties had settled down to a game of wait and see. About the most exciting thing to happen was a flying visit from the commander-in-chief and future president of Poland, Josef Pilsudski, on a tour of the front. The main attraction, as far as Hugo was concerned, was the open Cadillac he rode in, a gift from the people of the United States. After this the United States was high on his list of places to visit.

So Hugo embarked on a pleasantly lazy summer watching the border, in his sector a somewhat languid river called the Zbroutch, a tributary of the Bug. The men were quartered in a huge, abandoned estate on a hill—not unlike the one he imagined his uncle managed. The mornings were taken up with physical training. Afternoons were spent on the rifle range or with the machine guns in the fields. Every four hours the border patrol was relieved. Patrol duty was popular among the men since there appeared to be no soldiers on the opposite bank of the river. Peasants from the Ukraine crossed over, bought what they needed in the village on the Polish side, and returned. As a peace offering, they left eggs for the patrols. Before long so many were coming over, the soldiers collected the eggs on a blanket. Soon chickens, fruit, and vegetables appeared. The men lived like kings.

One of the regulars who crossed the river was a flaxen-haired lass with a captivating smile. More often than not, the smile was directed at Hugo, who began to note that its owner timed her shopping trips to coincide with his tours of duty. A number of soldiers had become attached to some of the girls, and vice versa, and Hugo, who at seventeen-and-a-half had not yet been with a woman, began to scratch his head. And the more he scratched, the more tied up in knots he became, until he could barely function at all. One afternoon, while absentmindedly pouring water into the machine gun, he made up his mind to act. A rendezvous must be arranged.

Incredibly, the next day, it was the flaxen beauty who approached him. She even had the spot picked out, and the time: soon after dark under a weeping willow some two hundred yards upriver. She would come alone in a boat that very night.

As he waited in the warm green tent formed by the drooping branches, Hugo was so nervous his teeth chattered. He shoved an army-issue Sherashefsky cigarette into his mouth, lit it, then stubbed it out. He'd heard the shouted exchange as a new patrol stumped down the hill, and now all was peaceful. He'd warned the boys—standard regimental practice—that a woman would be coming over, and taken the usual amount of joshing and queries as to his virginity (hotly denied). Every splash and lap of the river against the bank almost at his feet he attributed to her. At last the unmistakable squeak of an oarlock made him jump.

It sounded very close. He parted the green tresses of his hideout and saw the boat angling in on the current. A thin mist hovered over the water, and the sight of his beloved—in his mind she had become that—hunched over the oars, floating toward him, her hair concealed in an enveloping cloak, quite soothed away his tension. All his mother's stories, all the books he'd read, now it was happening to him: in a word, romance. And it was every bit as magical as he'd anticipated. Letting the willow fronds fall, he stood listening, and a great longing surged in him. A slight scrunch, and the boat nudged the muddy bank a couple of yards away. He would wrap his arms about her and kiss her full on the lips, holding her tight against his body so that their hearts beat as one . . .

A gentle rustling, the branches parted. Incredible. It couldn't be. No flaxen maiden here. No red lips. The cloak fell to the ground. "Disappointed, eh?" said the visitor, and grinned.

Hugo stood speechless. In two strides his brother was face to face with him, had reached out and was hugging him. Hugo held on, mechanically, then, gradually, returned the pressure.

"I heard you were asking for me." They stepped back, taking each other in. Hugo shook his head unbelievingly. This was it, the big moment, Viktor, found, here with him. He looked tougher, Hugo thought. Perhaps it was the scraggly beard that hugged his jawline, or a keenness of eye he hadn't had before. Fumbling in his pocket, Hugo brought out cigarettes, then struck a match that served them both.

They talked of home, and in doing so seemed to drop a scrim over the past, behind which familiar figures moved, but eerily, like ghosts. Viktor hadn't been back either. Maybe some day. Right now, he boasted, he was fighting against everything his father represented: the entrenched self-interest of the ruling class the old man served so unquestioningly, the very cause of all the misery around them. Though ironically the war had not turned out altogether bad, like a gigantic boil bursting in the face of the oppressor.

"Good for Poland at any rate," Hugo put in.

And Viktor smiled, shaking his head, disagreeing. "Don't you see, what you're fighting for is just more of the same: more war, more exploitation, more misery. Poland, Germany, Austria, France . . . As long as there's nationalism there'll never be peace."

"Then who are *you* fighting for?" Hugo challenged hotly.

"Not who, what. The brotherhood of man, if you like. It's got to start somewhere, and right now it's taking root over there, on Russian soil." He pointed across the river. "It's a chance in a millenium to put things right. We need you, Hugo. You're wasted here. Together we could do great things. So many times I've thought to myself, 'If only Hugo were here.' "

"What sort of things?"

"They're sending me north. There's a big move on to tie up the ports so the imperialist powers can't send arms and ammo against us that way. You and me, with our Polish, German, and Russian, could talk to the men, get them to see where their real interests lie. And who knows, we might even sign up as crew and spread our ideas all over the world, from port to port. We could set the world on fire with a new idea."

From port to port, all across the world. China, Africa, America, the two of them. The vision was mesmerizing. Already Viktor was talking as if it was within his grasp to bring it about.

"Let's go back now, together," Viktor encouraged; "There's an old tarp in the bottom of the boat. I'll throw it over you. They'll never notice. Tomorrow we'll be far away."

Tomorrow. Hugo snapped back to reality. Tomorrow he'd be doing physical jerks in the yard up on the hill. How could he go with Viktor? It was too sudden, too much like betrayal.

He pressed on Viktor all his cigarettes and watched the boat edge out into the current. Now, climbing the hill in the moonlight, he remembered one thing he hadn't given him: his coin. He cursed himself for a fool. Would there ever be another chance? Day after day, as summer slowly turned to fall, he looked for the girl with the flaxen hair. She never returned. With the fall came marching orders. North. He too was going north. North to Wilno, by train. More frontiers to defend, this time from the Lithuanians.

CHAPTER

10

.

EVEN before the arrival of the caviar and the unfortunate incident of the *blini,* Hugo had come to terms with the fact that any enjoyment he derived from Le Repas would be purely an oversight on the part of his host, the Baron. Apparently—despite tantalizing hints—Hugo was to be kept in the dark at the Baron's pleasure as to the reason he was there at all. As for Elie, hope of enlightenment and help from that quarter quickly faded. She had described the Baron as her boss, and she behaved accordingly.

But the affair of the *blini* alone would have ruined his meal. The waiter brought the caviar and was bowing out, murmuring, *"bon appetit,"* when the Baron waved him back. "Not so fast, *Liebchen,* with the *'bon appetit.'* I do not see the *blini.* Am I blind?"

"Monsieur?" The waiter was not sure he liked the appellation.

"Blini, peasant. You expect me to eat caviar without *blini?"*

"But Monsieur . . ." the waiter indicated a basket of thinly sliced ryebread.

"You call this *blini?"* The Baron, half rising from his chair, grabbed the basket and shook it under the waiter's nose. "Yes or no?" Several pieces fell out.

The waiter wisely did not commit himself. *"Un moment,"* he said, and withdrew.

The captain appeared. He did no more than crook an eyebrow. Hugo cringed inwardly.

"I requested *blini*," the Baron announced. "The waiter perhaps did not understand."

"He understood perfectly, Monsieur, but we have a small problem. We are a French restaurant."

"So?"

"The *blini* is, I believe, a Russian speciality?"

"As is caviar, my friend, which no properly civilized human being ate without he ate *blini*."

At a discreet signal from the captain, the waiter whisked the precious caviar to safety. "Monsieur would prefer an alternative?"

But the *blini* incident wasn't closed. The Baron watched the service door swish after the departing waiter. "Perhaps I should follow him and show your so-called chef how to prepare *blini*?"

He will too, thought Hugo, this man will stop at nothing to get his own way. The same conclusion had evidently been reached by the captain. His eyes swiveled, assessing the situation. People at nearby tables were trying not to stare.

"How about truffles? You like those," Elie piped up.

The captain allowed himself a grateful smile. "We have an excellent cassolette Sagan today, M'selle: truffles with mushrooms."

The Baron threw up his hands in a gesture of resignation. But when the cassolettes arrived, he cheered up at the prospect of a new complaint: where was the garnish of sliced calves' brain? The captain, summoned, explained that patrons of Le Repas generally preferred it without, and the Baron did not press the point. He contented himself with the remark that catering to the mass taste was the downfall of some societies and undoubtedly would be of this one, adding that the chef could do worse than slice up the brains of some of his colleagues next time the item was on the menu; the difference would not be noticeable. A comment the captain chose to ignore. Hugo had a feeling the Baron was saving his big guns for the entrée, and so it proved.

He had already noticed a couple of white-capped sous-chefs peeking out at them through the crack in the service door and assumed that the comment about calves' brains had spread to the kitchen, where revenge in some suitable form was being prepared. He himself was suffering acute embarrassment and would gladly have crept into the sarcophagus with the flowers. He recalled occasions where, because of unacceptable behavior, a table would be 'sent to Siberia' by the staff; in other words, ignored. As he toyed with his hors d'oeuvre and turned these thoughts over in his mind, his sense of the absurdity of life began to reassert itself. He chided himself for being so foolish as to have had expectations of this meal. Expectations lead to disappointment, as well he knew. Here he was, on the verge of extinction; when would he learn?

"It's not poison." Elie was watching, amusement in her eyes. Hugo took another tiny forkful. On the contrary, it was delicious. The Baron had devoured his cassolette, crust and all, in about three quick swoops. He too was watching, watching and sipping, chair pushed back, legs crossed, as if Hugo were some small dog or other animal performing a new trick with commendable skill.

The waiter hovered, somewhere between nervous and surly. He bent to speak in the Baron's ear. "The chef regrets that the roast goose in its entirety will not be possible, Monsieur."

The Baron waved him away. "Fetch here the boss. Why should I deal with underlings!" Tender roast goose was an item on the menu. The Baron had ordered a whole bird for the three of them, a reasonable enough request, it seemed to him. The captain reappeared, but the Baron waved dismissively at him too. "The big boss. Do I make myself clear?"

Next to appear, after a suitable delay, was the headwaiter. "If roast goose is possible sliced on a plate, then why is it not possible before it is sliced and put on the plate? Or do gooses here walk around already sliced? Please, do me the favor, explain.''

The headwaiter inhaled, and decided to take a conciliatory tack. Hadn't he smelled trouble from the first in this quarter, and was he ever wrong? Had the gentleman ordered ahead, he cooed, the chef would willingly have prepared the goose in the desired fashion. As it was, the geese—discreet emphasis here—for today's luncheon had been precarved to facilitate serving.

The Baron was not that easily routed. He took out his billfold, removed a crisp new fifty, and folded it as if he was going to smoke it. ''Do me the favor,'' he smirked, ''to have the chef stick one goose back together. Here I have promised my friends the roast goose. A gentleman's promise is his word, you know what I mean?'' Somehow, without eye contact, two hands found each other below table level.

When the goose arrived, the Baron insisted on standing up to 'carve' it, causing additional neck craning at nearby tables. ''How well I recall another occasion some years ago when the stuffed roast goose was on the menu.'' He laid several choice cuts from the breast on Hugo's plate, which the waiter was holding. ''We were all younger then, saplings, not seasoned timber, *hein?* In those days we bent in the wind. Sometimes we snapped. You know what I mean?''

Hugo blinked. He felt a slight buzz. Must go easy on the wine. One glass, max. Neither the reference to roast goose nor the intensity of the Baron's gaze made any sense to him. And those cheeky sous-chefs were peering through the door again. Well, the old boy had cooked *their* goose, for sure. He'd won that round, tidily. To bully an entire French restaurant into submission—and one listed in Michelin at that—that took balls. Roast goose? Sure, he went a long way back with roast goose. Roast goose and Christmas went together. His mother would pluck the bird, holding it tight between her knees, its long neck dangling, beak caressing the ground, down and feathers everywhere. Memories.

"One hundred years!" A new wine had been poured. The Baron raised his glass.

"One hundred years!" They leaned together and clinked. Hugo barely wet his lips.

An exquisite salad. A morsel of cheese. The meal was almost over. The Baron ordered coffee, decaffeinated for Elie, and pushed back his chair. The time for business had come. From the depths of his suit jacket he plucked a handful of cigars, passing one to Hugo, the very brand he'd sniffed just the day before by the railings of the cathedral.

"Sydney," Hugo pointed the cigar at Elie.

"You are very astute," she said sweetly. "We had hoped to surprise you, but you are too clever by far. As a matter of fact, it is thanks to your Sydney that we are here in Le Repas."

The captain, catching sight of the Baron with a cigar in his mouth, rushed over to their table. "Apologies, Monsieur, but in deference to our other guests, the restaurant does not permit . . ."

The Baron's contemptuous glance took in a swath of 'other guests.' For an instant he seemed about to protest. Elie stiffened. Then he shrugged, removed the offending cigar, and produced instead a crumpled packet of cigarettes. The waiter sprang forward with a light. As the first puff of smoke billowed across the table, it seemed to Hugo that the smell was a thousand times worse than that of any cigar. "It is precisely the Sydney," said the Baron, "who mentioned to Elie that you had many times expressed the wish to dine here. Eager as we are for your cooperation, we ask ourselves, why not? So, it is arranged." He took another pull, leaned back, and puffed contentedly at the ceiling.

"You must forgive us, American dreamer," Elie put in. "We had to do our homework. Find out all we could before the final approach. It is not an easy assignment the Baron has in mind. We had to be sure, you understand?"

Hugo understood one thing: very soon now they would realize their mistake, they would rise from the table, put on their coats and hats, and he would go home and continue

77

packing. His letter to Father Vince was weighing on his mind. He needed enough time to set down everything clearly. Probably, it would take several drafts before he got it right.

"So, *tailor-made, hein?* I like that." The Baron was enjoying himself. He seemed to see in Hugo some private joke or the memory of a good time. "And how is your health, if I may ask? A little heart trouble, perhaps? Not unexpected at our age. Otherwise, the clean bill, *hein?*"

"You have found all my little secrets."

The Baron savored this response, head cocked, eyes almost shut, until Hugo began to wonder what he'd said that was so absorbing. Suddenly the Baron leaned forward and jabbed his cigarette out in the saucer of his cup. "The main thing we have found is *you.*" The waiter came with the coffee and an ashtray. A busboy removed the saucer. "By the way, when did you last see your brother?"

"My brother!" Of all questions, this one Hugo least expected. "Well, it's been . . . It was years ago." He looked from one to the other. Why should he answer? Who did they think he was? "I think you have a different person in mind, perhaps some mix-up . . ." He felt guilty having to disillusion them after all the trouble and expense of the meal.

"You are Hugo T—," the Baron gave his full name, "son of Stephan, formerly customs inspector of Bucovina, and Liliana, née Lisowski. Sister: Odilia, whom you called Lusia. Brother: Viktor, a year or so your senior. Yes or no?"

"Yes." He shrugged. What else could he say?

"When did you last see your brother? Is that an unreasonable question?"

"Viktor?" The name—in his own voice, in his own ears—sounded forced, remote. "It was, oh, way back. Maybe nineteen twenty-three, nineteen twenty-four."

"In Paris, no?"

Hugo nodded. He didn't want to remember. Why should he have to?

"And you haven't heard from him since?"

78

"Why should I? We were refugees. On the move. In those days, families drifted apart."

"Then you've no idea about him, what happened to him, for instance?"

"We had no reason to stay in touch."

The Baron sipped noisily from his cup. "You might be surprised, that's all."

"We went our own ways." Hugo sat very straight at the table, very alert, his hands in his lap.

The Baron lit another of his foul cigarettes, puffed on it, and managed to look like a man with a very important secret. His hair—the little that was left—was plastered across the dome of his skull and escaped in tufts above his ears. It was a yellowish off-white, stained, Hugo surmised, by the smoke that clung around it. Come to think of it, his whole head looked smoked, like a ham. Though deeply furrowed, the flesh seemed oddly well preserved. He seemed ageless. "As I was saying," the Baron paused, watching for the effect of his words, "you may be surprised. He—how do you say—he changed his heart."

"Had a change of heart," Elie clarified.

"He's alive?" Hugo said. It was too late, much too late. There was nothing to be done now. An item of historical interest, that was all. "Where?"

"Back there, in the old country. He has a church. Perhaps you will not believe. He wears—how do you say—the holy collar." With a nicotine-stained finger, the Baron indicated his neck.

"A dog collar," said Elie.

Hugo found he was not surprised. Hadn't Viktor always been somebody's dog?

"For twenty years he is in Siberia. Hard labor, you understand? Building the canal. Nineteen fifty-six, they let him out. He is very quiet, very good boy, they think at first. He has small village church. No problem. But slowly, quietly, he is training young men, young priests, troublemakers in fact for the Party, and this small church becomes the shrine, the memorial, understand, to all Poles who perished in the

Soviet Union. This the Party does not like at all. They find embarrassing. To tell the truth, he has become like an idol, this man. Always they are looking for ways to destroy him. Not to kill, you understand, and create the martyr, but to kill the people's belief in him. Now, at last, they think they have found a way."

In spite of himself, Hugo was listening, and listening intently. It had ceased to be his brother's story that the Baron was telling; it was a good story in itself.

"In a short time," the Baron went on, "he is coming to Paris. For the first time since fifty-six this man is leaving his village in eastern Poland. He will attend some religious conference and so on and so forth, but most of all he will make publicity about the millions of Poles who disappeared, mainly after the so-called Hitler-Stalin pact. You follow?"

"What does this have to do with me?"

"Aha," the Baron directed a self-congratulatory beam at Elie. "We are coming to that. I must confess, by the way, I am a businessman. Once or twice a year, I contrive to visit Poland. My hosts there know I am not averse to a little hunting. The wild boar is plentiful in the eastern forests of Lubelska. While there this past fall, at a hunting lodge, I was able to visit your brother. Not that I knew then of the trap he is walking into in Paris. It has come to light only recently. But at that time, without knowing it, I discovered the way—how to say—to *spring* the trap." Sitting up excitedly he gestured with both hands toward Hugo, as if about to auction him off. "My dear sir: *you.*"

"I wish you would tell Monsieur Hugo exactly what his brother told you . . ." Elie began, perhaps to cover a momentary awkwardness, perhaps because she was afraid her boss had forgotten a key element in the story.

"Woman," the Baron regarded her sternly, "do not interrupt." The waiter, refilling the cups, permitted himself an unprofessional wince, turning it into a wink as he caught Hugo's disapproving eye. "As we were taking our leave, I pulled the old man aside. 'Father,' I said, 'is there any wish

I can grant for you when I get home?' Without a moment's reflection, he said, 'I am old. My days are numbered. Somewhere out there I have a brother. His name is Hugo. I would like him to know . . .' " The Baron paused, as if to recall the precise words.

Elie picked it up, " '. . . that not a day has gone by in all of fifty years when I haven't thought of him, and felt shame for the way I treated him.' "

For the first time since hearing Viktor's name that day, Hugo felt a pang of something close to affection for this long-gone part of himself.

The Baron broke the silence.. "If the question was just saving an old man's reputation, do you think I care? It's more than that. It's the priests he's trained, the cream of the crop, the most courageous and outspoken, some of them already paying with their lives. If they tarnish him, they stain the whole church; precisely what they want, these old-guard Party hacks. The church is Poland, whose citizens historically defend the eastern ramparts of the civilized world. Without the leadership of the church to guide and support it, the new emerging Poland we are witnessing will stumble and fall back into the clutches of these Communist traitors. Do you see what I mean?" Carried away with his rhetoric, the Baron dabbed his forehead with a napkin. His medals sparkled.

"So," Elie said brightly, "what do you say?" They fixed him with hungry looks.

Sure, thought Hugo, whatever harebrained scheme they had in mind, he'd go along. Why not? He would not be around to participate. "You'll have to give me a couple of days," he said, "to tidy things up."

CHAPTER

11

CURIOSITY may not be good for cats, but for Hugo T it was the very staff of life. One of his delights was to open the daily newspaper to see what his fellow earthlings had got up to in the preceding twenty-four hours. This curiosity of his did not extend beyond the grave, and though Father Vince had done his best to dangle before his friend's eyes some of the blessings in store for repentent sinners in the world to come—such as reunions with loved ones—Hugo remained skeptical. Had he believed, he might have looked forward to his rendezvous with the George Washington Bridge, if solely out of curiosity. As things were, he was beginning to dread it.

It had something to do with the lunch. Curiosity played a part here too. What did they want him to do, the Baron and Elie? They hadn't spelled it out. Such an odd pair, Hugo reflected. Why would she work for a man like that? A title hides a multitude of sins. Witness the famous Baron Gutmann, the Hungarian cardsharp, with his two accomplices, so-called "waiters." The judge at his fraud trial in Vienna played thirteen rounds of poker using Gutmann's method and found no way he couldn't win. That 'baron' got ten years.

Funny about Viktor, after all this time. The pang of nostalgia he experienced for his brother surprised him. Siberia! Perhaps it did him good, brought him to his senses. But how much of the Baron's story was true? Certainly there was a basis in fact, their pet name for his sister, for instance, Lusia. How many people would know that? Perhaps the fellow really had seen Viktor. At any rate, why speculate? The whole thing was cloud cuckoo land as far as Hugo was concerned. He had other fish to fry.

He must write a note for Elie: he was sorry, he'd changed his mind, gone to Chicago. Something along those lines. He didn't want them breaking down his door before Father Vince got there. Friday was the day they'd agreed on at the restaurant. They would come for him Friday. If they wanted him that badly, they'd have to fish him out of the river.

Around midnight Hugo fixed himself tea with honey and a dash of apple cider vinegar (his antidote to arthritis) and sat at the kitchen table to take stock. His packing was now virtually done, everything in tidy piles, clearly labeled for Father Vince to deal with. Tomorrow—when he was less tired—he would sit down and write the letter to Vince explaining everything. On his Friday visit, the priest would find it on the kitchen table. Then Thursday, depending on the weather, Hugo would set off bright and early to walk to the bridge, dropping off his keys at the rectory on the way. He would take it easy, stopping here and there as he fancied, remembering old times, saying good-bye. The walk might take all day.

Things to do tomorrow, Hugo wrote on his yellow pad, and underlined it. "Letter for Father Vince, Envelope for Keys, Letter to Elie (mail), Clean out Refrigerator, Visit Cassidy in the Hospital." He felt bad about Cassidy, even a little guilty. While Cassidy was throwing his life savings away and getting his head bludgeoned for nothing, his wife was probably thousands of miles away in Mexico not giving him a thought. The sooner Hugo could put him wise the better. He switched out the table lamp, gathered up the tea things, and was about to rise. On second thought, he pulled the pad toward him and made a final entry: "Jacques." If he had time after everything else, he'd go by Le Repas. If Jacques was on duty outside, maybe he'd find out from him a thing

or two about the Baron. Word would have gotten round.
What the hell. He was curious.

Dear Father Vince,
  (It was the following morning. Hugo sweated over
the most important letter of his life.)
  By the time you read this, I will be floating out
into the Atlantic Ocean to make a tasty Snack for
JAWS, unless I snag under one of the Piers and they
fish me out and I end up in the City Morgue cooling
my Heels! Can I ask you a big Favor? If I do get
"caught" for some Reason, and if you hear about it,
I would like my Remains to be cremated, in case
they try to put me in "Potters Field." I enclose an
Ad clipped out of the Paper a few Years back from a
Place in the Bronx that does Everything for $275
"No Frills." Perhaps the Price has gone up. If so you
will find over $500 in my Bankbook which I enclose
for all your Expenses. As you will also see, I made a
Will and had it notarized for $2 at the Bank leaving
Everything to you, the Contents of the Apartment
and so on.
  As to the "Penthouse," I have arranged
Everything with Labels, so that whatever you do not
want can be taken by St. Vincent de Paul or another
Charity. When SHE comes with her itchy Fingers, I
don't want her to get anything except Junque. The
Rent has been paid to the end of February so she has
no Excuse to come in; also the Electricity and Gas.
  I know you have another Opinion about what I
am doing, but I'm an old Man and have had my
Life. This is nothing to me. I have no Faith in
Hospitals or "Social Services." Look at the "Oldies"
you pass every Day struggling just to lift a Foot onto
the Sidewalk after crossing the Street. Imagine the
five flights to my "Penthouse" in a Year or two! Do
you blame me? I know you would try to talk me out

of it, and probably succeed. You see what a Coward you have for a Friend.

About my Ashes. If it comes to that, you can buy an Urn at Woolworths and keep them on the Mantlepiece at the Rectory with my Photo and a Sign saying "Before" and "After" as a Reminder of what will happen or a Conversation Piece. Or you can sprinkle them on my "Forty Acres," the tree-pit outside the street door, as Fertilizer. It would be interesting to see whether the Plants shoot up or die.

Please intercede with St. Pete so that he'll let me in. And so he'll give me a good Job. He probably won't give up to be Doorman so easily, so maybe just cleaning around the Lobby.

I am sorry to put you to so much trouble on my Account. Thank you for your Friendship during all these Years. Good-bye, Hugo.

P.S. If you don't need the Money in the Bank, on Account of no Funeral, why not throw a Party for old Hugo at Mama Leone's and take the Fathers to a Show afterwards. Oo la la!

Hugo completed a final draft of the letter, reread it catching a couple of misspellings, and attached to it the various documents mentioned. A great relief invaded him. He sat for a while at the table trying to think of some aspect he might have overlooked, and couldn't. All was ready. Was this how astronauts felt just before they launched into space?

By the clock on the kitchen dresser, he saw it was not yet two. Plenty of time to visit the hospital before dark, and even squeeze in the trip downtown. He stood at the window, contemplating the weather. Still dry, thank goodness, though soft gray clouds with ominous dark underbellies lowered in the west. An involuntary shiver passed through him as he wondered what tomorrow held.

Dressed warmly, not forgetting his umbrella, Hugo took the stairs slowly, stopping at each landing to listen. At one point he heard the thud of the front door; peering down the well he saw no one. He had to be extra careful now. Not only had he Mrs. Foley and Herself (plus her minions) to contend with, but, even more worrisome, Elie and her companion on the second floor. And the companion he hadn't even seen, except for his shoes under the door.

Approaching the second floor, he was of two minds: to pass by normally, as if he were going out, say, for milk and the paper, or to sneak by and risk raising all sorts of suspicions if he were caught. He settled on the former and was glad: a quick look back revealed the feet on guard duty. It crossed his mind that they were cutouts, or else why didn't they move?

At the hospital Hugo had little luck. He found Cassidy's door closed and a large gentleman in a security guard's uniform seated outside on a small folding chair reading a comic. "No way," this gentleman told Hugo several times. They seemed the only two words he knew. At the nurses' station, he asked the nurse on duty how Cassidy was coming along.

"Oh, much better. The bandages are off. He has his fish in there with him." She smiled brightly.

"The guard wouldn't let me in."

"Don't take it personally," she said soothingly. "Yesterday he wouldn't admit the doctor."

"What's the problem?"

She shrugged. "No problem. A patient can hire a guard if he wants to. Frank Sinatra had two when he was here."

"He's a celebrity. Cassidy's a waiter."

"He knows a lot about fish. You won't believe what he told me. There's a tropical variety where the female of the species can destroy a male fish it doesn't like just by staring at it. Like some fish you can't put in the same tank because they rip each other apart? This one can't even be in the same *room*. No kidding."

Hence the guard, thought Hugo, as he made his way to the elevator.

He took a bus downtown. It was way after three, and Le

Repas, as he feared, was closed, not to reopen till six. Still, there was another possibility: a sort of private club at the back of a greasy spoon where waiters of the area would while away the time between shifts playing backgammon and cribbage, shooting pool, and losing the tips they'd made at lunch. Hugo had gambled a few paychecks there in his time, and Jacques—in the character of Ricky, the inveterate nice guy—had once or twice had to bail him out. And vice versa. He couldn't claim to know Ricky well, more of what he called a "two by two" friendship. You each made two remarks and moved on.

"Hey, Ricky, how are you?"

"Jesus, Hugo, what's goin' on?"

"So how you bin?"

"What's doin', guy?"

Thus it might have ended. Except that Ricky was genuinely curious about what Hugo was up to, working the other side of the street, so to speak. In all his years as doorman at Le Repas, he had never once seen a known waiter enter the premises as a guest. And in such company, too. "So your rich uncle hit town? You seduced a teenage heiress? You won the lottery? What gives?" He made space for Hugo at a counter that served as a bar, though no booze was displayed.

"I was curious myself. I thought you might have picked up something. Who he was, for instance."

"Who who was?"

"The old guy I had lunch with."

"You're asking me to tell you who you . . . ?" Ricky cast his eyes to heaven, or at least to the pressed tin ceiling barely visible through the fog of smoke. "Jesus, Hugo, sometimes I wonder."

"I just thought you might have heard something. He made quite a commotion with the headwaiter."

"It's your marbles I wonder about, pal. So what did this guy do, pick you up on the street?"

"It's a long story. I just wondered if you knew who he was."

"He's not a regular, I can tell you that."

"I know—they put him by the service door."

"Who's the dame, that's more to the point? Fix me up with her, and I'll tell you anything." Two beers appeared. He pushed one at Hugo.

"Sure. I'll give you her number. But seriously, she called him Baron. That's all I know for sure. Did he look to you like a baron?"

"Unlikely, I'd say, considering who made the reservation."

"Who?"

"The fuckin' Russkies. The Mission of the Soviet Union to the United Nations."

"You're kidding." Hugo was so surprised he took a swig of the beer.

"Old Cod"—the headwaiter's less than affectionate nickname, derivation: Cash On Delivery—"wouldn't have stood for it, I heard, only the ante was inflated so much it took off by itself. Those foreign diplos forget what bills are for, and in this particular case, they had galloping amnesia." He glanced around. "They say the Cod has a numbered Swiss account these days, purely for the convenience of the customer . . ."

But Hugo wasn't listening. All the way home on the bus, he was trying to work out the connections. Even though it was rush hour and traffic was at a crawl, by the time his stop came he still hadn't made any, none that made sense, that is. As he started wearily up the stairs, the shadow under the second floor door aroused rather different sensations than before. Fear, for one. Suddenly it seemed he was a prisoner in his own home.

CHAPTER

12

EVEN the day before, Hugo couldn't have imagined that the thought of walking down stairs he'd descended ten thousand and one times would keep him awake half the night. He'd have been less worried if he hadn't had the sensation on his way downtown the previous day that he was being followed. At the time—it was before his talk with Ricky—he'd ascribed it to nerves. Later, he began to wonder.

He'd noticed the man on the bus because he was reading the *Post* the wrong way up, at least the front page headline was upside down: SEX FIEND. Nothing else was striking about him—probably an immigrant, Hugo thought, learning the language. Finding the restaurant closed, he'd hesitated under its awning before deciding to take a chance on the club. Retracing his steps, he passed Sex Fiend staring at his reflection in a store window, and as he turned into the avenue saw him heading his way. No way could the man have entered the club—you had to be a known face for that—so he wouldn't have seen him with Ricky. Perhaps he'd waited outside and caught the same bus uptown. Or it could just have been a coincidence.

At this stage Hugo couldn't take chances. The options he considered ranged from climbing down the fire escape (with the long drop to the street at the bottom) to disguising himself as an ayatollah with a towel tied around his head. Then it struck him: if going down was so tricky, how about going up? Father Vince used to say that when his family moved in, he'd been passed through a window from their old apartment in the adjacent building. From Hugo's roof, which was flat, he could step across to the flat roof next door. It was worth a try.

The door to his own roof was secured with a bent skewer, Herself being too cheap to install a proper lock. On sunny summer days, Hugo liked to take a book and a blanket up there, and usually a kitchen knife with which to raise the skewer in case he got locked out. So he added a knife to the small array of things going with him: the half-bottle of scotch (decanted into an Aunt Jemima pancake syrup bottle to fit in his coat pocket), the Franz Josef piece in its plastic case, his pills (one left), his wallet, and, of course, his keys and the envelope addressed to Father Vince with, "A spare set from Hugo," inscribed on it. And, in lieu of his cane, the swordstick. The letter to Elie he'd mailed the day before. It would arrive later that morning or the next day, Friday.

Hugo stood at his sink for the last time, washing his breakfast cup and saucer. "You're going to miss me," he said, addressing the roaches hiding within earshot. He donned his winter coat and his cap with earflaps, but decided against galoshes, which made his feet swell. It had rained during the night, but the radio forecast an unseasonably warm day. He made sure he'd flushed the toilet and that the gas was off, and tied up a plastic bag with a few small items of garbage to be thrown out. After double-checking that his letter to Father Vince was in place under a paperweight, he let himself out and locked the door behind him.

The wooden steps to the roof creaked horrendously. Hugo resisted the temptation to look down the well lest somebody might be looking up. Once outside he took a deep breath of what passes for fresh air in New York City. It felt good. The day was soft and gray, and he sidestepped the few puddles in the roofing felt left by the rain. Feeling brave, he climbed over a low dividing wall and approached the little hutch that housed the neighboring door. He pushed. It was unlocked.

Strange, to be descending stairs he'd never climbed. Like spending money you hadn't earned, perhaps. He met no one. The nine-to-fivers would have left already. Out the front door he turned right to avoid the chicken eyes of Mrs. Foley, even though it meant walking an extra block. At the rectory he sealed his keys in the envelope and dropped them through the mail slot. So confident was he that his ploy had worked and that no one had seen him leave, he almost abandoned the little ruse he'd thought up overnight. But since it hardly took him out of his way, he went ahead anyway. Entering the nearby hospital by a side door, he rode the elevator to four as if to visit Cassidy. Then he rode down and left by the main entrance.

A few minutes later, waiting to cross Park Avenue, Hugo took stock. He'd been so caught up in planning his escape from his penthouse that he'd lost sight of the greater escape he was undertaking. Here he was, launched inexorably, no turning back. He looked south down the great sweep of the avenue, its medians set with Christmas trees, its lights changing from red to green, to the blur of the Pan Am Building. Such a familiar view, and he'd never see it again. Yet instead of regret, a kind of peace invaded him, pushing out all the bustle and worry of the past few days, so that he stood through several changes of light oblivious to the clangor of the traffic.

Entering Central Park, Hugo's mood of calm, almost of resignation, stayed with him. Not even the shrieks of schoolchildren playing tag on the grass disturbed it. He leaned for a while against a stone balustrade overlooking the Bethesda Fountain and the lake. There was no wind, and all around gray skeletons of trees reached up into the soft, gray sky. It was the dying season. A photographer was setting up a shot of a model in a scanty summer outfit. Hugo wondered how the model could stand the cold. Next summer's fashions. His private preview. How styles had changed in his time.

He walked on around the lake, like a country gent enjoying the amenities of his estate. Every few yards he stopped and leaned on his swordstick, the better to appreciate some new marvel: the perfect circles on the smooth face of a puddle, the wet, black bough of a tree, the slow pirouette of a dead leaf, the bursting brightness of some berries. For a short time, he sat in a Japanese-style summerhouse at the water's edge, attracting a flotilla of ducks that drifted away when their hopes proved groundless. If only he'd brought some bread. Normally, by this time the lake was frozen over. The ducks must be happy.

What Hugo didn't notice was a cyclist who was having more than a fair share of trouble on the road some twenty yards away. It might have struck him as odd that the man— or woman, the obscuring helmet made it difficult to tell— first let air out of one tire and pumped it up, then did the same for the other. Then appeared to repeat the process. But Hugo was absorbed by the ducks. Had he noticed the troubled cyclist, he'd most likely just have felt sorry for him.

Meandering north, Hugo began to feel hungry. He knew a comfortable coffee shop with a nice men's room on Broadway in the Eighties—if it hadn't been replaced by a trendy ice cream parlor or a health spa—and set his course for it. As he left Central Park and worked his way west down gloomy side streets, he felt the weight of Franz Josef nestling in his pocket, and it put him in mind of his brother. If Viktor was in trouble—and it seemed he was—was there nothing Hugo should do about it? Perhaps Viktor *had* changed. Perhaps . . . But no. It was too late. He increased his pace as if to put the thought behind him.

The Mermaid Restaurant was on a Broadway block that had somehow been overlooked by developers. In other words, they had looked it over and were biding their time. Hugo had lived in the neighborhood on his *official* first visit to New York in the forties, when you could rent a room for five bucks a week. He had moved out when his large Irish landlady had made advances he considered life-threatening, otherwise he'd be a millionaire, the prices these places were fetching today. He slid gratefully into a booth, wiped the drip from his nose, and craned around.

There it was, the familiar yellow landmark. On his infrequent visits over the years, Hugo looked forward to the dynamic little waitress from Sofia with the beehive hairdo. They'd hit it off famously, and she'd recounted the dramatic story of her escape with her small son from Bulgaria and her husband. Well-meaning friends had tried to wean Dimitriana—that was her name—from the embarrassing (to them) affectation. Hugo frankly admired it, and understood. The beehive reminded her that she was an American.

"What trouble you in now?" a crackly voice whispered in his ear. Dimitriana handed him the menu.

"Corn muffin toasted, tea with lemon."

"You hear what I say?"

"Ask no questions, hear no lies."

"So who they after? Nobody else come in. I am telling them with eyes shut, just by smell."

He glanced around. "Telling who?"

"Our friends from secret police. This one who come in, he is on your heel. You watch, I take order. Opera cake. Always opera cake they are having. You know why? Most bourgeois item on menu."

Hugo watched her taking a man's order at a booth near the door. He looked harmless enough, middle-aged, clean shaven, brown leather jacket, a small-time salesman or city employee. Dimitriana returned with the corn muffin. "Opera cake," she snorted, managing to combine triumph with scorn. "Bulgaria, no. I think maybe Ukraine."

When Hugo came back from the men's room, she had fresh news. "He is talking into small telephone," she whispered.

Dimitriana prided herself on being an expert on the dark underside of Communist bureaucracy. She'd observed them for years. She'd been married to one. They had shadowed her even in New York. She knew they didn't sit around in dingy cafes for the fun of it. "Okay," she said, "you forget here your hat. You come back. We see."

When it was time to go, Hugo left his hat on the seat. He walked to the end of the block, turned round and started back, almost colliding with the man in the brown leather jacket. Dimitriana produced the hat. "You take care," she crackled.

Hugo walked west toward the river and the park that hugs its bank, to get away from dingy streets and stretch limousines with dark windows that might vaccuum an old man up in seconds like a dust ball. He felt confused and bitter and vulnerable. How had they known? If, indeed, it was *them*. He mustn't look. He mustn't appear suspicious, turning this way and that at every corner. He needed to think, to gather his wits together and make a plan. Fumbling in his pocket, he came up with his bottle of heart pills and popped the last one into his mouth.

The river was steaming, as the warm air hit the cold water and the elements danced together in billions of tiny particles up into the hazy light. At least that's how Hugo saw it. Perhaps, when the dancing ceased, and the particles relaxed, his head would clear and he'd think of what to do. Meanwhile, he walked, watching the river till the path tunneled down under the elevated highway that runs up the west side of Manhattan, and he found himself at the water's edge. The sky widened, the world opened up, and he smelled the sea air he knew so well.

Up ahead two people seemed to be fishing. He couldn't see clearly—they were some way off—but they had rods and were paying attention to the water. Fishing, in the Hudson, in the dead of winter! Then way in the distance, wraithlike in the mist, he saw it, the twin-pinnacled bridge. Hugo stood at the railing, his hands in his overcoat pockets, chin tucked into his scarf, earflaps hanging loose, gazing at it. When his hands emerged from the pockets, in one was the Aunt Jemima pancake syrup bottle full to the top with whiskey. He unscrewed the cap, took a quick pull, and smacked his lips. Just what the doctor ordered. He replaced the bottle and walked slowly toward the fishermen. As he approached, he saw that they were black. Ordinarily, this might have caused him a twinge of alarm. Today, he was grateful. It seemed unlikely that the people Dimitriana had warned him about would be black.

Hugo sat on a bench some yards away and settled down to some serious planning. Since the bench was set back somewhat from the water, he could see a considerable stretch of pathway left and right, and so far nobody was in sight. He was beginning to hope that the whole thing was a false alarm. Dimitriana was jumpy, even paranoid, over such things. She had fled from a vindictive husband who had had her pursued and tormented for years right here in New York. And who could blame her? What with Hugo showing the strains of the previous days, and a Ukrainian happening to walk into the restaurant behind him . . .

Out of the corner of his eye, Hugo saw movement. A man had strolled to the exact spot at the railing where, minutes earlier, he'd had his drink. The man was looking across the river toward New Jersey through binoculars, like a bird-watcher. Where were the birds? There weren't any. No birds out there, not even a boat. Some planes—hardly more than sounds—that was all. From the other direction, a jogger had appeared and was doing warm-up exercises. In front of Hugo was the river, on either flank the men. Squeezed, like a hunted hare. Surrounding tactics. How beautifully they'd pulled it off, those Russian Borzois. Myshka, my Myshka, good dog. The hare hadn't a hope. Hugo pulled out the bottle, another swig. Behind him he heard the rumble of traffic on the highway. It was sending him a message. He knew what he had to do. The highway ran along out of sight of the path, on an embankment planted with trees and shrubs and grass. Clutching at bushes and tufts of dead vegetation, Hugo made it to the road.

Cars move fast on the West Side Highway because there are no lights to slow them down. No way could Hugo cross the southbound stream of traffic, not that he greatly cared. He stood by the roadside with his raised stick, leaves and mud clinging to his coat, looking like some latter-day Moses trying to part the Red Sea. At last a car pulled over and stopped, not a yellow cab but, at that point, who was fussy? "The George Washington Bridge," Hugo urged, as soon as he could get the door open.

"You got cash?" asked the driver, laconically.

"Plenty," gasped Hugo, and collapsed on the back seat. The car swerved into the traffic, heading south.

CHAPTER

13

HUGO T spent the coldest winter of his life patrolling the frozen River Dvina, at that time the Russian border, some fifty miles northeast of Wilno. It was so cold that watches were relieved every half hour. In the spring the Red Army counterattacked—"Urrah! Urrah!"—and chased the Poles all the way back to Warsaw. But a last-ditch stand, with women, old men, and children scooping out trenches, and help from the French, somehow reversed the Polish fortunes. During the retreat Hugo lost his shoes. After delousing and the issuing of new uniforms—an American one for him this time—the regiment rested at Bialystok, where Hugo was picked out by his company commander for NCO school. But he'd had his fill of war for the time being. Demobilized, at nineteen he was already a veteran campaigner.

The exceptionally hot European summer of 1921 found him in Gdynia measuring logs. The logs arrived by train, were measured in three places and dragged by oxen to the new harbor being built by the Polish government on the Gulf of Danzig. There they were rammed into place by steam engine. Gdynia at that time comprised just a few houses, in the biggest of which, the Inn Under the Oak, Hugo rented a room. It was an undemanding life. Of an evening he would sit at a trestle table under the spreading branches of the ancient oak and banter with the locals who spoke an old Slavic dialect he found amusing.

One evening after work, he was sitting as usual with a beer under the tree and noticed a woman approaching carrying a small suitcase. To accommodate the tree, the road split forming an island; she would pass quite close to him if she kept coming, which she did. Being a well brought up young man, Hugo rose and greeted the traveler, whom he saw now to be about his own age, and she returned the greeting.

"Have you come far?" he asked, noting her dusty shoes and the sweat that stained her dress.

"From Danzig." Ten or twelve miles down the coast.

"And have you far to go?"

She shook her head, eyeing him with obvious relish, which confused him a little. "This is the end of my journey."

"You are visiting friends in Gdynia?" Clearly she didn't live here. She had fine, intelligent features and her Polish was that of the city, yet she was simply dressed without makeup or obvious jewelry.

"Perhaps I'm visiting you," she said, and laughed when she saw the look on his face. "Here, isn't this for you?" From her suitcase she took an envelope and handed it to him.

He turned it over. Sealed, but otherwise blank. "Oh yes, it's definitely addressed to me." Clearly there was some mistake.

"No, go on, open it," she protested, as he tried to hand it back.

Hugo shrugged. Carefully, with a knife from the table, he slit along the flap. Inside were a few scrawled words on a sheet of paper torn from a notebook. "I owe you. Enjoy yourself. Viktor."

He didn't, at first, understand. "My brother! But how did you know who I was?"

"It's not hard to guess."

He looked down at the piece of paper, and up at its bearer, relaxed, smiling, so sure of herself. It can't be, he thought, he's crazy. Then a faint suspicion crossed his mind: she's in on it. Quickly, he pulled out a chair. "Please, you are tired, just sit here a minute. I'll bring some beer."

Viktor must be out of his mind to do a thing like this. Had the girl agreed? How long was she going to stay? How on earth had Viktor traced him? These things tumbled around in his head as he made for the inn. Thank God, yes, they had an extra room. It was in the attic, but it had a bed. He took it for the girl.

Viktor, she told him, had put into the port of Danzig on a boat—he had some menial crew job with one of the international lines—but it had only docked for one night. How he'd known Hugo's whereabouts was a mystery that Liesl— the girl—could not shed light on. She insisted she was just a messenger who'd met Viktor on the boat. As to how long she planned to stay, a day, a week, it didn't matter. She was on holiday. Eventually, she would make her way back to Hamburg, to her job as a schoolteacher.

Gradually, Hugo relaxed. Living with soldiers for a couple of years, he'd had little chance to talk "properly" to a woman. But by the end of dinner, he felt like a pro. She clearly relished his tales of life in the Polish Army and became appropriately solemn at the (slightly exaggerated) accounts of his close calls with death on the battlefield. She seemed content with her room, and he went to bed in an excellent frame of mind, very much looking forward to the morning—which was Sunday—and to showing Liesl around. He had it in mind to have the kitchen pack a picnic lunch, which they could take up the coast to a sandy beach he knew of.

The night was hot, but for Hugo not unbearably so. His corner room had two windows, which allowed for a slight breeze. Stretched out naked on the sheet, he was soon snoring peacefully. He awoke in a still-dark chamber to a wonderful sensation centered in the region of his groin but pleasurably suffusing his whole body. For a while he lay, drowsy and immobile, not wanting to spoil the dream; and only gradually did he become aware that he was not alone.

99

Something soft and caressing was stretched beside him, not unrelated to the way he felt. Soon he heard a voice whispering close to his ear, "It was so hot up there, I couldn't sleep." Hugo fished around in his mind for the name that went with the voice, failed to find it, and drifted back to sleep with the overriding sensation that it didn't much matter.

In the morning he appeared for breakfast to find that Liesl had beaten him to it. In neither look nor word did she give the slightest sign that anything had happened. Not even when the innkeeper's wife asked perfunctorily how he'd slept, and he'd replied "Pleasant enough dreams," did she betray a thing. How do two people end up in each other's arms? Usually when one of them engineers it. And Liesl's chance was soon to come. They walked the couple of miles to Hugo's sandy bay and sat on a log watching the tide coming in. "I'm learning to swim," he confessed, shyly.

"Then I'll give you a lesson," she didn't miss a beat. "Perhaps you'll become a sailor like . . . well, like your brother."

As it happened, Hugo had on his swimming trunks under his trousers. She tucked up her dress and they waded into the sea. Soon he was earnestly attempting the breast stroke, holding onto Liesl with one hand and maneuvering in a circle around her. It was while she was showing him how to float on his back that the accident happened. Either she leaned back too far and lost her balance, or tripped on something, or—most likely—neither. Whatever it was, she was down, she was wet, and she kept going out to sea in a powerful backstroke of flailing arms and kicking legs. Hugo stood in the water and watched with frank admiration, relieved when she turned and waved and started back. As she floated alongside, she grabbed his legs, and over he tipped with a yelp. After that a free-for-all of spluttering, splashing, laughing youth developed as Hugo made for dry land as best he could.

Liesl stayed the full week, and not a night passed that she didn't sneak downstairs and stretch her body alongside

Hugo's on the sheet. When she left to go home, she wrote out an address where he could reach her if he ever came to Hamburg.

"So the Jew has pushed off," the innkeeper's wife snapped the day Liesl left. "And none too soon. I told Maria to give the room a good airing out."

The Jew! Hugo was stunned. He'd no idea Liesl was Jewish. The Jews in the Bucovina were quite different, with their funny clothes and hair, keeping to themselves in their own villages. No mistaking *them*. "How do you know she's Jewish?" he challenged.

"How do I know! How do I know the cat likes to curl up next to the stove. I know."

"So what if she is? What's wrong with that?"

"Ach, the poor beardless baby," she appealed to some laborers smoking in a corner, gesticulating with her brawny arms, "is it not a fact that they're the ones who've brought all this misery down on our heads?"

The smokers growled their various assents to this judgment, and Hugo stalked out. Crossing the road he fancied the inn resounded with mocking laughter.

Next day—Sunday—still confused and angry, he pocketed all his savings from the meager clerk's pay and walked to the little resort of Zoppat, five miles down the Danzig road. Here, at the casino, he lost every *zloty* he had at *vingt-et-un*. Walking back alone and hungry in the gathering dark of an August coming to its end, the thought of suicide first entered his mind. He asked God for a sign, "If You are anywhere around, show me what to do." Entering the village, he couldn't believe his eyes. There on the road were two hard rolls. Here was his meal until the next day, indeed, the next payday. Had they fallen from a bakery cart and lain undisturbed all day? How else did they get there? Later, thinking over the incident, he read more into it than a meal. He saw a profession. In the restaurant business one could be sure of food, of pay, and sometimes of lodgings—enough to keep a person traveling. St. Paul had his experience on the Damascus road. Hugo's was on the road between Zoppat and Gdynia. In years to come, long after the Faith had been ironed out of him by life's cruel nursemaid, this was one incident he couldn't quite account for.

On the subject of life's cruel nursemaid, it wasn't long before the Polish government contracted out the job of building the new harbor to a private firm, and Hugo was discharged. He made his way south, stopping here and there to find work, ending up almost at the Czech border in the town of Bielsko-Biala. Here, at the Café Baur, he spent the winter making sandwiches (and money), and in the spring moved to nearby Kattowitz, the coal mining center of eastern Silesia, recently awarded to Poland by the peacemakers. The Hotel Opawski, where he got a job as a porter, may have sounded Polish, but it was run with military discipline by a former Prussian major who came down to work in riding attire. It was Hugo's task to keep his shiny black boots polished.

Some of the waiters at the hotel commuted across the nearby German border by showing special ID cards. When, after six months, Hugo thought he'd saved enough for his purposes, he borrowed one of these cards, crossed the border—the guards were not strict—and mailed it back to the hotel. His first employer in Germany, as was required, registered him with the police. The job—at the Hotel Four Seasons in Breslau—lasted three days. As a foreigner, and a hated Pole at that, he was told to leave the country. Instead, he took the train and went deeper in. Police or no police, he was determined to reach Hamburg.

Jobs under any circumstances were hard to come by in the Germany of the nineteen-twenties. As the boundaries shrank, the country filled up with refugees. In station after station, Hugo saw them lying in long rows on the floor. As if that wasn't bad enough, inflation was sky-high. A loaf of bread cost ten thousand marks one day, twelve thousand the next. Printing presses could hardly keep up. One day in Breslau, Hugo saw an old hag on the street burning a handful of thousand-mark notes, one after the other. "Crazy old witch," someone remarked. "Who's crazy?" came a reply from the little crowd that had gathered to watch. Probably her life savings, now worth a few eggs, thought Hugo. Luckily his own Polish money was very high, and thanks to his Austrian upbringing, he passed for another refugee.

Hamburg that October of 1922 seemed to Hugo like a city walking on eggshells, and crunching quite a few. The police were everywhere—checking papers, rounding people up—and so were the unemployed, standing in grim lines for handouts. There were rumors that a Communist takeover of the port was imminent and that Red sailors had already seized a number of ships. Workers openly sported the blue cap and red five-pointed star of the Party cadres. Hugo wondered about his brother: where was Viktor in all this?

He was surprised that the address Liesl had given him was in a rundown district near the waterfront and even more surprised when the house turned out to be that of a coffin maker who lived above his business. "Ask for Willie W," Liesl had written. The coffin maker, a small bent-over man with a three-day-growth of gray stubble and enormous hands, didn't move from his lathe when Hugo entered. The man held Liesl's note in his free hand so long that Hugo wondered if he could read. Finally Hugo asked, "Are you Willie W?"

The man indicated that he was not, but that he would send someone to inform that gentleman of Hugo's arrival. In the meantime he was welcome to doss down in the storeroom at the back. Odd as this gesture seemed at the time, it came to make perfect sense. It was three days before a boy arrived to say that Willie W was waiting.

The meeting took place in a small park some half-hour's walk from the coffin maker's. Hugo's silent young guide pointed to a man standing by a pond with his back to them, then slipped away. As Hugo approached he saw the man was feeding ducks, watching them flapping and jabbing at each other for crusts. Hugo was wondering how to announce himself when the man, without turning, said,

"They eat today. Tomorrow they will be eaten. Such is life. Not so?" Hugo stepped forward. "So we meet at last, my dear Hugo." He threw a crust far into the pond, provoking pandemonium. "I've heard so much about you."

"From Liesl?"

The man called Willie W at last turned his head. "Yes, quite so, from Liesl." He seemed to think this was funny, though it was hard to tell, his face was so muffled in a scarf, hat pulled well down over the eyes. It was indeed a raw day.

"I've just arrived from Poland." It occurred to Hugo that this man was Liesl's brother. From all he could tell, they looked about the same age.

"Unfortunately Liesl is away at the moment. But she told me to expect you and to do everything to help you. I suppose the first thing you'll need is a job."

"Easier said than done. The police are not very cooperative."

"These things can be arranged. Now what sort of thing can you do?"

"Hotel work, restaurant work. But really, anything."

"I'll see about it. And Otto, you are comfortable with him for the time being?"

"He's most kind."

"Yes, a good man. Doesn't say much, but reliable. One of the family, you might say. Oh, and Hugo, please, one small favor. I would like you to cultivate a mustache. I think it would be very becoming. In fact, Liesl herself mentioned this to me. 'If only Hugo would grow a mustache.' What do you say?"

Hugo was astonished. "Of course," he stammered, "Why not?"

"You know your way back? Good. I will contact you about the job quite soon." He stuck out a gloved hand and they shook. "Till then." As Hugo left the park, he looked back. The mysterious Willie W was still feeding the ducks.

The return journey lasted two hours because Hugo took a wrong turn and found himself on the Reeperbahn. Shock, amazement, disgust, and intense excitement were his emotions as he walked quickly past the endless bordellos, beer halls, and "contact cafés." The prostitutes all but manhandled him—if that's the word—into their establishments. As if they could smell the *zlotys* in his pocket. He dared not stop and ask the way for fear of being overwhelmed. Lucky, perhaps, that he had Liesl on his mind.

A week went by—of waking up to coffins piled around him, of helping Otto lift and carry and hammer. Business seemed to be booming. At last the boy came. The journey was longer this time, and partway by tram. Hugo made sure to remember the route. At one point a man boarded the car and took a seat beside him, and though Hugo tried to ignore him, he sensed the man was looking at him. "It's coming along nicely," the man said. It was Willie W.

Hugo blushed, fingering the growth on his upper lip. The boy had vanished. Seeing the mysterious Willie in full face for the first time, the freshness of his skin, the disturbing paleness of his blue eyes, Hugo realized how close in age they must be.

"So, the job. It's in a bar. Cleaning up and so forth, bartender's assistant. Nothing much, but it's a start."

"What about the police?"

"No problem. An after-hours club, you follow? Doubtless the police have been bought off. The important thing is the bartender, to see if he likes you. That's where we're going. Just tell him, 'Max sent me.' "

"Max sent me?"

"Don't mention me. And another thing. You're Polish. You don't speak much German. You fought the Reds. You don't care for Yids. Got it?"

"But why?"

"You'll get the job. The place crawls with disgruntled ex-officers of the German Army. You know the type. They might be happier if you don't understand all they are saying."

"Any idea when Liesl will be back?"

"Ah, Liesl, yes," again the implied smile, "we expect her very soon. Next week, as a matter of fact."

Hugo's first night on the job at his club as he called it—it didn't seem to have a name—was almost his last. The bartender took him down to the cellar to show him how to tap a beer barrel, asking if he'd ever done it before. "Oh, sure," said Hugo, afraid to sound inexperienced. His attempt was disastrous. The gadget slipped out of his fingers, and the pressure went toward the ceiling. He learned some new cusswords that night. But the incident served him well in the light of his next meeting with Willie W.

Willie was delighted Hugo had got the job. He asked him, as a favor, to report any conversations of a suspicious nature. Once the tale of the ill-tapped barrel got around, it proved the perfect cover. As Hugo went about his work, washing glasses behind the bar and wiping tables, club members treated him like their pet Polish idiot, a role he found he was good in. Indeed, the talent that surfaced here he was later able to employ at the Théâtre de Châtelet in Paris, where he signed on for a season as an extra.

Hugo was terribly excited at his new cloak-and-dagger role and the realization—he had wondered at all the secrecy—that Willie W was an agent of the forces of law and order. Perhaps Liesl was in the same business. It seemed odd for a schoolteacher to be away so long when the schools were open. What a team they would make, himself and Liesl, tracking down criminals across Europe. He bought two tickets for the famous Circus Busch for his next day off, hoping she'd be back by then. Meanwhile, he reported daily to Willie, who seemed fascinated by even the most trivial-sounding exchange Hugo picked up among the German officers and showed a particular fondness for names and addresses. Since Hugo didn't get off work till four in the morning, the meeting would take place at a different prearranged spot in the late afternoon. In case the news was so hot it couldn't wait—such as a plot to assassinate the mayor at noon on the steps of City Hall—Willie made Hugo memorize a street address at which he could usually be found. On no account was he to come there for any other reason.

One afternoon when the bottom seemed to have fallen out of the sky, Hugo, dripping wet, entered the cafe that was the day's rendezvous. And there, sitting beside Willie in a booth, was Liesl. They must have just arrived, because her hair was plastered to her head, reminding him of the swimming lesson at Gdynia over a year ago. But as far as anything else went, it became clear that here was a different Liesl. They shook hands rather formally, Hugo having no option but to sit down opposite.

"So," she said, "you've grown a mustache. Congratulations." It was like a big sister talking.

"You see," Willie W put in quickly, "I told you she'd like it."

The worst moment came when Hugo produced the circus ticket. She smiled. "How sweet of you. I really don't think I can. But you never know," she added, seeing his face. She put the ticket in her pocket.

The next day at the circus he waited in his seat, still hoping. Willie's presence had put a damper on things, that was it. It would be like old times with just the two of them. Moments before the start, when the clowns were still warming up the audience, a woman slipped into the empty seat. It wasn't Liesl, that's all he knew. In the intermission he bought her lemonade and a chocolate pretzel. They made polite conversation. The second half featured a sketch called *Der Sprung uber den Grossen Teich* (The Jump over the Big Pond), about life in America, which he enjoyed in spite of himself. He took it as a sign. He had come to Hamburg in search of something that wasn't there. Now he must move on.

At their next meeting, Willie admitted the truth. "You see," he said, rubbing the side of his nose with his index finger, "you could say she is already married. Naturally, I thought it best for her to break the news herself."

"Why didn't she?"

Willie shrugged. "It is difficult situation."

Three days later, at the club, Hugo picked up a red-hot piece of news, the sort that couldn't wait. A break-in was planned into the armory of the occupying power, which in Hamburg meant the British. It was to be that very night. With the stolen weapons, an attack would be mounted in the morning on Red House, Communist Party headquarters in the city center, and the building razed with everybody in it.

Hugo could hardly wait for the last patron to leave so he could clean up. His usual routine was to go to an all-night cafe near the club, enjoy a coffee and some food, and catch the first tram out to where he was living. Luckily, the address Willie had given him wasn't as far away, maybe an hour's fast walk. It turned out to be a small, rather shabby tenement building with a little yard overlooked by two balconies, off each of which were two doors. The ground floor seemed to be for storage. Willie hadn't given him a house number, and the iron staircase rattled as he climbed. Checking names on the first balcony, he heard a hiss from above and leaning out saw Willie's head and beckoning hand. Hugo ran back along the balcony and up the stairs to be confronted by the rest of Willie, who'd slipped an overcoat over his pajamas and was frantically signaling for quiet. Far too excited by the urgency of the matter, all Hugo could do was blurt, "News, big news!" At which point Willie seemed to surrender and draw him into the flat.

After that it was hard to say in what order things happened. Hugo remembered standing in a dark hallway, the open door behind him, in front of him the mass of Willie's overcoat blocking the passage. Then, over Willie's shoulder, appeared the face of Liesl. A startled face. Yes, he was sure of that, because for a moment he'd thought, well . . . But only for a flash, because back there somewhere he heard, more than actually saw, his brother Viktor. And Viktor had spoken his name.

So that was it. Hugo ran. When finally he slowed to a walk, he had little idea where he was. Here and there people were trudging to work. A tramcar rattled past a few streets away. Perhaps out of force of habit, he boarded the next one that came along and sat miserably in the back, his chin buried in his scarf, trying not to think. After a while—the tramcar had filled up and almost emptied again—he realized he was in the Saint Pauli district near the waterfront, from where he could find his way back to Otto's. He got out. A few streets away was the Reeperbahn, and it was well-known that a glass or three of schnapps numbed the brain most wonderfully. Fog was creeping up from the river between the houses, and he fancied he heard the sirens sounding their lugubrious warning.

Almost forty-eight hours later, before the first light of dawn, Hugo managed to drag his unwieldly self to the door of the coffin maker's. He never knew it, but his orgy of booze and sex had saved him from a second encounter with his brother. Viktor had sat in wait in the storeroom, resisting nourishment and sleep, not uttering a word. In his pocket was a new Ortgies pistol, loaded. Two hours before Hugo's return, Viktor gave up and left. Was it out of fear or concern that Otto pressed on Hugo the few belongings he had and showed him the door?

An hour or so later, Hugo sat in a dingy waterfront cafe with the previous day's paper spread out in front of him on the counter. The robbery of the armory by a secret fascist cadre, the assault on Red House, it was all there. They hadn't exactly razed the building, but grenades hurled over its defences had made some nasty holes. Several people had died, with many wounded.

Among the dead was Liesl. But Hugo was not to know this till fate, in the shape of Willie W, caught up with him again.

CHAPTER

14

"LOOK man, how much you got there?" The driver of the gypsy cab didn't in the worst way want to cross the George Washington Bridge. Hugo, dollar by dollar, was trying to persuade him to change his mind. He'd gone as high as thirty, no takers.

He counted slowly: "Sixty-five. I don't know why I brought so much."

"Okay. Gimme sixty, fi' dollar tip."

"That'll clean me out."

"Okay, hol' the tip."

"You may as well have the lot. I won't be needing it."

The driver looked round sharply. Up till then he'd been negotiating in the rearview mirror. "You goin' de whol' way, right? All de way to Jersey?"

"I'll tell you when to stop."

"Man you not gonna jump?"

Hugo managed a smile. "That's my business."

"No deal. De whol' deal's off."

Hugo gazed wearily through the car window toward the bridge. He'd done it before, doubtless he could do it again, though his legs were already protesting. He opened the door of the cab. "How much do I owe you?"

"Hol' on, man. You gonna do it anyway, right?"

Hugo peeled off two tens and held them out.

"You gonna do it anyway, right?" the driver was almost turned around in the seat.

Hugo said, "It's a free country."

"Okay," said the man, "that'll be sixty-five."

Hugo hadn't walked more than ten paces when he realized the cabby had not only taken his last dollar, but gone off with his swordstick too. He half-turned, then plodded on. Let him have it. Weird that the last person you talk to on earth should be a perfect stranger. Not so weird, in New York, that he should be a crook. When he reached the pedestrian ramp, he paused again. A couple of quick pulls on the bottle. That should do it. He started across. The bridge in the still-rising mist looked somehow less daunting than before, and the surface of the river was as smooth as thick, green glass. It was the shuddering and shaking from the traffic that unnerved him so. Another swig. He held up the bottle. Two-thirds empty. True, he'd had a drop in the cab. He glanced around. He was alone on the walkway. Seemed like he'd shaken them. Not much they could do now, anyway.

Hugo took his time. In the shelter of the first great tower, he paused for another nip and again examined the bottle. Better leave the rest for a last big gulp at the very end to get him over the railing. Best idea he'd had in years, bringing the scotch, and all thanks to Father Vince declining to take it to the rectory. If he ever found out what a help he'd been to old Hugo, the poor man would chalk up a lot of Hail Marys. Oops! Hugo stumbled. Have to keep a hand on the railing. He was beginning to feel hot and tugged at his scarf to loosen it. Was it really February? To his left, in the haze, he sensed a brightening, as if a great white searchlight were burning its way through the atmosphere. Even the sun wants to see old Hugo jump. Was this the spot? Better push on; another fifty yards or so should do it. He shuffled on.

Now his eyes were playing tricks on him. He couldn't focus. Everything was conspiring to atomize him, like he was inside a big blender. The roar and shake of the bridge, the bright white orb of the sky, up, down, around, all pulsating together. He kept his left hand on the rail and shook his head vigorously. When that didn't work, he dealt it a couple of hard blows with the palm of his hand. It only made things worse. Hold hard, Hugo, it's now or never for you. Loosing his grip on the railing, he felt in his pocket for the bottle and staggered as if on a ship in rough seas. At last he got the top off and the neck to his lips. Now for the railing, which seemed higher than he'd counted on. If he leaned and just rolled over, that should do it. Lean and roll. God-dammit! Something was forcing him back. Hands were pulling at him. Instinctively, his right hand went to his coat pocket for the ammonia. It came up with something sharp, the kitchen knife. He jabbed wildly. The last thing Hugo felt was an explosion in his head, like a firecracker on the Fourth of July.

"American dreamer, are you awake? American dreamer!"

First just the voice, then when he opened his eyes—or eye, only one wanted to cooperate—the face of Elie, bending over him. Hugo reached a hand up to his blind eye and felt a bandage. What had happened?

Elie's face dropped out of sight. He heard talking. The next time he opened his eye, he saw two faces and smelled something. He sampled the smell and arrived at Bay Rum with a garlic base. The Bay Rum he found both reassuring— it went back with him a ways—and disturbing, on grounds very much more recent. Finding it a strain to keep the eye open, he let it close. So, he thought, they got me.

Elie said—and this was on a subsequent visit, without Bay Rum—"You know, American dreamer, how naughty you've been? The Baron is very disappointed." She was trying to help him sit up. "There, is that comfy? You gave us all a big scare. Do you remember?"

Hugo remembered nothing after the fireworks on the bridge. He was angry. Why should he answer questions? They were the ones with all the explaining to do.

112

"You promised to cooperate, remember, at the restaurant? Don't say you've forgotten."

With a bunch of tricksters like you? Never.

"Just think where you'd be now if we hadn't been driving by."

Just where I meant to be, that's where.

"I'm sorry about the nasty bruise." She touched the dressing. "Snagov let fly after you surprised him with that knife. He's on a very short fuse, that one. Still, it could have been worse. Here, have a look."

He took the proffered mirror and saw a pirate, the bandage wound rakishly over one eye. And something else wasn't right. Instinctively he put his hand to his lip. His mustache. It was gone.

"You're even more handsome without it," Elie said. "You'll see. Wait till the bandage comes off."

Hugo bristled. What right had they to shave him? Where had they taken him? How long since the bridge? What did they want?

"Poor dear, you must be starving. I'll fetch some lunch. The Baron will look in later. He's very concerned." She leaned over, plumping up a pillow, "Listen to me, American dreamer," an almost pleading intensity had crept into her voice, "it's three days, a week at most. Then you'll be as free as you ever were. Believe me. No harm will come to you. I'll make sure of that."

She seemed to be saying, You can trust me, even if the others are a bit unreliable. He'd fallen for it once. Not again.

The lunch was indeed most welcome. There couldn't be much wrong with him, Hugo decided, if his appetite was so good. He looked for clues to his whereabouts among the items on the tray—the room itself was utterly bland, with no outside windows—basic Horn & Hardart type stuff like beef stew and carrots and canned peaches. All the same, something was different that he couldn't put his finger on. Perhaps the design of the plastic fork? It didn't seem like a hospital, though he wouldn't rule out the infirmary at the Soviet Consulate on the East Side or their estate on Long

Island. After she'd cleared away the dishes—for all Hugo knew it was three o'clock in the morning—Elie showed him to the toilet. All very modern and uninteresting. Then she had him walk around in circles for exercise while she made up the bed. She also promised him a shower.

He was wearing a blue hospital-issue style robe over yellow-and-brown striped pajamas. Slowly, it dawned on him that the pajamas not only looked like a pair he had at home but were, in fact—he stopped to check the laundry mark—his. "These are my pajamas!" he exclaimed.

"Any objection?" Elie looked up from the bed.

"No, I mean, yes, I . . ."

"We want you to feel quite at home."

"You mean you . . ."

She went over to the closet and slid open the door. Inside Hugo saw not just the clothes he'd been wearing on the bridge, but the raincoat, suit, tie, even the ill-fitting black wing tips that had gone missing from his apartment.

"You're a bunch of thieves," he managed to blurt. He recalled the lingering smell of aftershave in his kitchen and the sound of the door closing as he looked down the stairwell. "Thieves and kidnappers and liars. You should be locked up."

But Elie's attention was fixed at a point over his shoulder, and when he turned, Hugo saw the Baron standing against the closed door in his black homburg.

"No, please, continue," the Baron waved an unlit cigar, "I have the skin like the elephant." He was looking very dapper in charcoal-gray pinstripes with a rose in his buttonhole. "That Snagov, that bloody fool ape. They shoot for less in the old days. Do you hear me?" glancing at Elie, "Unwind it, woman. We haven't got all day."

"You better sit for this." She eased Hugo into a chair and set about unfastening the bandage as the Baron watched. When it was off, they examined his head in silence, the Baron moving around, observing from different angles.

"From here is fine," he announced. "Please, no no," to Hugo, "don't move. Do me the favor."

Elie went and stood beside him. "But you can't say this angle or that angle like a cinematographer."

"Silence," he commanded. "How long did that bloody fool doctor say? One week minimum, more like two?"

"We haven't even got a week," Elie protested.

"Don't tell me what I already know," stormed the Baron. He began to pace, "That Snagov. His days are numbered. It will give me the greatest pleasure to wring out his fat neck."

Elie handed Hugo the mirror. He saw a dark bruise spreading like a stain from his right temple down to his ear lobe. There was some swelling—not as much as he'd imagined from the Baron's ranting—and the side of his face was painful to the touch. From the looks of it, the sideburns under the bandage had a couple of days growth. But the eye felt fine.

"So, we paint it," barked the Baron, "Is that the possible solution?"

"You mean cosmetics? We could try," Elie sounded doubtful, "It might be a bit risky."

"Above all, don't do anything risky, *hein?* My God, woman, everything we do is risky! You call yourself a ..." he stopped short. "Please, get a job in a beauty parlor." Holding the door ajar he motioned her to leave. "Imbeciles," he swore, before it had quite closed, "nothing but imbeciles they send me." He lobbed his hat onto the bed and pulled up a chair. "So, to business. By the way, all we are trying to do is hold you to your agreement. Please, if you have changed your mind you have only to say so."

"It's you who changed your mind."

"How so?"

"Pretending to be one thing and being exactly the opposite."

"My dear Hugo. Evolution. In this world we are forced to adapt to circumstances. You, above all, know that."

"Speak for yourself."

"As stubborn as ever, I see," the Baron pushed his chair back and contemplated his companion through half-closed eyes, the way one is taught to look at art. At last he nodded as if arriving at some difficult conclusion. "Yes. I still think a mustache suits you better."

"Then why did you shave it off?"

"For approximately the same reason I asked you to grow it, so many years ago."

Hugo felt as if someone had tossed a grenade into his mental processes. There was a moment or two of horrified silence, then it exploded. "You're Willie W."

"Willie, Fritz, Dieter, Max . . . there've been so many. If you say Willie, then I believe you."

Hugo stared unbelievingly at the shrewd, deeply etched peasant face, so changed from the smooth young bureaucrat's of sixty years ago. If he'd not been told, he'd never have guessed, so deep in its leaden coffin was that part of his life buried. "It was wintertime. You were feeding the ducks."

"Just like yourself, yesterday in the park."

"Only yesterday?"

"The day before, what difference does it make?"

"You said, 'I want you to grow a mustache.' It was our first meeting." Hugo shook his head as memory cut through the years.

"But it suited you, *hein?* I was right."

"I did it for Liesl."

"Liesl! I'm surprised you remember her."

"You don't forget the ones you kill."

"We were young. It wasn't your fault. She should have told you. I pleaded with her to tell you. You want to know why? I wanted to keep you. You were my best agent, Hugo, even if you didn't know it. In the end, the way it worked out, it was perfect. What did we get: a half-dozen martyrs, including Liesl—young and beautiful and female—the most valuable sort. A cause feeds on martyrs, my dear Hugo. And on fear. Thanks to you with your sharp ears, within days three times that many fascist leaders were blown to pieces in their beds. People said, 'Those Reds can sting.'

"So when, the following year, came the possibility for an even bigger sting, I said to myself, 'For this I must have

Hugo.' And there you were, in Paris. And today, again, for the most daring coup in my career, I say to myself the same thing. No one else will do, only Hugo. Again, as it happens, in Paris."

Hugo sat transfixed. "You're a devil, that's what you are."

"On the contrary. This time we are on the side with the angels."

"You mean you retired from that gang of murderers?"

"No one retires from the G.P.U. apparat or its successors, if that's what you mean. But at my age it's advisable to keep one foot out of the grave."

"You have some nerve," Hugo said.

"We will only borrow you for one week, a brief respite from Eternity, so to speak. And as I mentioned, you are irreplaceable. Hence, the mustache had to go."

"Why?"

"In Hamburg, long ago, it helped set you off from your brother, Viktor, who was wanted by the police. In Paris today, its absence will help them to confuse you with him."

"Paris! And if I refuse to go?"

"My dear Hugo, that is an impossibility. You are already there."

CHAPTER

15

PARIS.

From the breast pocket of his jacket, the Baron brought forth a blue United States passport. Opening it at Hugo's own photo, he passed it across Hugo's line of vision like a conjurer setting up a trick. Then he turned a few pages and repeated the process in very slow motion. "Police Nationale. Charles de Gaulle. France," he recited, and a date, and returned the document to the safety of his pocket.

Hugo remained silent.

"An old man in a wheelchair, nicely dressed in a suit and tie, sedated because of a heart condition, with of course the doctor's certificate, returns with his granddaughter to visit his family here in France one last time," the Baron intoned, boastfully. "Not bad, eh? And, perhaps, not so far from the truth after all."

"*Viktor?*" Hugo whispered, "Is that what you're saying?"

"Aha," the Baron was pleased, "the tunnel is becoming light, *hein?* If all goes well, you will not so much *meet* your brother as *become* him. You follow me? But of course not. By now you are completely out to sea. So let me explain." The Baron picked up the cigar he'd been toying with, looked at it, sniffed it longingly, and returned it to his pocket. From another pocket he produced a crumpled pack of cigarettes, extracted one, and tamped it on the table. Suddenly, he jumped up muttering some sort of oath, and went to the door. "Woman!" he yelled. A moment or two later, Elie appeared. After a brief exchange, the Baron turned to Hugo. "In a little while, in more comfortable surroundings," he said, and left the room.

"He's a slave to nicotine, that one," Elie observed dourly. "Everyone has a weak spot. His worst torture would be to sit in a room with a packet of those foul cigarettes dangling just out of reach. The doctor won't let him smoke in here. It's the sick room."

"Where are we?" Hugo asked, not expecting an answer.

"You mean where in Paris?" She smiled, "Don't ask me, I only work here."

Soon he was showered and dressed in his gray suit. The shoulders didn't seem as tight as he'd remembered. Perhaps he'd shrunk. Elie admired it, and he explained about the jacket. "Just be glad he brought matching pants," she said, dabbing ointment on the bruise. "That Snagov is as thick as gravy. Which must be why the Baron keeps him."

"But he managed to find my passport."

"I'm afraid that was me. *Starting Right with Milk Goats* made a perfect hiding place."

What an old fool he'd been. The shoes were as roomy as he recalled. "He didn't bring an extra pair of socks, I suppose?"

She promised to find some. "I'm going to have to blindfold you, loosely because of the bruise. Don't worry, I'll steer you. And don't forget what I said; just go along with the Baron. It's no big deal. In a couple of days, you'll be free."

As a canary, he thought, in a cage.

Several doorways and passages and a creaking old-fashioned sounding elevator later, Hugo found himself standing in a small sitting room blinking against the daylight that flooded in through two unshaded mansard windows. Elie had withdrawn, and the Baron was rising from a comfortable-looking wing chair by a flickering fire. He went over to the door, opened it, looked out, closed it, and locked it.

"It's snowing," Hugo remarked. He suddenly realized that the white rectangles of sky were alive with falling snowflakes. The little stone balustrades along the bottom held snowcaps about two inches high.

The Baron lit a cigarette, inhaled deeply, and belched smoke in every direction. "Here we can talk," he pronounced, "without—how do you say—the candid camera." He looked at the cigarette between his yellowed fingers and smiled. "Sometimes it is good to have the vice, no? Come." He led the way to the fire and pulled up a chair for Hugo. "Believe or not as the case may be," he said, once they were settled, "this time I *am* with the angels. You too I am offering a place beside the angels, take it or leave it." He might have been flogging heavenly real estate.

Some angels, Hugo thought.

"Everything I tell you before about your brother Viktor is holy truth. Everything. In day or two he is coming here to Paris," he glanced up at the window as if Viktor might at that very moment be flying past. "I tell you, he is walking into the trap. Aha, you say to yourself, perhaps I too am walking into it. Here is a man known to me many years ago as Willie or Max or Fritz, at that time successful G.P.U. apparat agent, who even today is glove in hand with the Soviets, who tries to fool me with some cow and bull story about the Jagiello Society and the Committee for a Free Poland. Why should I trust this man? My dear Hugo, I confess. I am no baron. I have no castle in Silesia. My father was merely a coal miner. I myself, aged fifteen, toiled alongside him in the pits, struggling to fuel the Kaiser's war machine. Whatever I was then, what I am now is a Polish patriot, pure and simple, who is being given a chance to strike a blow for the new Poland."

Anything less pure and simple than the man sitting before him in the armchair Hugo was hard put to imagine. "But supposing I am not such a patriot, and my brother's affairs don't interest me. What then?"

The Baron leaned forward and flicked the stub of his cigarette into the fire. It made a hollow ping. The flame was decorative. "That is your business. I will not stand in your way. I should think, by the by, that you'll find the Alexander

Bridge here in Paris by far more agreeable than the George Washington with all those noisy trucks. More dignified, if you know what I mean. And of course the excellent Snagov will run you down there in the car at your convenience.

"You'll not send me back to New York?"

"Impossible. After the trouble I had convincing my bosses to bring you here, how could I explain your leaving so abruptly? But let me outline the part I had in mind; something of a cameo role, but a vital one. Perhaps you'll change your mind. I always thought highly of your acting abilities, remember?" The Baron brandished the cigarettes at Hugo and lit another, dragging deeply. "It's just the old, old story. As old as your Garden of Eden. Headlines: man caught eating the forbidden fruit. Big trouble. You understand? In this case Viktor, your brother, is photographed in a Paris brothel. None of your suspicious doctored photos here. The official press. The real thing. In a few hours the story is in all the Polish papers. In every way, the Reverend Father Viktor is finished. Kaput.

" 'Hold on, not so fast,' you say. 'How to get such a priest into a brothel?' Not so easy. Average priest is not like average party functionary, Snagov for instance. Show the door to that knucklehead, bam! He's in there like a boar in heat going at it. Am I right? 'Oh,' say the bosses, 'then what are we going to do?' And this is where yours truthfully holds the key. Because none of them knows what I know. None of them knows that this old Polish priest, somewhere in the world, has a doppelgänger. In other words, my dear Hugo," the Baron blew a perfect smoke ring, "you."

Hugo was catching on. Disguised as his brother, he was to be photographed in a bordello. "But how would this help Viktor, and at the same time save Poland?"

This detail the Baron had anticipated. He leaned forward in his chair, beckoning to Hugo till their noses were almost touching. "Next day, when it's all over bar the shooting," he said in as near a whisper as he could muster, "we will have our little press conference, you and me. The entire plot will be exposed. Viktor the priest will return to Warsaw not to shame and degradation, but to the hero's welcome, maybe even the ticker-tape parade U.S.-style. The Communist Party of Poland and its secret police will be caught with the pants down once and for all.''

"And what about you," Hugo enquired. "It seems to me you won't be too popular around here."

"All taken care of," the Baron winked, "if worse comes to worst, Australia is very big place to get lost in. Also, I understand, is very beautiful bridge in Sydney harbor." He sat back, every line of his face exuding cunning, a sorcerer observing the effect of some heinous incantation on his apprentice.

The apprentice, for his part, was weighing his chances of escape. The prospect of being alone and penniless on the streets of Paris—if that was really where they were—appealed to him even less now than it had sixty-some years ago, when, as a young man, he first experienced it. In the middle of winter, too. He doubted he could survive. Yet anything seemed preferable to his present set of keepers, all mad. And as for Viktor, assuming he existed, Hugo didn't see how he could help him. Sitting there in the beam of the Baron's enthusiasm, with the snow steadily falling beyond the windows, he knew he was trapped. But traps are designed for the aggressive and the implacable. To all outward appearances, Hugo decided, he would go meekly along.

"I must thank you," he said, "for saving my life." In an odd sort of way, he meant it.

On the question of Viktor's whereabouts, light was shed by a newspaper clipping that Elie brought to the sickroom some hours—perhaps even a day or two—after Hugo's interview with the Baron. It announced the arrival in Paris of various church dignitaries to attend a convocation on human rights and the Christian conscience, or some such topic. The writer's description of Viktor jibed with what the Baron had said: "the populist priest who spent twenty years in Stalin's labor camps and has made his church a shrine to the thousands of Poles who have disappeared in the Soviet Union." It went on to refer to him as "a thorn in the side of

Polish-Soviet relations'' and ''an early supporter of Solidarity within the Catholic Church, the inspiration of many of
the young activist priests in the movement today.''

"Why did you change your name?" Elie wanted to know.
Viktor's name, in the paper, retained all its Czech sibilance.

"Easier on the tongue, I suppose." He hadn't changed it,
not really, just shortened it to accommodate headwaiters.
He was working in England at the time.

It was clear to Hugo, from the stench of Bay Rum if
nothing else, that Snagov had virtually taken up residence
in the adjoining room and was guarding him around the
clock. Every so often he would saunter in and, leaning
against the doorjamb, contemplate his charge for ten or
fifteen minutes on end, a fox watching a turkey. Hugo imagined him licking his chops and wondered what tasty mor-
sels he'd been promised and by whom. The knife wound
he'd dealt him on the bridge had been to his left forearm,
and for a while he'd carried the arm in a sling. The wounds
inflicted by Cassidy had healed, leaving an ugly red welt
across one cheek. Poor Snagov. He was itching for revenge.

Hugo felt cocooned in time and space, not dead, yet with
few of the responsibilities of the living. In an appendix to
life, as it were. While his captors were clearly concerned
that he would try to finish what he'd begun on the bridge,
he himself felt no such compulsion. That old life had been
neatly tied up and dispatched. It was over. There was no
going back. Oddly, it had ended without the anticipated
plunge into the cold waters of the Hudson. How had his life
ceased without the life in him being extinguished? He was
beginning to find it all rather interesting.

Elie was virtually his only contact with the outside. Snagov didn't count, and the Baron had not reappeared since
their meeting. With the first flush of anger behind him,
Hugo began to take more objective note of her. And despite
all that had happened, he found that his first impression
held. Which made her involvement with the Baron as unlikely as it had seemed the first time he'd seen them together
at Le Repas. Then one day she walked into the room carry-

ing a bundle of clothing. "Try these things on," she said, abruptly, "I'll wait outside."

So much for modesty. Hugo knew he was being observed round-the-clock on video monitors. He'd located one of the cameras right over the bed. Stepping back into the room, Elie looked him over critically. The suit—for that's what it was— fitted perfectly. In a dark-blue serge with no discernible styling, it showed signs of wear around the turnups and the jacket pockets. A tiny wooden crucifix was pinned to the left lapel. Elie produced a clerical collar. "We're not quite sure about this," she held it tentatively, "It might not be 'appropriate.' "

"Is this . . ." Hugo swallowed hard, "It's not Viktor's, is it?"

"The Baron is very thorough," she flashed a professional smile.

"What will be expected of me?" he asked, sensing that time was running out.

"I told you. Absolutely nothing. Perhaps they'll take a picture, and that's it."

"In the bordello?"

"So that's what he told you. I wouldn't count on it, if I were you. Let's have a look at that bruise." He removed the jacket and she dabbed talcum powder on the side of his face and stood back. "Does it hurt?"

"Not so much."

Later Snagov came and lounged in the doorway. Lightly, he passed his fingers across his throat.

CHAPTER

16

HUGO drifted south like a tourist, spending the last of his Polish money and seeing as many sights as he could. By the time he reached Mainz on the Rhine, he could no longer ignore the irritating pain in his private parts and went to see a doctor. The cure for clap was excruciating, but it seemed to work. It relieved him also of the rest of his money. A week later Hugo walked across the French border into Lorraine and, as nobody stopped him, kept on walking. He spent an uncomfortable night in a woodshed, but the sound of French cocks crowing in the dawn roused him to the feeling of a new beginning.

His first job was at a dance hall on the outskirts of Metz, making the floor shine for Saturday nights. After Christmas he moved to Strasbourg and found work as an apprentice waiter at the Hotel Victoria. Alsace-Lorraine was celebrating its return to France after forty-eight years of being German, and politicians came down from Paris to pose in open cars in front of the hotel. When, after an argument with the wine-steward, Hugo had to quit, then and there he decided to head for Paris. It was the spring of 1923, and as the train clattered over the tracks, and he looked out the window at the countryside coming to life, Hugo felt the sap rising in his own veins.

Unfortunately, Paris was not quite ready for him, or vice versa. With his rudimentary French, the waiter's job on the

Champs-Élysées he'd set his heart on proved elusive. He found himself instead working for the biscuit factory Pernod, distributing square tin boxes to small stores and groceries on a tricycle. On the lid of the carrier basket, he pasted a city map and soon learned to pedal his way around the old streets of Paris from the Place de Châtelet where the factory was situated. As a foreigner working in Paris, Hugo had to report to the police in the arrondissement in which he lived: the Ninth, since he'd moved into a cheap rooming house off the Place de Budapest behind the Gare Saint-Lazare. He was fingerprinted, had his picture taken, and was issued a *carte d'identité*.

With his evenings free—he got off work at five—Hugo decided to try his hand as a thespian. After attending a performance of *Around the World in Eighty Days* at the Théatre de Châtelet, he stopped by the box office and asked if they needed help. He was immediately signed up as a nonspeaking extra with four costume changes a night. The pay was a pittance, but Hugo was happy to feel himself part of the theatrical world of Paris.

Happy until, leaving the theater by the stage door late one June night, he was waylaid by a man stepping out of the shadows. "Congratulations, *mon ami*." Hugo felt the squeeze of fingers on his shoulder almost before he heard the voice, "I always knew you had talent. You will go far." It was Willie W.

Hugo shook himself free. "Only as far as my bed, tonight," he said curtly.

"Then let me put my taxi at your disposal." He steered Hugo toward a taxicab that had been idling nearby and assisted him into it, at the same time giving the driver the address of Hugo's own apartment.

Climbing in himself, Willie W sat back against the upholstery, all smiles and pleasantries. Even now it was hard to believe that he was not some minor bureaucrat in a government department. So much so that Hugo wondered if the conclusions he'd jumped to in Hamburg that fateful morning hadn't been a bit hasty. Possibly Willie W was with the police after all. Then where did that put Viktor? The permutations were endless. He kept thinking of Liesl's face in the dark passage, the startled look in her eyes. And Otto— silent, supportive Otto—pushing him out like a leper. Whatever it was, something had been very wrong. Of one thing he was certain, he didn't want anything more to do with Willie W. Why had he come all this way to bother him?

As if reading his companion's thoughts, Willie W interrupted a monolog on the beauties of Paris by night to exclaim, "But you're wondering why I have reappeared in your life like this when you thought you had left me far behind in Hamburg?"

Hugo admitted as much.

"I don't mind telling you, my dear Hugo, that in my heart I have the soft spot for you." They spoke in German, as before. "In fact, I feel very bad about the way things turned out between us. You left so fast and so effectively that there was no chance to thank you for the excellent work you did, or, indeed, to compensate you adequately for services rendered. Oh, I know there was no discussion along those lines between us, but we always like to settle the score, you understand?"

"I'm not sure I do understand, or even want to," Hugo put in, but Willie raised a gloved hand. He was wearing the tailcoat and white tie of a fashionable evening theatergoer.

"So finding myself in Paris for a few weeks, and mindful of your often-stated wish to come here, I thought I'd look you up and express the thanks that circumstances so rudely robbed you of in Hamburg."

The taxi had pulled up at the rooming house off the Place de Budapest. "How did you know where I live?" Hugo demanded.

Willie W jumped down. "Aha," he all but wagged his finger, "it's in the nature of my work to know where people live. To tell it briefly, I'm here to investigate the activities of a notorious gang of international criminals. Naturally the police opened to us their records of registered foreigners, and naturally I looked for you."

"As an international crook?"

"As someone to settle up with. As someone to whom something is due."

Behind them the taxi driver yawned loudly. Hugo took his cue, "I need my beauty sleep. I have to be up at crack of dawn."

Willie W got back into the cab. Before shutting the door, he said, "And that's precisely where I think I can help you. A man of your talents, my dear Hugo, shouldn't be delivering biscuits on a tricycle. Don't worry, I'll be in touch."

But Hugo did worry. He watched the cab till it disappeared into the Rue de Clichy, then turned and let himself into the building. He worried all the way up the dingy, smelly stairs, and at last he worried himself to sleep in his little iron cot of a bed.

September found Hugo wiping tables at a place off the Boulevard des Italiens. The theater had closed for the summer and coincidentally he'd found a job as *débarrasseur*, or busboy, at the Hotel Montreal. Not that he hadn't looked for something better. Every day he read *Le Matin* and *Petit-Parisien* and his French was much improved. But he was dispirited. He'd been setting aside as much as he could, not a lot, for his dream of going to Le Havre whence the trans-Atlantic liners left for America, yet on his day off, for several weeks running, he'd played the horses at the "Bois," and lost. He'd just cleaned the last sidewalk table and stacked the chairs and was about to quit for the day when he noticed that a man had sat down in the now roped-off area. "Pardon me, Monsieur, lunch service has ended."

The man turned. It was Willie W. "My dear Hugo, isn't it time you got a decent job?" He dismissed Hugo's stammered response. "Go and get changed, and we'll talk about it."

They walked to the Grand Hotel with its big outdoor cocktail lounge facing the Opéra. As usual it was bubbling with tourists. "Here are available the best cigars in Paris," Willie

W boasted, "and the most expensive." The job he had in mind for Hugo was in the nightlife section of Montmartre. An opening for a waiter existed at a famous nightclub called The Capitol. He advised Hugo to apply without delay and to play up his Russian.

"Max sent me?" Hugo enquired.

"This time, Igor," Willie W kept a straight face, "Report to the headwaiter. It pays well."

"No eavesdropping?"

Willie W's face took on a pained expression.

"Then why are you doing this?"

The pain deepened. "My dear Hugo, how can you be so crass? I told you, I do not like to be in debt. Possibly that look of skepticism on your face has to do with Viktor and the girl. Perhaps I should explain." A waiter brought their drinks. "Your brother is a man I have to keep an eye on. The girl is my eye on your brother. There, does that help?"

Hugo closed his eyes. "You make my head spin. All I know is that once I had a brother. His name was Viktor. And now I don't."

They finished their beers in silence.

"If I were you," said Willie W, "I'd go after that job tonight." He stuck out his hand. "Perhaps we meet again. In America, *hein?*" When Hugo blushed, he said, "You see, I know all your little secrets."

Was it Liesl he'd told that to? Who else.

It took Hugo a while to get used to working in black tails and white tie. But before long he found that the pockets in the back were a perfect hiding place for a roast chicken or half a filet mignon, which he would munch in the locker room when he didn't like what the cooks dished up for the help. The atmosphere of The Capitol was a heady mixture of flamboyance, luxury, and corruption. At first Hugo was shocked at some of the tricks the owners got up to. One scheme involved a wealthy American, a Mr. Johnson, who came twice a week and would order champagne for the whole house. He had a table set next to his on which were placed the empty bottles. At the end of the evening—usually in the morning—he called for his bill. Mostly he paid three times what the guests consumed, because the waiters were told to sneak empty bottles from the cellar onto the table.

Hugo soon developed his own scam. As the junior waiter, it was his job to serve the band, six African-American jazz musicians. At 10:00 P.M. they would order dinner at a table near the bandstand and pay Hugo direct, and he would pay the cashier. Usually he kept something back. At last he was making good money and saving quite a bit. Less and less frequently did he think of Willie W and wonder what sort of a payoff he had in mind. Perhaps he'd misjudged the man. The weeks went by, and he ceased thinking about him altogether.

His Russian, too, came in handy as far as tips were concerned. The Capitol was a favorite gathering spot for all sorts of countesses and duchesses who'd fled Moscow and St. Petersburg after the Revolution and were looking to snag some rich husband or just play around. Their less fortunate compatriots—who hadn't had the foresight to bring with them the family jewels or paintings—were reduced to taking jobs as chambermaids and taxi drivers. It was rumored that the woman in charge of the ladies' powder room was a grand duchess.

In the second week of November, Willie W reappeared. It seemed so like a chance encounter that Hugo was caught off guard. He'd read in the papers about a production of *Boris Godunov* at the Opéra and overheard several animated discussions at The Capitol concerning the title role, for which no ordinary basso voice would do, only a basso profundo. It was this basso profundo that intrigued Hugo. As it turned out, he was standing so high up in the "pigeon coop" he could scarcely see the stage, let alone hear anyone on it.

Exploring the building in one of the intermissions, he heard his name called from across a crowded corridor. Willie W greeted him like a long lost friend, enquired solicitously after the job, and insisted on buying him a coffee.

"What a happy coincidence," he exclaimed, "I was just thinking to myself, should I or shouldn't I pay a visit to my friend Hugo and ask him for a tiny favor. And just as I decide no, he has suffered enough, he appears before me to speak for himself. And the job?" he put in quickly, sensing Hugo's hesitation, "If you're not completely satisfied . . ."

"It's fine," said Hugo.

"Just a matter of passing on a message, a few words in someone's ear, you're sure you wouldn't mind?"

"No no, I'm very grateful to you."

"Good, that's settled then," said Willie W as the warning bell sounded. He named a cafe on the Rue Pigalle that Hugo passed on his way to work. "Tomorrow, then."

And really, it didn't seem to be all that much to ask. The Capitol had a couple of rooms at the back that were rented for private parties. One such party was to take place on the Thursday of the following week: an annual dinner of the surviving officers of one of the regiments of the Czar's army. *"Jahrliches Liebmahl der Offiziere,"* as Willie put it in German. Hugo would be one of two waiters assigned to the dinner of perhaps fourteen or fifteen men round a single table.

Willie produced a menu card written in Cyrillic under the insignia of the regiment. He ran a finger down it. Herring with garnish. Pirozhkis. Soufflé of pike. Salade olivier with game. Goose with red cabbage. Roast pork. Cheese. Coffee. Ice cream. Vodka. Liqueurs. Wines. Between the pork and the cheese, he jabbed an index finger. "Exactly here," he told Hugo, "they sing the regimental song. Everyone will be a bit tipsy. The song has four verses. The second verse begins, 'Our cross and our sword/Call us to good deeds!' When you hear this, reenter the room, approach the guest of honor, and whisper in his ear the following message . . ." Willie W broke off and looked Hugo up and down. *"Mein Gott,* if they stand up for the song, you may have a problem."

"Why?"

"The guest of honor is extremely tall. That's how you'll

know him: the tallest, thinnest man in the room. Forty-five. Mustache. Graying. You go up to him and you say, 'General, your wife is on the telephone. An urgent matter.' You open the service door for him and he leaves. Close the door. Do not follow him out. Understand?''

"Yes."

"What do you say?"

" 'General, your wife is on the telephone. An urgent matter.' "

"Which door do you open?"

"The service door."

"Excellent."

"But will his wife be on the telephone?" Hugo asked.

Willie W expelled cigar smoke towards the Rue Pigalle. "This general, understand, he is crazy in love with his wife."

"General, your wife is on the telephone. An urgent matter." The lines chased each other round in Hugo's head like a game of tag. A couple of times he caught himself repeating them aloud as he went back and forth to the kitchen. They had just served the goose with red cabbage and poured the *Château-Yquem*.

Right away he'd realized who the guest of honor was. He didn't know him by sight, but the name on everyone's lips was very familiar. General Baron P. N. Wrangel had taken command of the White Russian regiments when they were evacuated to the Crimea near the end of the Civil War. Units of the Polish Army had marched south, Hugo included, to discourage the Russians from turning west, and Hugo had followed the career of Wrangel in the papers ever since. The General had made a valiant last stand against the Reds and eventually shipped his entire one hundred and forty thousand man army across the Black Sea to safety in Constantinople. From there it dispersed through Europe. Quite recently, Wrangel had founded in Paris the fiercely anti-Bolshevik Russian All-Military Union, ostensibly to help the men of his émigré army find jobs. Rumor had it that its real mission was to overthrow the Soviet government and install the late Czar's uncle, the Grand Duke Nikolai Nikolaevich, on the throne of All the Russians.

Hugo found the general to be quite as imposing in person as by reputation. As tall as Willie W had described, his bearing and features were of such nobility that one would surely have followed him blindly into the most hopeless battle. His eyes had the steady gaze of a searchlight. Hugo had been trying to avoid them all evening. And while his fellow ex-officers drank copiously and were beginning, red-faced and sweating, to undo the buttons on their jackets and loosen their belts, the general had hardly touched his wine. Was this exalted warrior in league with the likes of Willie W? Or was Willie W the hunter, stalking a very grand prize indeed?

The pork was going down. Suddenly, it struck Hugo that he had been the world's biggest fool, that the whole reason for his getting this plum of a job was for this moment alone, the moment that was hurtling towards him: "General, your wife is on the telephone. An urgent matter." He was being manipulated like a marionette. What to do? Go through with it, as he'd promised? Continue serving the meal and do nothing? Whisper a warning to the general? Whatever happened, he would hand in his notice that very night. He wouldn't even wait to be paid.

The new wine was being poured, a *Médoc*. In his nervousness Hugo knocked over a glass. It stained the white linen like a wound, but nobody seemed to care. If the song started, should they wait to clear the pork or go ahead anyway? His colleague wasn't sure; he thought perhaps they should wait. Already someone was leaning toward the general, showing him a piece of paper, presumably the words of the song. Since it wasn't his regiment, he wouldn't be expected to know them. Hugo looked around the table. Was one of these Russians a Judas? Had one of them sold out to Willie W just as he had?

They were in the middle of clearing the pork when the

singing started. Quickly, Hugo piled some dishes on a tray and disappeared through the service door. The kitchen was down a passage to the right. Also down to the right, but closer, were the dishwashers. To the left were the locker rooms and beyond them a loading bay giving onto an alley. Hugo dumped his tray on the counter and hurried back. Between the clatter of the dishes and the inebriety of the singers, he couldn't make out the words. One of the dish-washers, a shifty-eyed youth, lounged in the passage pulling on the dregs of a cigarette. There is no telephone out here, Hugo realized, as he pushed through the door.

For all he knew the second verse had already started. Nobody was standing. Most of them couldn't. The general was following along on the sheet but not singing. He seemed quite amenable, almost relieved, when Hugo leaned to whisper in his ear. "General, your wife is on the telephone. An urgent matter."

At the word, urgent, the general leapt to his feet. No way could Hugo have beaten him to the service door. And before he quite realized what was happening, the general strode past it round the end of the table and left the room by the main entrance. Few of the singers even noticed him go. Tears were streaming down their cheeks for the lost glory of battles long ago.

> Wherever Fate leads us,
> To exile and battle or to a feast
> In the love of our regiment we find strength
> Which can conquer the world!

Hugo bustled about clearing the table and serving the cheese that his colleague had fetched from the kitchen. He hardly knew whether to laugh or cry at the unexpected turn events had taken. And what would the general say when he came back, having found no phone call from his wife? In a few minutes the general did return, and took no more notice of Hugo than he'd done before. He appeared to be explaining his absence to his host in a relaxed, even genial manner.

Hugo set out the coffee cups, and made two or three trips to the kitchen. Nothing seemed amiss. As soon as he could after the party had broken up, he left. He would hand in his notice the following day and try to collect his wages.

It was three o'clock in the morning when Hugo sneaked out the front door of The Capitol into the raw November night. Employees were supposed to use the back door, but for some reason the thought of the dark alley made him uneasy. For the same reason, he did not take his usual route home, but a more roundabout one, frequently glancing behind him as he walked. He approached the rooming house from an unaccustomed direction. A light shone in the concierge's window as he let himself in. She poked a tousled head into the hall. "Gentleman came asking for you about an hour ago. Said he'd wait, so I showed him up."

Hugo broke out in a cold sweat. "Can you describe him?"

"Nicely spoken. I could see he was your brother, or I wouldn't have let him in."

Slowly, he climbed the stairs. His legs moved but his head felt like a jammed intersection at rush hour. He fumbled with his key, but the lock was already turned. The familiar yet strange figure of Viktor half lay on the bed, his feet up, his hands in the pockets of his overcoat. He looked pale and unwell, or perhaps it was the faintly greenish glare of the light in its shade.

"I'm glad it's you," Viktor said. "Please lock the door."

Hugo did so, took off his hat and started to unwind his scarf.

"Don't bother," said his brother. "We're not staying."

Hugo sat down on the one chair. He fumbled in his mind for something to say, but came up blank.

"Remember the time you laid into me because of the dog? Myshka, wasn't it? You might want to try that again now. It's my fault. I should never have let you go through with it. It's not as if you were one of us."

Hugo knew at once what he was talking about. "What was the plan?" he asked.

"Kidnap Wrangel. Put him on trial in Moscow. He has a

lot to answer for, that one, and knows it, which is why he's so hard to catch. If Max—that's Willie—had pulled this one off, not just Dzerzhinsky, the head of the Cheka, but Stalin in person would have thanked him."

"But he didn't."

"He blames you, Hugo. You are the official scapegoat, the turncoat, the monarchist lackey. Which is why you have to disappear fast."

"What's he going to do?"

In answer Viktor's right hand slid from his pocket. "This." He tossed a shiny pistol onto the blanket. "The ultimate loyalty test. Abraham and Isaac, Cain and Abel, what have you. It flatters Max's sense of divinity."

"He expects you to . . . ?" Hugo gaped at the weapon.

"Not for the first time. A year ago I might have. I waited for you in that roomful of coffins for almost two days, this gun in my hand. You never came. Max believed me then. I wonder if he'll believe me now."

"You mean you were going to shoot me?" Hugo managed to force the words out.

"No one retires from this game, I'm finding out. Once you are dealt in, no matter how lowly, you keep playing. Or die. Shoot you? I suppose I was. I'm not sure. I was deranged. You see, there was Liesl."

"Yes," Hugo laughed a hollow laugh, "there was Liesl."

"She was killed, you know, in the attack on Red House. Blown to bits by a grenade." As Hugo listened in horror, Viktor explained what had happened. "It was my fault. I took you for granted. I was so convinced I could recruit you."

"And now?"

Viktor looked at his watch. "Pack your things. There's still time. For you, that is. The Marseilles train leaves at six from the Gare de Lyon. Go to the Messagerie Maritimes office at the port. Ask for the Chief Steward of the *Sphinx*. It's a tourist ship. There are always galley jobs available. Hellish tough work but a good place to lie low. She sails for Alexandria in a day or two. A nice warm Mediterranean cruise. And Hugo, if you ever run into Max again, remember, it's him or it's you." Hugo was already throwing his things into a cardboard suitcase. "Is there a back way out of here?"

"No."

"Then take my coat and hat. And leave me something for the concierge. I'll settle with her in the morning, in case they come asking."

"What will you do? What will happen to you?"

"We're swimming in shark-infested waters, Hugo. Perhaps I'm losing my appetite."

Jogging south through a France stretching itself in the faint light of a November morning, Hugo sat muffled in the corner of the carriage. His thoughts were of Viktor, and of the life he was making for himself. Would he ever see him again? Then he remembered the coin somewhere among the jumbled things in his suitcase. He might never have a chance to return it.

CHAPTER

17

SO there is a life after death. This was Hugo's first thought on opening his eyes. His second thought—uncannily accurate—was that they'd buried him alive. The small dark space he occupied had about it the chilling dankness of the tomb, also perhaps the smell: dead flowers in slimy water. He was sitting very low to the ground, his legs stretched out before him. Looking up he saw a pale white light outlined in the gloom just above his head, the shape of a tiny church window. And while his body seemed exhausted, as after strenuous activity, his mind didn't seem able to give an account of itself.

Then he recalled the doctor. The doctor had come to see him to look at the bruise. Instinctively, Hugo raised a hand to his face and was a little surprised to feel an earflap. He had no recollection of putting on his hat—or the overcoat he was wearing. Positively his last memory was the doctor bending over him, and over the doctor's shoulder the face of Elie.

Where was he? What had they done with him? He moved a foot and heard the clink of glass on glass and moved it again. Bottles. He leaned forward just enough to grab one. (Funny, he was wearing gloves.) Empty wine bottles. Unbelievable. Drink had never been his problem. He groped. Nothing to hold onto, to pull himself up by. With difficulty he managed to twist around in his seat and was surprised to find his knees sinking into a soft cushion. Leaning on the chair's backrest, about to push off and up, he found himself gazing at a sizable crucifix. Above the crucifix, a stained glass window in blue, orange, and white illuminated clusters of dusty cobwebs. Beneath it, on a little altar, lay a smashed vase spewing plastic flowers onto an altar cloth, ancient with dust. And on a plaque, level with his eyes, were the words: REGRETS ÉTERNELS.

All this Hugo took in rapidly. In hardly less time than it takes to say "buried alive," he had pushed open what proved to be narrow double doors and stumbled into the light. He found himself in a miniature city of stone, a shantytown of masonry. And on each crumbling sepulcher and lichened wall crouched a cat. A parliament of cats, concentrating on something outside his line of vision. Those nearest him glanced around but quickly shifted their attention back to the main attraction. Jaded cemetery cats that they were, they'd had their fill of the living dead.

Hugo looked around in utter bewilderment. Life's twists and turns were nothing new to him, but surely this was the Big Daddy of them all. Tombs, tombs, and more tombs, all shapes and sizes, most of them taller than himself, blocking his view in every direction. Perhaps they went on forever. He ached. Oh for a good hot soak in a tub with Epsom salts. He was cold, but not as frozen as he might have been, thanks to his warm clothes, which, now that he could see them properly, were the same ones he'd worn that final day on his walk to the bridge. Same shoes even. As if he were in a play with frequent costume changes. The charcoal suit from Gimbels with the overlarge black shoes went with the fake fire and the windowful of falling snow. He looked around. Yes, it might have snowed here, say within the past week, and then rained. In angles of deep shade frozen patches of gray lingered on.

Hugo made his way along a narrow passage between the tombs. He was curious about the cats and what so captivated their attention. And then he saw it, thirty or so yards away, two people engrossed in some sort of ritual. As he moved closer, threading his way among the monuments, barely acknowledged by the cats, most of which were black, Hugo made out an old man and a woman. Spread out on surrounding gravestones were plastic bags, cans, and bottles. The couple busily spooned food out of large containers into smaller ones, chatting desultorily as they worked. A veritable soup kitchen for cats. Hugo waited at a respectful distance to be acknowledged. Nothing doing. Finally, he called out, "Pardon me, Monsieur, Madame, is this France?"

The pair glanced not at Hugo but at each other, and went on spooning. He moved closer, "Are we in Paris?"

Again, the exchanged glance, which seemed to say: here's a live one. Hugo was about to give up and wander off through the cats when the old man spoke up. "Are you lost, Monsieur?"

Before he could answer, the woman chipped in, "We saw you arrive. And then he left without you. We wondered what was going on."

"The problem is," Hugo began, wondering how he was going to explain the inexplicable, "the problem is that I have no idea how I came to be here, or even where I am. No idea at all. I found myself inside somebody's sepulcher, over there," he pointed.

The woman glanced in the direction indicated and continued to dole out cat food. "I said to my father when you arrived, There goes a man so burdened with grief that he cannot even hold himself upright. Lucky for him he has such a devoted son. Then, when your son returned alone, I said to my father, That's strange. Where does he think he's off to?"

"And I said," cackled the old man, "That's what I call a cheap funeral."

The woman shushed him.

"But I have no son," protested Hugo, "and I'm not in mourning for anyone."

They'd heard a vehicle drive up the hill, they explained—oh, an hour ago—and the slam of a car door. Shortly thereafter, through a gap in the tombs, they'd had a glimpse of a stocky young man escorting a small old man through the cemetery, half carrying, half dragging him. A few minutes later, the young man had run back, and they'd heard the car drive off. This was indeed France, Paris to boot, they assured Hugo, the Père Lachaise cemetery to be precise. Yes, the month was February. The old man offered Hugo a swallow of brandy from his hip flask, and it tingled right down to his toes. They wished they could do more, but the house was already full of convalescing cats. "They get into the most terrible battles," the woman complained, "and leave each other half dead. We pick them up in the morning. The hospitals won't take them."

Not only cats, thought Hugo.

"If you wait here, I'm sure he'll return," she continued soothingly, as if to an old man with Alzheimer's.

Waiting for Snagov—the name leapt at once to Hugo's mind—was exactly what he wouldn't do. "Sure," he said mildly, "thank you, I'll just go back and sit tight." He retraced his steps until he knew he was out of sight. Instead of making for his old sepulcher, he kept going, looking for a respectful spot to pee in. He didn't really think that Snagov would come back. Most likely the Baron had ordered his henchman to lose Hugo somehow good and proper, and this was friend Snagov's idea of a joke. Perhaps he was supposed to take the hint and go six feet under. Soon he came to a cobbled roadway wide enough for a car. Beyond it stretched more graves as far as the eye could see. He'd been to Père Lachaise sightseeing on his last visit to Paris, back in the twenties, and knew how big it was and how many famous skeletons it harbored.

A heap of damp leaves and twigs smoldered in the gutter, acrid smoke blending with the steam of Hugo's breath. Neat piles of logs were stacked at intervals along the road, the stumps of branches, white against the dark tree trunks, showing where they'd been pruned. A few leaves still clung on overhead, fluttering against the washed-out sky. Here and there a burst of color—orange glads like a fire—animated the somber grays and greens. A bowl of pink ceramic roses looked, from where Hugo stood, like someone's intestines.

Wandering on, Hugo found a discreet spot (not that anyone was looking) in the angle of some steps, part of a system of terraces marching up the hill, when he heard a sound like distant machine-gun fire approaching. Peering out, he saw a car climbing rapidly toward him, its tires rat-tat-tatting on the cobbles. He pulled back quickly, but just beyond him the car crunched to a halt. Almost simultaneously two doors slammed and two voices started talking at once. In Polish. Snagov and Elie.

They've spotted me, he thought, looking desperately for cover. Then reason asserted itself. Hold on: they were arguing. In another lifetime, back in Manhattan, he'd stood on the stairs of his building and heard those same voices raised accusingly. And thought it was a lovers' tiff. *Too late schmart.* He listened, trying to disentangle the dialogue.

Elie: "How many times do I have to tell you? He's finished, he's in disgrace, he's been called back to Warsaw. From now on, you listen to me, bonehead, or you'll be heading east yourself. Now, is this the place?"

Snagov: "Who's the bonehead? I just do what I'm told. And look how I suffer."

Elie: "Is this the place?"

Snagov: "Of course. I told you. Red and white carnations, like a cross, and the ribbon said, *'A notre Cousine Cherie.'* "

Elie: "Look, *'Le temps passe, le souvenir reste.'* Are you sure it was carnations?"

Snagov: "They were red and white."

Elie: "In a cross?"

Snagov: "A cross, a circle, what's the difference?"

Elie: "What exactly do you remember?"

Snagov: "I tell you, I was in a hurry. Supposing he'd come to? What would I do? Talk football? I didn't even have my pistol."

Elie: "He's wanted *alive.* Clear? If he's dead, I wouldn't give a kopek for your own chances. Clear?"

Snagov: "But Max said . . ."

Whatever Max said and whatever Elie thought about it was drowned in a staccato drumming of car tires on cobbles, this time coming down the hill. Hugo waited for the inevitable smash. But whoever it was applied the brakes in time, and the rain-slick cobbles exerted the required friction. A smell of burning rubber drifted over the scene. A short silence, then the crunch of steps on the path. Hugo pulled well back. If they came his way, he'd be caught like a deserter in front of a firing squad.

The footsteps stopped, and an avalanche of abuse poured from the Baron's mouth in four languages. Hugo, flattened against his wall some ten yards away, winced at the scrunch, thud, grunt of what sounded to him like a right royal pistol whipping. Snagov, the victim, groaned and screamed enough to make the dead sleeping all around think that perhaps Halloween had come early this year. From the sound of it, he was reduced to a blubbering heap.

"Okay, what happened?" the Baron said at last.

"Was that really necessary?" Elie demanded icily.

"Not you," growled the Baron, "this dog." And from the retching gurgle, he must have kicked Snagov in the stomach.

"He drove to the Alexander Bridge," Elie spoke up, undeterred, "as instructed by you, or so he claims. It seems that even at seven o'clock in the morning one can't just go throwing people into the Seine without attracting attention. In this case a passing police car. Snagov composed some story about the old man having to vomit and passing out from too much vodka, and flashed his diplomatic immunity badge. They followed him anyway. He drove around aimlessly for an hour until they got bored and went for breakfast. Then he saw this place, and it seemed like the perfect solution, the best idea he'd had in years. So, mindful of your injunction, he dumped our friend in somebody's family vault and raced back to the house for instructions."

"What injunction?"

"You told me not to bring him back," Snagov erupted.

"You'd cut me open and tear out my guts if I brought him back, and feed my liver to the dogs."

"Enough from you," the Baron snarled, "I'll settle your hash later. But I'll tell you one thing right now: if you don't discover him fast, you'll be sausage meat by lunchtime. That's a promise."

"Think," Elie appealed. "Don't you remember anything?"

"Cats," said Snagov. "A whole mess of cats."

"Cats?" echoed the Baron. "*Dummkopf.* That's over there. I passed them. Hundreds of them."

"We're on the wrong road," groaned Elie.

"Fan out and we'll walk back, checking everything. That way we'll turn him up. And keep quiet. You remind me of a bunch of chimps."

Hugo heard them moving off and relaxed. He'd give them five minutes to get out of sight, then skedaddle. The whole of Paris was at his disposal. Paris on no dollars a day. Interesting, to say the least. At last peace descended. He looked around. Moss and lichen swathed everything in a living pall of green in this older part of the cemetery. Below him a beech tree bared its magnificent limbs to the sky. A pair of black-and-white birds, tail feathers trailing, squawked from branch to branch. On a nearby grave stood a vase of ceramic violets and a china notebook, its pages edged in gold, a corner of the top one turned down bearing a single word, *Regrets.*

From all he'd overheard, Hugo gathered there'd been a split in the ranks, with Snagov taking the heat from both sides. The Baron apparently had consigned Hugo to the waters of the Seine—so much for the talk of a press conference and a one way ticket to Australia—whereas Elie wanted him back alive. What had gone wrong? What about Viktor? Had the whole operation been called off?

Hugo tensed. He flattened himself against the wall, and sniffed the air. Yes, it was stronger now. His reflexes weren't playing tricks. Who else smoked that execrable tobacco? He listened, both ears cocked, for a sound, the crunch of gravel, the snap of a twig, a cough. Only the birds in the trees and the distant roar of the city. But that smell— surrounding him little by little in a paralyzing embrace.

CHAPTER

18

THEN it came, the confirmation he'd been listening for, the squeak of a car door. Now footsteps in the road. Tentative, as if someone was looking around. Moving away, up the hill, into silence. The smell too was gone, dropping its entwining coils at his feet. Hugo looked with fresh eyes at the scene around him knowing that at any moment the Baron could appear—above him, to his left, somewhere. If he'd seen the cats, chances were he'd talked to the cat people. He'd know that Hugo was on the loose, and that the last place he'd be was where Snagov had left him. The others were wasting precious time, and the Baron knew it.

So Hugo scanned the area as if his life depended on it, and what he saw he didn't like. Some three paces away, a tree had thrust its way up from the depths of a tomb, shouldering aside with its now hefty trunk a massive slab of stone and leaving a gap big enough for, well, for Hugo to slip through, though all he could see to slide into was a triangular wedge of darkness. By the girth and straightness of the trunk at its point of exit, he reckoned it had a few feet to spare before its roots buried themselves in the earth, though what else might be lurking in that space, alive or dead, he didn't care to speculate.

Nor did he have the time. One last, frantic, searching glance convinced him. Had there been a mausoleum near enough, even that would have been futile, the obvious place for the Baron to look. He had no option. One, two, three. He crouched beside the tree, the hole as dark as ever. Picking up a loose piece of masonry, he dropped it down and put his ear to the gap. No splash, just an echo. A fate worse than the Baron, to drown in someone else's grave. Sitting next to the tree he squeezed his hips through the hole, lowering himself, lowering and lowering till all that was visible from above were the fingers of two gloved hands on a slab of gray stone and the top of a brown corduroy cap. For a moment he felt like a trapeze artist without a net. Then his shoes found solid ground. Or so he thought till he worked out his position. It wasn't the ground, it was the far side of the hole. His body was straddling the space.

Experimentally, he loosed his grip, first one hand, then the other. He was wedged. Only then did the full horror of his position hit him. This was no simple grave. The stone marked the entrance to some long disused family vault. He thanked his stars for his Reeboks with their rubber grip. In the black shoes, he'd have been lost. And once down there with the coffins, fat chance of ever coming up. Another skeleton for Père Lachaise. He groped to his left, feeling the bark of the tree. It too seemed to angle across the width of the hole. With his left foot, he probed along till he had his heel on the tree trunk and the flat of his foot on the wall of the vault. Then he levered his top half onto the trunk and brought up his legs. On the far side of the trunk, he felt the end wall of the vault. He was safe. Relatively speaking.

For a while he lay there panting, amazed at what he'd accomplished. Not so long ago, he was fussing over five flights of stairs in New York, and here he was in Paris performing gymnastic feats that would curl the hair on men half his age. There was life in the old bones yet. Thanks to the tree. For thirty, forty, fifty years it had been growing, perhaps from a chance seed that had lodged there the last time the vault had been opened. Against all odds, but following its natural instinct, it had made for the crack of light, pushed through and pushed and pushed and imperceptibly set the slab of rock in motion. Two growths, himself and the tree. One moment together. What sort of planning was that? Father Vince would call it Divine.

Hugo's head was an inch or two below the rock slab. On either side of him—on either side of the tree—light filtered down, and when his eyes accustomed themselves to the gloom, he saw that the walls of the vault were of bricks roughly set in mortar. Below him, the void. He was just setting his mind to the eventual task of getting out, when he heard something. A hard object falling and bouncing down the steps above him, landing not too far from his head. A stone dislodged by a foot, perhaps. Yes, someone was slowly coming down those steps, from terrace to terrace, a ponderous theatrical tread, inexorably descending, coming for him. He was watching the whole time, thought Hugo. He's the exterminator and I'm the bug that crept into the crevice. What chance do I have? I might as well give up.

How typical of this man, this modus operandi, and how essential to his surviving all these years as a secret policeman. The minimum expenditure of energy, the shuffler on the dance floor who keeps going long after the pyrotechnicians have burned themselves out. The chess master, preparing the ground, biding his time, manipulating the pieces, then pouncing. The bully who knows precisely whom he can dominate and who must be dealt with by other means. Only this time, it seemed, something had gone wrong. Viktor's warning in that bleak rooming house off the Place de Budapest came echoing back. *It'll be him, or it'll be you.*

No more heavy steps. He must be standing there, just a few yards away. Doing what? Why the delay? Hugo fancied he could hear breathing, until he realized he could: his own.

"My dear Hugo, so this is where you were hiding?" The voice was so close, it might have been whispering to itself. "Now where would you have gone from here, *Liebchen?*"

Just as Hugo reached the conclusion that the Baron *was* talking to himself, he also reached another. The man's sharp eyes had seen where he'd been standing—perhaps the freshly scuffed moss had given him away. The Baron would now be scanning the vicinity from that spot. It was just a matter of time before he guessed correctly. Hugo could almost feel those laser eyes piercing the rock above his head.

And then, like clouds over the sun, a deep shadow fell across the vault. Hugo braced himself for what he didn't know and could never have anticipated. Something shot past him in the darkness with explosive force. He cringed and closed his eyes and when he opened them the shadow had passed. A wild ringing filled his ears, and as it died away he heard below him a scuffling and a squeaking. Then, above him, the sound of voices.

"What do you think you're doing?" Elie seemed out of breath and angry.

"Shooting rats," said the Baron, with more honesty than perhaps he intended. "One of my favorite pastimes. So, you found him?"

"You know very well the answer to that." From the road came the cough cough of a car starting up.

"Comrade Snagov is in a hurry?"

"Perhaps he's not as dumb as you think."

"Then do me the honor to ride with me."

"Perhaps I'm not, either."

"I have the morning paper," the Baron said, enticingly. "I couldn't have written it better myself. And the picture is completely convincing."

"I'm sure they won't have sold out."

"Suit yourself," barked the Baron, "but don't get any fancy ideas, *hein*. You and I, M'selle, we swim and sink together."

"You promised not to harm the old boy. Do you think I'd have cooperated if I'd known it would come to this?"

"A word of advice, *Liebchen*. Many times in the past people congratulate themselves that they outsmart me. I ask you, where are those people now?"

Hugo heard the slam of car doors and the whine of the engine reversing at speed downhill. He fervently wished the Baron would leave, too. He was cold, and the little strength he had left was rapidly ebbing. The prospect of ever getting out seemed dimmer by the second. What was the Baron up to now, he wondered. So silent. Like a cat at a mousehole.

"Do not sit on the tombs, Monsieur." The firm, precise voice belonged to one of those self-appointed guardians of graveyard etiquette. *"Monsieur,"* the warning was repeated with emphasis.

Apparently, it worked, because the next thing Hugo heard was the car moving off over the cobbles. He listened till he could hear it no more, then stuck his hand through the hole and waved. Perhaps the woman who'd spoken up was still somewhere nearby. He shouted for help several times in French. His voice against the underface of the rock sounded—to him—deafening. To get out the way he'd got in was out of the question. He simply hadn't the strength. Sooner or later someone else must come along, and he'd try again to attract attention.

Gradually, Hugo became aware of a noise from far away. It was, he now realized, a human voice, very faint, rising and falling, almost a chant. Perhaps a burial was in progress, or someone was praying aloud over a grave. As the sound got nearer, Hugo caught little snippets: references to Napoleon, to France, dates, campaigns, anecdotes. Surely a tour guide. A guide implied an audience. Relief was on the way. Hugo stuck his hand out of the aperture and wiggled it for all he was worth. The guide droned on. General this, *Maréchal* that. No one seemed interested in a disembodied wiggling hand. Perhaps the tree was in the way. *"Au secours!"* he yelled, *"Au secours!"* Dates, campaigns, battles. Aha! Running footsteps. A child's light tread. "Get me out," cried Hugo, "I'm stuck down here."

The footsteps stopped abruptly.

"Help!" Hugo cried again.

The footsteps resumed, fast, going away. *"Maman, Maman,* someone dead is talking."

No stampede of excited adults followed this announcement. So far as Hugo was aware, no one even glanced in his direction. The raconteur didn't skip a beat. His voice was fainter, moving away. Battles, generals, *La France.*

"*Maman,* look, the corpse is waving good-bye."

It was indeed. Hugo had discovered a handkerchief in one of his pockets and was brandishing it as energetically as he could. *Maman*—no doubt against her better judgment—must have glanced in the direction the child was pointing. Her screams brought the whole group running to see what the matter was. The guide was forgotten, and little Eric found himself the center of attention. Kneeling on the stone, he lowered his head into the darkness where it appeared to Hugo hanging upside down like some grotesquely carved lantern. Everyone was talking at once. A man's head replaced the child's. Eventually, after much haggling, a decision was reached: the stone must be moved.

But how? They shoved, they pulled, they levered. Eric almost fell in. At last it budged. An inch, two, six, a foot. Finally, Hugo was hauled out and brushed off. Everyone had a theory about what he was doing there, none came near the truth. Had anyone actually asked him, they wouldn't have believed it anyway. The guide, a bearded professorial type in a camel's hair coat and Greek fisherman's cap, looked anxiously at his watch. Having tolerated the rescue, he was in no mood to be further detained. Illustrious French generals and *maréchals* waited in their tombs, not to mention his mistress in the Renault.

"*Enfin,*" he picked up his briefcase, "a person of your years shouldn't be wandering around here without a guide. It's dangerous." Flourishing his cane, he marched off down the hill followed by his flock. Soon the dirgelike voice was intoning again: generals, battles, dates.

"Eric!"

Eric, who had lingered, reluctantly trotted off, several times looking back. After all, Hugo was his discovery. A talking stiff is a lot more interesting than a bunch of bygone generals. The corpse, for its part, sat alone on a tombstone contemplating a future far from rosy. He had rejected all offers of help because it wasn't in his nature not to. But what *was* he to do? Sooner or later he'd have to eat. A wash and a shave would be nice. A bed for the night. All of which cost money. He checked his pockets. In his overcoat an American quarter. In one inside jacket pocket his reading glasses. In the other—surprisingly—his passport. In a small inside pocket below that—exactly where he'd put it—the little plastic pouch containing the Franz Josef hundred crown piece.

He could, he supposed, go to the American Embassy. They might have emergency funds available to help stranded citizens. Perhaps they'd put him on a plane to New York. But his life in New York was over. And how would he possibly repay such a loan? No way. Whatever happened, he had to get away from the cemetery. Sooner or later they'd be back, maybe with dogs. Nothing was beyond the Baron.

The first thing about Paris that came to mind was the metro. It was warm. He could sit. He could think. There must be a station nearby. Hugo picked his way between the ranks of the dead, avoiding the main thoroughfares. He felt lightheaded, not quite in the world, and was happy to see a sign, MESSIEURS, next to the gates. He went in, took off his hat and gloves, and splashed water onto his face. His comb was in its usual place in the top pocket of his corduroy jacket, and as he ran it through his white hair, he gave himself an encouraging wink. Things could be worse.

A woman in a flower shop directed him to the nearest metro. Walking up the busy boulevard, Hugo wondered how he was going to pay the fare. In New York you could be arrested for turnstile hopping. He hung around a newsstand near the entrance wondering what to do, and this brought to mind what the Baron had said about the morning paper. *The picture is completely convincing.* He glanced at the front pages of various dailies. Then he saw it. A photo of a man with a face he had very recently seen. It had winked at him from the *Messieurs* mirror in the Père Lachaise cemetery. And spelled out in bold type below, THE PRIEST AND THE PROSTITUTE.

With scarcely a second's thought, Hugo snatched up the paper, plonked down his quarter and disappeared down the stairs to the metro. Sheer momentum carried him through the turnstile and onto the platform. Nobody called him back. Settling himself on a seat, he fumbled for his glasses and prepared himself for the worst.

Furtively, not daring to think, he turned to an inside page for the story. "Ambulance men carry heart attack victim Father Viktor T out of the male brothel off the Rue Sainte-Anne," read the caption under a larger version of the same picture. Worse even than he suspected. The photographer had caught the priest in profile as the stretcher was lifted through a doorway. Only it wasn't a priest at all, it was Hugo.

Some minutes after three o'clock this morning, [the story began] an ambulance was summoned to an address in the Rue Thérèse off the Rue Sainte-Anne in the First Arrondissement where a man was reported to have suffered a stroke. The man turned out to be Father Viktor T, a priest well known in Poland as a vociferous Solidarity supporter, and the place to be a hotel where male prostitutes, who solicit sex on the surrounding streets, habitually take their customers.

Father T, who is said to be at least eighty, arrived in Paris from Warsaw a week ago for a convocation on religion and human rights attended by church leaders from many nations. He was scheduled to address the convocation this morning on the subject of the millions of Poles who disappeared inside the Soviet Union in the years since the Hitler-Stalin pact of 1939.

According to a press release put out by the convocation, Father T spent twenty years in Stalin's labor camps. In 1956, on his release from a Siberian gulag, he enrolled in the Catholic university at Lublin. Subsequently, he was ordained a priest.

Father T, a virulent anti-Communist, was assigned a village church in a remote section of eastern Poland. To this church he attracted young activist priests whom he trained to work for the overthrow of the regime. A number of his protégés died in the years before Solidarity came to power, in circumstances which have never been clarified.

Father T's visit to Paris was believed to be his first ever to the West. Since his induction he has strictly confined himself to his parish, not even traveling as far as Warsaw.

Nobody at the convocation could be reached for comment.

No one at the hotel in the Rue Thérèse would agree to an interview. A man who described himself as a local resident said, "You see them going in and out at all hours. Some of them are a bit old for it. Sooner or later it was bound to happen."

The Rue Sainte-Anne and the Rue Thérèse. Too many years had passed since Hugo delivered biscuits in the First Arrondissement. He would have to ask. He looked around. On his right a man with a fiercely jutting black beard who was mumbling about *La France* drank wine from a square plastic bottle. On his left a woman was filling small bags with peanuts and hanging them on a portable display rack. Hugo watched as she licked her fingers to pick up each new bag. Perhaps her bulk, which overflowed the seat like a cascade, made her look sympathetic. He leaned across. "Pardon me, Madame."

CHAPTER

19

THE nut lady hadn't heard of the Rue Sainte-Anne or the Rue Thérèse. She herself—when she had filled her bags—was traveling to her usual station at the Châtelet in time for the evening rush hour. If Hugo would accompany her and perhaps hold her rack, they would surely find someone to direct him more precisely. Hugo obligingly held the bags open while the woman filled them, but after a while he found he couldn't keep his eyes open and dropped a couple. At her suggestion he stretched out uncomfortably across three seats, using his coat as a mattress, and despite the trains coming and going a few feet away, he was soon fast asleep. When he woke up, the nut lady was gone.

It took a minute or two for Hugo to reconstruct his life, at least the last few hours of it, and another minute or two to straighten the kinks out of his body. Depressed, he slumped down in the seat, thrusting his hands into his jacket pockets. When he drew them out, in each hand was a packet of nuts. Looking from one to the other he was amazed, not so much that they were there as at the feeling of déjà vu they engendered. Two bags of nuts, two hard rolls on the road from Zoppat to Gdynia. He was young. He'd been gambling. He was hungry. And there they were. How often, over the years, he'd told the story, claiming that the incident had sparked off his career as a waiter. But there was a deeper parallel that forced him now to think harder and more disagreeably. Why was he on that road at all? And why was he sitting now in the cemetery station of the metro? Because of Viktor, the Viktor he'd last seen here in Paris in the rooming house behind the Saint-Lazare station on the night they'd exchanged overcoats.

His bearded neighbor was proffering the square bottle, mumbling incoherently. In vain Hugo countered with the nuts, then ate some himself, crunching the shells between his palms. It would be dark outside by now. He knew what he had to do. Another woman had taken the nut lady's seat, small with a pointed nose and tightly belted raincoat. "Excuse me, Madame." She looked up, a little defensively, and he quickly put his question.

The woman knew the area, her work taking her to certain establishments in the neighborhood, though not till near the end of her rounds. She had a bucket at her feet full to the brim with objects wrapped in silver paper. Flowers, she explained, bought cheaply at the end of the day from florists near the cemetery. She made them into posies to sell in certain clubs and restaurants where she was discreetly admitted, in this way making enough to support herself and her aged mother.

"But be careful," she admonished Hugo, after giving him precise directions. "There are plenty of unsavory characters in that vicinity, particularly late at night." He didn't tell her that it was precisely these characters that he was hoping to meet.

How kind everyone was, thought Hugo, as the train sped along in its tunnel and he clutched the silver-wrapped posy the woman had pressed on him, all the more firmly as it seemed like a talisman for the new course he had embarked on. He sat knee to knee with a fat old Chinese lady holding a pink budding branch of apple blossom. For the New Year? Was it that time already? He'd learned the Mandarin for Happy New Year from his laundryman, but decided not to risk it, considering his unkempt appearance. Across the aisle was an ancient Frenchwoman in a coat of black Persian lamb such as was rarely seen nowadays, on her lap a pot containing three pink hyacinths. They'd come a long way, he'd wager, these three old people with their flowers and their memories, and of their stories surely his was the strangest and least predictable.

Emerging from the metro at Pyramides, Hugo crossed the broad Avenue de L'Opéra and walked toward the lurking mass of the Opéra itself, barely distinguishable in the distance in the confusion of lights and vehicles. Paris. He felt for the first time that he was really back. Following directions, he plunged down a side street, which proved to be the Rue Thérèse. It was darker here, narrow and hushed. He pulled down his earflaps and slowed his pace. People scurried by with closed evening faces, thinking of home and warmth no doubt. Hugo walked on.

When he came to the Rue Sainte-Anne, he stopped, puzzled. He'd expected something along the lines of Manhattan's Eighth Avenue—garish signs advertising male burlesque, seedy rooming houses above seedier bars, kids loitering, cars slowing down, cops watching, an atmosphere of sleaze and drugs. Or at least the subtler, more intense cruising scene of parts of the West Village, with its specialty bars and quaint townhouses. What he found himself in was a crossroads of gray stone buildings drained of life, a desert of small offices closed for the day. More mysterious, many of the signs were in Japanese. Nothing remotely resembling his idea of a male brothel. He stopped under a streetlamp and pulled out the paper, trying to distinguish some background feature in the photo that might provide a clue. It could have been anywhere. He reread the text, noting the mention of a ''hotel where male prostitutes take their customers'' and that ''no one at the hotel in the Rue Thérèse would agree to an interview.'' In vain he looked around for a hotel.

Crossing the Rue Sainte-Anne, Hugo continued down the Rue Thérèse, wondering what to do. He had no backup plan. Finding the place, he'd thought, would be the least of his problems. He was on the edge of a void. Just as the direst thoughts began to grip his mind, he realized that he'd walked straight past the very small lobby of what conceivably *was* a hotel. Through the glass door he could see a carpeted vestibule and a little desk on which stood a vase of flowers. As he watched, the head of a woman appeared from behind the flowers. She was talking on the phone. The scene looked most unlikely.

Swallowing his doubts, Hugo pushed against the door. It was locked. He pressed a little white button, and the woman looked up. Instead of releasing the catch, she came out from behind the desk and confronted him through the glass.

"Is this where the priest died last night?" Hugo stammered unwisely.

"Speak up," she scolded, "What is it you want?"

"Do you remember me?" he said, changing his tack. "I was carried out last night on a stretcher." Fumbling for the newspaper, he held it up to the glass.

"You're drunk," she said. "Go away."

"Isn't this a hotel?" Her attitude annoyed him. "I would like a room, please."

"This is a respectable house," she shot back. "Be off with you, or you'll be spending the night at the police station." She walked purposefully back behind the desk and picked up the phone.

In the light from the door, Hugo again studied the photo. What little of the background was visible tallied with what he saw before him. The door was glass, because whoever was holding it open—the head was cut off—was partially visible through it. What now, he wondered. Wait for someone to go in or come out? And freeze to death. He wandered back the way he'd come. On the Rue Sainte-Anne a young man was standing, smoking a cigarette. Hugo went up to him. "Do you live nearby?"

The man nodded, stamped out his cigarette, and pointed down the street.

"Did you hear about the priest they took away in an ambulance last night?"

The man shook his head, his face was covered with pimples.

"From that little hotel round the corner. It was in the papers."

"They charge too much, that hotel—it's robbery," the man volunteered. "My place, it's basic but it's comfortable. What are you interested in, Monsieur?"

Only then did it dawn on Hugo that he was being propositioned. Not wishing to offend the young man, and at the same time marveling that anyone would opt for intimacy with such a forlorn-looking specimen, he stammered something about waiting for a particular friend.

"Could be a long wait. There's not much action around here till later."

"I'll come back."

"You could wait at my place. It's warm. It won't cost you much."

"To be quite honest," Hugo declared honestly, "I haven't a centime to my name."

The man shrugged, "Please yourself."

Hugo fled. He went from street to street, turning this way and that at random, feeling sorry for himself. Eventually, light and the sound of music spilling from a doorway drew him in. In a church, dimly lit, a scattered crowd was listening to a trio of saxophonists. He found a seat tucked away in a corner and between the warmth and the mellow timbre of the music was soon asleep. A hand on his shoulder woke him. "The church is closing now." An old man in a black suit was bending over him. Everyone else had left. Hugo stood up, a little too quickly, and sat back down. He felt dizzy. "Have you anywhere to go?"

"Yes, thank you Father." Was the man a priest? Whatever he was, Hugo didn't want his charity. Was there no depth to which he could fall, he wondered in some remote recess of his mind, before he would ask for help? As the door swung to behind him, he did regret not asking directions back to the intersection. What did it matter what the old man thought?

As luck would have it, he stumbled upon the Rue Sainte-Anne before very long and followed it toward its sister, the

Rue Thérèse, and the closer he came to the meeting of these two ladies, the more hopeless loomed his quest. He even began to have bitter thoughts about the fool Snagov, on whose lumpen-headedness could be blamed his present predicament. If Snagov had done his job, he, Hugo, would now be peacefully obliterated instead of cold, hungry, penniless, and footsore on a dark street at eleven o'clock at night in search of a male prostitute, who, come to think of it, might have been as much an actor in that role as he himself had been in the role of a Polish priest.

As Hugo approached the intersection, he saw two men break off a conversation and one of them disappear into the Rue Thérèse. Something about the encounter—its exclusiveness, its abrupt end—alerted him, and he took a good look at the remaining man, and, as he came abreast, stopped and greeted him.

For a moment Hugo thought he'd been mistaken. The fellow was clearly surprised. He had a gym bag slung over his shoulder and the lithe build of a welterweight, perhaps an athlete coming from a late workout. Nevertheless, after a moment's pause, he returned the greeting and was moving off when Hugo held out the newspaper. "Excuse me, Monsieur, but would you know anything about this?"

The man cocked his head to look. " 'The Priest and the Prostitute,' " he murmured. "Do you mind?" He took the paper from Hugo and, moving to where the light was better, read the entire piece. "Yes," he said, handing it back, "as a matter of fact, I do."

"Would you have any idea where I could find the, the . . . ?"

"The prostitute?"

"It's not by any chance . . . ?"

The man smiled. He had a nice smile, Hugo decided. "No, I'm afraid not. But no problem, if it's ecstasy you're after, I'm sure I'll do as well. Though I couldn't guarantee the stroke."

Hugo blushed. "It's really just a few questions, if you wouldn't mind . . ."

"Anything at all, anything. How long would you need, do you suppose?"

"Oh, just a minute or two, I . . ." A little late it dawned on him: there was a price tag.

"That's just the way it is," the man gestured helplessly, seeing Hugo's confusion, "Time is money, as they say."

"How much would it be for . . . ?" He didn't know why he was asking, to stall perhaps.

"A moment? Three hundred francs."

"Three hundred, but that's . . ."

"Fifty dollars," the man said. "You're an American, yes?"

"But I don't have anything like that."

"How much do you have?"

From his overcoat pocket Hugo produced the posy the woman had given him. He peeled back the silver paper and shyly presented it. "That's it. That's all I have."

The man took the little bunch of flowers and admired it. *"Mon dieu,"* he laughed, "the last of the true romantics." He looked at Hugo with new interest. "And what's your part in all this?"

Hugo pointed to the paper. "See that man in the photo. That's me."

After a great deal of comparing, and many exclamations of disbelief, the man—who introduced himself as Michael, pronounced in the English way—agreed that the likeness was pretty convincing. And as Hugo told his story, he became more and more intrigued. Finally, when Hugo reached the end, Michael said, "I'm glad I didn't get mixed up with that. It had the smell of a fish market."

"So you do know something?"

"Oh sure," said Michael, "They came to me waving a stack of money. It made me nervous. The sort of deal that lands you in the Seine—how do you say in the States—with concrete feet? If you're looking for the guy they ended up with, well, I don't know just when we'll be seeing *him* again."

161

CHAPTER

20

PIAF was singing.

Ah! Quand il me prend dans ses bras
Il me parle tout bas
Je vois la vie en rose . . .

Watching those expressive eyes, the pallor of that thin face, the scarlet lips and fragile tilt of the body, Hugo had to remind himself that it was not only not Piaf, it was not a woman. The words were being mouthed, the sound on tape. So much that was unreal had happened to him since the George Washington Bridge, this latest episode seemed quite in keeping.

Hugo T had his share of the mindless homophobia you'd expect in a man of his age and experience. Then, lo and behold, appears Michael, a veritable St. Bernard to rescue him from the snowdrift into which he had plunged. He had first come to that corner, Michael confessed, when he was thirteen. He would soon be thirty. He had given it the best years of his life and had won there some famous victories, notably, six years ago, against heroin. With heroin you could stand outside all night in the cold and not feel a thing. That had been a tough one. He had survived heroin, he was not sure he would survive Mitterrand and the Socialists. Business was better in the former political climate when sodomy was *interdit*. With the "anything goes" atmosphere of today, things were slow. Some of his friends, boys of seventeen, eighteen, nineteen, had not been as tough or perhaps as lucky. He'd seen them die. And now along comes this new guy, not even French, two or three months on the corner and already he's dragging its name in the mud, giving it a reputation that will drive decent people away.

Not that Michael sympathized with the Church. That aspect didn't bother him. He was a free-thinker himself. In his opinion the church deserved a bit of bad press. It had kidnapped God and shut Him up in a building. "I believe in a God who doesn't live in a church," he said. Priests weren't all hypocrites, either. He knew one who came regularly to the corner to make sure they were all right, and had even stood bail for Michael and given him a character reference the time he was arrested. But this new guy, togged up in shiny black leather with handcuffs dangling suggestively from his belt, was bringing rough trade into the neighborhood, attracting a bad element. No wonder they'd gone to him with their vicious little scheme and their filthy money.

How did it happen, Hugo had asked.

Michael knew only that late one night a car had come nosing down the Rue Sainte-Anne and, after a brief discussion, the German—yes, he was German, the new guy—had got in. (Nothing now about Michael being offered first refusal, Hugo noted.) As far as Michael could tell, the driver had been the only one in the car, and the German had sat up front next to him. He'd assumed the driver was a man, though being some yards away, muffled and in shadow, Michael couldn't absolutely swear. He didn't see the German again that night or the next, and on the street rumors began to circulate. In fact he hadn't seen him since. He himself had been away the previous night but had heard that the German, in full regalia, had been observed escorting a client from a car into the hotel on the Rue Thérèse, and that shortly afterward an ambulance had showed up. Seeing the paper and hearing Hugo tell his story had brought it all together in his mind. As for the German, who was known as Rolf, Michael didn't know where he lived or even his real name. He would try to find out. In the meantime . . . He looked distressfully at Hugo, then his face lit up. "My mother had an uncle who went to America. Perhaps he has come back."

So, it was decided. Hugo would go home with Michael. And since Michael lived some way away with his sister and usually went out on the first metro of the morning, the six o'clock, a place had to be found to park Uncle Hugo. And before he was introduced to any of Michael's friends, Uncle Hugo had to be spruced up a little bit. Which is how he came to be sitting under a statue of Molière while Michael stroked his cheeks with a razor he carried in his gym bag.

"Molière," Michael exclaimed, shaving perilously close to Hugo's nose, "a man like that makes me proud to be French."

Hugo's thoughts were more concerned with whether or not they might be arrested. A couple of gendarmes strolled by but barely glanced at the strange sight, perhaps quite normal in Paris.

Michael walked his new relative to a discreet club behind the Palais Royal where he appeared to be well known. The coat-check lady, who Michael said was a former prison matron, promised to keep an eye on Hugo. There were two bars, upstairs and downstairs. Michael installed Hugo on a stool at the obscure end of the downstairs one, bought him a cognac and orange, whispered a few words to the bartender, and left. No one seemed overly impressed by Hugo's incongruous presence, and after a while he relaxed, sipped his drink, and watched a handful of serious young men pirouetting narcissistically in front of mirrors on the tiny dance floor. He was surprised and touched when the coat-check lady brought down a plate of cold cuts and salad, procured from God knows where, and set it before him. Later, just as his struggle to keep his head off the bar fizzled, chairs and benches were assembled and the floor show began.

Ah! Quand il me prend dans ses bras
Il me parle tout bas
Je vois la vie en rose . . .

After that he really couldn't keep his eyes open, and the coat-check lady, mercilessly accusing him of overimbibing, installed him on cushions in the farthest reaches of her tiny domain, where he snored away the wee hours till Michael's return.

He dozed too on the metro. Michael lived at the end of the line near one of the eastern gates of the city. His sister would be no problem, he assured Hugo. She'd go along with the uncle business. As for her husband, the less he saw of Hugo the better. He drove off early every morning to his job as a customs inspector at one of the airports, getting back in the late afternoon for dinner, TV, and bed. A man of few words who believed that the mouth was made to put food into.

Inquiries about the German had not, Michael reported, turned up much. He'd been seen going into the hotel in the Rue Thérèse, but no one could absolutely swear he'd been present when the stroke victim was carried out. Michael would have to find out which bars he frequented and see what he could pick up there.

The morning was gray and chill with a light snow falling but not settling. Early commuters shuffled by as they made their way up a street of small shops and eating places. At a bakery Michael picked up a couple of baguettes, and they turned into a starkly contrasting complex of tall, forlorn-looking blocks of flats set at odd angles to one another. Entering one of these, they took the elevator to the sixth floor. Michael got out his key, motioning Hugo to wait. He found himself on an open balcony with a number of identical doors opening off it. A double stroller and a scattering of toys suggested small children, making him suddenly feel awkward and out of place. He'd been so intent on his own pursuit that he'd not taken into account the burden he'd be to a busy family, particularly one with kids, something Michael hadn't mentioned.

Then Michael beckoned him in, and the sister at once put him at his ease. "You are now part of our family," she said firmly, taking his coat. She was older than her brother but with the same olive skin, curly hair, and appealing brown eyes so that he wondered if they weren't part Arab. The husband had already left and the twins were not yet awake, so Hugo was given the run of the bathroom. He emerged in a borrowed bathrobe to the smell of coffee, and it crossed his mind that the world was not such a bad place after all if you didn't expect too much. For years he'd lived in hope, had not imagined life without it. Now, beyond hope, he'd entered a state of weightlessness where things moved toward him of their own accord, where no rights existed, not even the right to hope. It would take a bit of getting used to.

Later, as Michael slept in an adjacent room, Hugo sat on the living room sofa that was to be his bed. He had a job that made him happy: keeping an eye on a couple of gurgling one-and-a-half year olds while their mother was off doing the laundry, including his. In the afternoon Michael got up and went shopping. He came back laden with groceries and handed Hugo the morning paper folded to an inside page.

NOT GUILTY CLAIMS PORNO PRIEST. That was the headline. The subhead said, TALK CANCELED. Hugo read on. "Father Viktor T, whose photo—taken as he was carried from a hotel frequented by male prostitutes and their clients after suffering a stroke—appeared on the front page of yesterday's edition, has issued a sweeping denial of the allegations. 'He was in his room here all night,' said a spokesman for the octogenarian Polish priest, describing the allegations as 'absurd.' Father T, along with many of the delegates to the International Convocation on Religion and Human Rights, is staying at the Hotel Select on the Boulevard Raspail. Asked if Father T could have left the hotel without being seen, the spokesman admitted it was possible but said there was no reason to doubt the priest's word.

"Asked if being photographed elsewhere at three o'clock in the morning was not reason enough, the spokesman said that photographs had been known to lie and that Father T, on account of his courageous stand on behalf of fellow Poles who had disappeared inside the Soviet Union, had many enemies eager to discredit him.

"The spokesman added that Father T was in excellent health for a man of his age and had not recently suffered a stroke. He challenged this newspaper to give the name of the hospital to which the priest allegedly was taken and to produce the young man with whom Father T was said to have had relations.

"Asked why Father T had not made himself available to the press to comment in person on the charges, this reporter was told that the priest's main concern was to not distract from the proceedings of the convocation by inflaming an already overheated issue, and for this reason he had asked that he be excused from delivering his address entitled, 'Perestroika for Dead Poles?' as scheduled.

"Information leading to the whereabouts of the prostitute seen entering the hotel on the Rue Thérèse in the predawn hours of the night before last will be treated by this newspaper in confidence. A reward will be offered."

Hugo looked up as Michael came from the kitchen. "Did you read it?"

Michael nodded. "I'll try again tonight. Should dig up something."

. . . *to produce the young man.* . . . The words stuck in Hugo's head, and reassured him. Surely it meant he was doing what Viktor would have wanted. He had read the reportage. He had also noted the subtext. Whatever conclusions others came to about that photograph, Viktor himself must have guessed whose face it was. Yet he'd said nothing. Yes, Hugo told himself, the next move definitely belonged to him.

That evening Hugo woke to the sound of television. He had stretched out on the bed in Michael's room after Michael left. Rubbing his eyes, he stumbled into the living room. The husband had returned. He was sprawled on the sofa and his eyes were open. Hugo addressed him, "Good evening, Monsieur," and got no reply. He tried again with the same result. Hearing sounds from the kitchen, he edged around the sofa and looked in there. The twins were being fed.

"Don't mind him," their mother remarked, pointing her chin at the door. "It's the strain of acting polite all day long and listening to so many lies, not even good ones. He'll be better tomorrow. It's his day off."

Hugo helped himself, as directed, from a casserole in the oven and sat eating at the kitchen counter as the twins in their mother's lap sucked greedily, one at each breast.

"What'll happen to him?" she suddenly burst out, so that for a second the babies lost their moorings. "I worry all the time."

"Your brother?"

"He thinks he's young and invincible, but soon he'll be middle-aged. What sort of a life will he have?"

A growl from the living room saved Hugo from the impossibility of an answer. Michael's sister disengaged the twins and dumped them on the floor, where they set up a howl, and busied herself preparing her husband's espresso.

What sort of a life do *you* have, Hugo wondered. Getting down stiffly on hands and knees, he made puppy dog noises, then pretended he was a train. It didn't help.

CHAPTER

21

NEXT morning, along with the baguettes, Michael brought an early edition of the paper. Hugo had been up for some time, and while Michael was in the shower and his sister was brewing coffee, he leafed through it. PRIEST WAS SOVIET AGENT blared the headline. The accompanying picture was a more closely cropped version of the original one with Hugo's head dramatically circled in red.

A caller, alerted by our coverage of the affair of the priest and the prostitute, claimed that he recognized the photo of Father Viktor T as being that of an agent provocateur of the notorious G.P.U., forerunner of the K.G.B., and that the man had been active in Paris in the twenties.

A spokesman in the press office of the International Convocation on Religion and Human Rights did not deny the accusation. He pointed out that the priest, in the biographical sketch provided to the convocation, describes himself as ''a former member of the Communist Party'' who, in the years following the First World War, ''worked in the underground apparat in the capitals of Europe to destabilize democratically elected governments.''

According to the caller, who declined to give his name for fear, he said, of reprisals, but who spoke in thickly accented French, Father T worked for TRUST, a front organization set up by the G.P.U. in the twenties to infiltrate anti-Soviet émigré groups, and personally planned and participated in a number of kidnappings and murders including that of the White Russian general, Baron P. N. Wrangel, a leading anti-Bolshevik who, the caller claimed, was poisoned in Brussels in 1928.

Father T was a protégé of Felix Dzerzhinsky, the caller stated, a fellow Pole and founder of the hated Cheka, who recruited him in 1920 during the Bolshevik war to destabilize the new nation of Poland and used him later in his extensive European spy network.

Asked if, in his opinion, Father T had put his old loyalties behind him, the caller said it was an open question, and that if not, Father T would be in an excellent position to sabotage the work of building the new Poland, just as he had done back in the early years.

Reminded of the twenty years Father T had spent in exile in Stalin's labor camps, the caller agreed that it looked very convincing, but that perhaps this was the way it was supposed to look.

Asked to elaborate, the caller said that he did not wish to be too harsh on an old man who clearly had personal problems of his own, which would bring about his undoing if nothing else did.

This newspaper's request for a full, fair, and exclusive interview with Father T was denied. The priest is said to be in seclusion at his hotel.

"Can it be true?" Michael asked.

Hugo had read the piece through carefully twice, then sat with the paper on his knees in a kind of reverie, his thoughts roving along far-off, sparsely trodden paths. The question startled him. "Yes, yes, much of it, possibly. But then . . ." That regimental dinner party—he could see it now in every detail. Had Viktor, in the end, done the job? Had he, on G.P.U. orders, murdered Wrangel? And if he had, could Hugo pass judgment? Hugo who, five years earlier, hadn't the guts to disregard the Baron's request to deliver that message? A message he knew to be dangerous? Hugo ran away. Viktor stayed.

"Are you all right?" Michael sounded anxious. "This anonymous caller with the heavy accent, I suppose they made him up. It's an old trick, no?"

"I'm not so sure they did," said Hugo. "I've a good idea who it was. Power is not so easily surrendered."

Michael picked up the paper. "It can't be true, all this."

"Why not? We're talking about things that happened before your *father* was born. The things you think now, will you think them fifty years from now?"

"Fifty years! He'll be lucky if he's alive in five." His sister brought in the coffee.

Michael ignored her. "News of our German. I found his hangout. One of those basement torture chambers on the Left Bank. They haven't seen him in three or four days. Unusual, I gather. But he did hint to a bartender about an all-expense-paid trip to Morocco. Acted like he had money to throw around."

"They'll never see him again," said Hugo.

Later in the day, Hugo sat on the sofa keeping an eye on the twins. Michael was sleeping, and his sister had seized the chance to go shopping. Perhaps Hugo did close his eyes for a minute or two, because when he looked up he saw the husband had come in and was eyeing him with a certain amount of absorption. On his lap he had the morning paper.

"So you're Uncle Hugo from America," he remarked genially, settling himself more comfortably and brushing away one of the twins who was trying to climb up his leg.

Hugo's instincts of self-protection were roused. This was the first time the man had so much as acknowledged his existence. "You are most kind to have me to stay."

"But the honor is all mine," the host protested, and Hugo, sniffing sarcasm, found the words suspect. "Doubtless back home in Texas, California, or is it Florida . . ."

"New York City."

"Ah yes, in New York City, you are by now a successful

171

businessman, a banker perhaps, or a judge, retired of course with time and money at your disposal, free to travel the world.''

"More time than money," Hugo put in, and they both laughed, Hugo nervously, the husband with cynical exuberance so that he had to dab his eyes with a handkerchief. The twins, also giggling, crawled into the kitchen.

"And your luggage, no doubt a matching set by Vuitton or Gucci, I presume you left it at your hotel for the time being?"

Hugo smiled agreement, not liking the drift things were taking. Then he rallied. "And when you bring your family to the States, Monsieur, I will put my executive jet entirely at your disposal. Disney World, the Grand Canyon, Yellowstone National Park, the colorful New England fall, Fifth Avenue, Washington, D.C., my people will cater to your every whim." He could see that the man was a little shaken, though not for long.

"Monsieur," he reached to straighten a nonexistent tie, being still in his pajamas, "I must warn you that I am a customs inspector for the Republic, and as such . . .''

"So was my father," exclaimed Hugo.

"I beg your pardon?"

"A customs inspector. Though not for France. For the Emperor Franz Josef."

"Then I need hardly remind you . . .'' the inspector raised his voice in an attempt to regain control of the conversation, but Hugo seemed not to hear him.

"Of course in his time there were no airports like you have now."

"But there were still cheats, Monsieur, and there were still liars." The man leaned forward, his eyes, strangely dilated, assumed a messianic fervor. "You know what they call me, Monsieur? They call me The Dog. Why? Because I sniff out a liar at twenty paces. In the very way a man approaches me, I know if he's going to lie. You, for instance, Monsieur. Perhaps you *are* somebody's uncle, but not my wife's mother's." He rose from his chair, waving the newspaper. "You want to know what you are? A phony Polish priest, a Stalinist spy, a corrupter of the young men of France. If I did my duty, I'd turn you in to the police. However, all I have to say to you is this: get out of my house!"

This last injunction was upstaged by a reverberating crash from the kitchen, as of saucepans tumbling out of a cupboard. The shrieks of the twins started up like sirens. Michael, blinking away sleep, put his head out of his door just as his sister's keys rattled in the lock.

That afternoon Hugo accompanied Michael on the inbound metro. Through several stations they sat side by side in silence. Finally, Michael said, "What are you going to do?"

"Don't worry about me," Hugo replied bravely. "Anyway, my life is over. If people as old as me have the impertinence to still hang around, we deserve whatever comes to us."

"Paris is not like New York," Michael said. "Here you can always find a meal and even a place to sleep. People are more generous, if you know where to look."

"How do you know about New York?"

"New York? I lived there for almost a year. I had a friend who had a French restaurant. When he died he left me his bulldog and his cat. Then the dog died. The cat pined for it for months. Of course if I'd learned the language I might not have been so lonely."

"And you, you're not afraid of sickness and death?"

Michael tapped his head. "I'm more afraid of sickness up here." As he stood up to get off at the *Centre de Relaxation* where he worked out every afternoon, he slipped a piece of paper into Hugo's pocket. "So you know where to reach me. Oh, and these may come in useful." He held up a bunch of metro tickets and pushed them in too. Then before Hugo could protest or even thank him, he brushed him lightly on both cheeks and was gone.

Hugo came up out of the ground in the Place de Châtelet from where he had once delivered biscuits on a tricycle. The late afternoon traffic swirled around him. In those far-off days, the speed limit had been fifteen kilometers an hour. It would take a brave tricyclist to venture forth in this maelstrom, he thought, as he let himself be jostled along in the rush-hour crowd. Finding himself on the Rue de Rivoli and having no particular plan or clear intention, only a whisper from the prompter's box that he was determined to ignore, Hugo boarded a bus. Sometimes he found that the simple act of getting on the first bus to come along and riding it, perhaps to the end of the line, served wonderfully to compose the mind. The passing scene, the antics of fellow passengers, the chance to be alone with one's thoughts and in motion, whatever the reason, it wove a certain spell. Now, looking out on the street from the curve of the back seat, he thought, What is a city but a pile of bricks and mortar containing things down to the minutest hairpin on a lady's dressing table? For an instant he saw Paris in all its vulnerability, open to conquerors, and he began not to fear it as much, but almost to pity it.

The bus had turned, but instead of crossing the river, continued along the Right Bank. On an impulse Hugo got off. Drawn by the sight of an old friend, the *Tour Eiffel,* rising into a somber sky, he walked onto a bridge and stared westward over the Seine. He was all alone in the crowd, as alone as the *Tour Eiffel* and almost as old. Placing his hands on the wrought iron balustrade, Hugo leaned over and stared into the murky water. Not quite all alone. Someone's eyes were on him. He straightened up. A man was watching him, a businessman perhaps, in a well-cut overcoat and carrying a briefcase.

"What bridge is this, Monsieur?" The man was so close, Hugo felt the need to say something.

"The Bridge of Suicides," the man replied, "the Alexander III." He raised his hat, smiled sadly, and was gone, a blur in the moving current of men and women. Had he lingered he'd have seen the old man's face—perhaps it called to mind the face of someone he knew—pinken with self-reproach under its fur-lined cap. How delicate our associations with our fellow beings, the incident seemed to say, yet at what peril discounted or ignored.

Whatever the man with the briefcase felt, it seemed to Hugo that the prompter had come out of his box and confronted him. Before he finally quit, he had to do one thing. Indeed, until and unless he did it, he probably would not be allowed to pass from the scene. He would indulge himself, he decided, to the extent of putting it off till the morning. Which left the approaching night. Perhaps because of what Michael had said about places to sleep, Hugo felt in his pocket for the paper he'd slipped in there earlier. To his amazement he held in his hand two tightly folded hundred franc notes. He was rich. Rich enough to afford something to eat, a cheap hotel, and breakfast. Beyond that, the big question mark in the sky.

Hugo headed north through the now-lighted city bound for his old neighborhood, at one time synonymous with cheap lodgings. How much had it changed, he wondered. In some respects, he discovered, not much. After a tiring walk and a couple of wrong turns, the Gare Saint-Lazare, floodlit and vast, loomed before him. Behind it, in the Place de Budapest, he passed some two dozen men standing like blighted pine trees on a dark hillside, transfixed by a single point of light, the entrance to *Le Sex Shop*. The old rooming houses by the looks of it had been upgraded, but further on, in the Rue Blanche, he found a little hotel advertising *"Tout Confort"* and *"Calme,"* just what the doctor ordered.

Before reaching for the light switch in his bare room, Hugo felt in his pocket for the plastic case holding the Emperor Franz Josef. A pity that he hadn't got it shined up, he thought, rubbing it vigorously on the blanket.

CHAPTER

22

THE sun, streaming through gaps in the curtains, nudged Hugo awake like an insistent cat. The night before, when he finally closed his eyes, he'd dived so deep into the pool of unconsciousness that even the poorest souls have recourse to in the backyards of their minds, that worries, dreads, decisions all were washed away. He came up smiling. The mood was short-lived. Today he would find Viktor and hand Franz Josef back to him. Leaving his room he noticed a sign on the door: *EN CAS D'INCENDIE, GARDEZ VOTRE SANG-FROID*. Before twelve hours had passed, he would need all the *sang-froid* he could muster.

Out on the street, Hugo hugged the shady side. He moved warily, ostensibly just an old man out for a morning stroll, and marveled at the sheer normalcy of life around him. A man polishing a brass doorknob, a woman wiping the marble counter of a *boulangerie,* boys walking to school with satchels on their backs, a maid flicking a yellow duster from a second-story window. At his age, this was all he wanted out of any day. Yet fate seemed to deny him even the simplest pleasures. He bought a paper and, in an effort to dispel the gloom, settled himself in a corner *pâtisserie* with a *tatin* and a pot of tea. Not till he'd sipped the tea and sampled the pastry did he open the paper.

MYSTERY BODY LINKED TO PORNO PRIEST. The story jumped out at him as he was half afraid it would. The first thought to cross his mind was that Viktor's dead body had turned up somewhere. As he read on, relief mingled with horror. The corpse of a young man had been fished from the Seine at the Pont D'Issy. It was clad exclusively in black leather, arms handcuffed behind its back, and bore no identifying papers. A wad of bank notes, estimated at six thousand francs, was found in an inside pocket. A single gunshot wound in the back of the head was given as the cause of death, leading to the hackneyed description, "execution-style killing." Based on the clothing and a preliminary pathologist's report, the body was thought to be that of a male prostitute dead for at least twenty-four hours.

The reporter then rehashed the affair of the Polish priest, reminding the reader of "the K.G.B. connection"—as it was now termed—and the fact that, according to an eyewitness, a man who fitted the description of the deceased—tall, fair-haired, and clad in black leather—had been seen entering the hotel with the priest a short time before the ambulance was summoned. The piece ended by quoting a spokesman for the Convocation on Religion and Human Rights as saying (lamely enough, Hugo thought) that Father Viktor T was "unavailable for comment at this time."

Hugo finished his tea and sat deep in thought as Parisians came and went buying their morning loaves. For him, the mention of the six thousand francs clinched it. The unfortunate German had got no closer to Morocco than Hugo had to the promised land of Australia. He shivered and glanced uneasily around, then chided himself for extravagant fear. If he was the needle, then the whole city of Paris was the haystack. Or better still—since the Baron must know Hugo had his passport—the whole world. What would he do, Hugo asked himself, in the shoes of that shrewd exploiter of human nature? Assume, quite likely, that Hugo would try to contact his brother, if only to borrow money. This he must bear in mind.

He had memorized the name of Viktor's hotel as reported in the press. It was across the river on the Boulevard Raspail. Returning to his own hotel to ask directions, he discovered that a bus from the Rue Blanche would deliver him in the course of time to his destination.

It can truthfully be said that, of all the bus journeys Hugo T had undertaken in a long career, this one—from the Rue Blanche to the Boulevard Raspail—was at once the most agonizing and the most exhilarating. The blue sky and brisk sunshine of the day served to sharpen the gleam on already burnished emotions. It seemed in Hugo's imagination that his life was running backward and that soon he would be meeting with Viktor in that early morning overcoat exchange off the Place de Budapest. And what made this flight of fancy almost believable was the vengeful shadow of Baron Max, the shadow that then, as now, dogged their footsteps and dominated their actions. All round the Mediterranean, in Naples, Saloniki, Constantinople, Alexandria, Algiers, and Tunis, wherever he went ashore, Hugo had eyes in the back of his head, convinced that Max would be waiting. Not till the thirties when he joined the U.S. Merchant Marines did he manage to banish Max from his mind. And now he was back.

As the bus moved up the boulevard, Hugo kept watch. The Hotel Select proved large, faceless, and rather shabby, the perfect choice, he thought, for a religious convention. He pushed through a revolving door into the lobby, a rectangular room with fake marble pillars and green drapes. A number of earnest-faced folk with name tags wandered around; at the desk a knot of luggage-toting foreigners, perhaps human rights activists, had the receptionist pinned down under crossfire. Not an encouraging scenario. Hugo withdrew to a vantage point to await his moment, keeping a sharp eye on the door. At last the human rights group stumped off and the receptionist lifted a weary visage from her computer terminal to look into a pair of smiling blue eyes in the nicest, kindest little old face she'd seen—well, since yesterday. And that was the odd part about it.

"I'm here to see Father Viktor T," Hugo began.

"He checked out."

Seeing her puzzled look, he added, "I'm his brother."

Now she understood. "But he left yesterday."

"Yesterday?" He was already turning away, not wanting to believe her.

"One moment, Monsieur. His brother, of course. There's something . . ." She found what she was hunting for and passed it across, an envelope. "He left that."

"For me?" Hugo held it gingerly.

"You're his brother, no? You must be. For an instant I thought he himself had returned."

The envelope was sealed, the words "For Hugo" written on it. Trembling with anticipation Hugo picked a chair in a far corner, sat down and tore open the flap. Inside was a map. He put on his glasses and saw that it was part of a street plan of Paris. Scrawled across the bottom were some words in Polish: "In case you need to contact me." Facing it to the light, Hugo examined the map, which looked like a cheap tourist giveaway. A point on the Boulevard Raspail was circled, presumably the hotel. Another circle with a cross marked a spot in the middle of the Seine between the two bridges that connect the Left Bank to the Ile Saint-Louis. Between these two points stretched a long arrow. Hugo held the map extremely close, shifting it slightly to catch the light. No getting away from it: the spot indicated by the second cross was right in the water.

Returning to the desk, Hugo waited in line till his turn came again. "Pardon me," he asked the receptionist, "but would it be possible to speak to someone from the convocation?"

"They've mostly left already," she glanced distractedly around the lobby. "Was there anyone in particular?"

"Perhaps who'd know about my brother . . ."

"They weren't meeting here, you know. Perhaps someone at the conference center could help you, though I doubt it. It ended yesterday."

"I don't suppose you know where he went?"

"Oh no," she looked at him pityingly, "it was all hushed up, to avoid the press. They got him out through the kitchen."

"This letter," he held it up, "he gave it you himself?"

She shook her head. "It must have come last night."

For a moment he hesitated, then, mumbling thanks, made way for the next in line. Back in his corner he pulled out the map and street by street plotted his journey.

The denizens of Paris, responding to the urging of the sun, had taken to the parks in droves. Hugo did not hurry as he traversed the Jardin du Luxembourg. The gloom of the morning had lifted, replaced by an inexplicable sense of peace. Sometimes he paused, missing his silver-topped cane, but mostly he strolled. Past benches crammed with old people like sparrows on a telephone wire, past a couple kissing with such refined relish that they couldn't possibly be married, past office workers with hastily assembled lunches, past kids roller-skating and a group of men heaving heavy silver *boules*. He walked under the chestnut trees, bare and leafless, that he'd first seen so many years ago bursting with green, and felt sad. At a bistro between the Pantheon and the Boulevard Saint-Germain he stopped for a bite to eat, then decided to splurge and spent every last franc he had on an apéritif, steak *pommes-frites,* and a princely tip for the waiter. After all, he told himself, you can't take it with you.

Now, standing among the postcard sellers on the quai looking down at the river and across it to the Ile Saint-Louis, Hugo had to smile. Because right below him, secured to the bank by their cables, were three barges. So Viktor, old sailor that he was, had ''gone to sea'' just as Hugo had done when trouble threatened. He made his way carefully down the long ramp so that the first bridge loomed darkly above him, casting a long, cold shadow. Walking upstream by the water's edge, he scrutinized first one barge, then the next. Only the third seemed to have any life about it. Over and above the lazy squelch, squelch of its rising and falling in the water, he heard the low buzz of a generator.

Hugo strolled alongside the boat, some thirty-five yards from stern to bow, painted black and a dull red. Through the glass windows of its raised cockpit he made out various nautical instruments and the glint of brass in the sun. A gap in the curtained porthole of a low cabin area revealed part of a lighted room with what appeared to be the horns of animals mounted on the walls. It looked decidedly cozy down there, and he couldn't help picturing the two of them, himself and Viktor, reunited in its warm, water-rocked embrace. What would he say, he wondered, how greet his brother, in what language? He hoped he would find him alone.

The balance of the boat consisted of a long, low area roofed over with tarpaulin, presumably for freight. Propped against it was an old bicycle. On the cabin roof, a number of pot plants had not survived the winter, and were drooping out of their containers like victims of a mass execution. Keeping them company was a Christmas tree whose needleless branches, draped with a vestige of tinsel twine and two glass balls, suggested some old, neglected courtesan.

Hugo stepped aboard, and not seeing any way into the cabin, walked around to the river side. A lifeboat dangled over the stern. A sign by the cockpit door said, ATTENTION CHIEN DE GARDE. Just to be sure he wasn't trespassing, he went back and tapped on the undraped cabin window. No response. He tapped louder, watching eagerly for a face. Nothing. It occurred to him that Viktor was deaf. Opening the cockpit door, he climbed in. There, on a comfortable chair, slept a ginger cat.

The space, in the sunlight, felt like a greenhouse. But the smell—no wonder the cat was smiling in its sleep—was like a Polish restaurant. "Hello!" Hugo called down the steps that led to the cabin. "Anybody home?" The cat opened an eye. The cabin itself was as cozy as he'd imagined. Around the walls, besides the mounted horns and antlers, were prints of sailing boats. A table with a jolly check cloth was set for two. Against one wall was a sink and next to it a stove. On the stove was a frying pan, and in the pan were chunks of succulent kielbasa. Hugo felt the edge of the pan. Still warm. At the end of the room a short passage gave onto three smaller rooms, two containing double bunks neatly made up and the third a bathroom with two clean towels.

Whoever had been cooking the sausage, it seemed to Hugo, had nipped out for something. Bread perhaps, or milk, or a bottle of wine. He looked around for a fridge but didn't see one, and opened drawers of cutlery and utensils and cupboards containing cans and dry goods. Everything was in perfect order. Even the knife that presumably had been used to slice the kielbasa was put away. As he looked around, it began to dawn on Hugo that for his brother to come to a place like this was rather odd. Who lived here? Why stay in Paris at all? He fetched out the torn piece of map and read again the cryptic message. "In case you need to contact me." But of course, he had jumped to conclusions. The most he could hope for here was someone who was in touch with Viktor, perhaps knew how to reach him in Poland or wherever he was. A disappointment and a relief.

The garbage container was under the sink and even that was practically empty, just some wads of paper towel. He gave it a shake to see what might be underneath, and froze. It wasn't anything he could see, it was the smell. He lifted a handful of paper and looked into the bottom of the can. Those foul cigarettes. He had walked blithely into a trap. For a few seconds Hugo's brain seemed to go into reverse. He dropped the trash can and made for the cockpit steps.

Too late. Footsteps sounded on the deck above. Hugo ran to the window, but the steps were rounding the stern of the boat. Perhaps it was the kielbasa that put the idea into his head, but the next thing he knew he'd grabbed a knife from a drawer and slipped it into his pocket. The thought of hiding came to mind, but he rejected it. Too old for fun and games. Whatever his fate, let it come, the quicker the better.

The first he saw of the newcomer was a black-gloved hand stroking the cat, which arched its back into the pressure. Then came heavy shoes descending and the swish of a fur-trimmed overcoat. And soon the whole man was standing there with just the table between them.

"Liebchen!" the Baron beamed and gave a slight bow. "So! Romantic, *hein?* Dinner for two under the bridges of Paris." He set a bulky string bag on the floor beside him.

Hugo said nothing. His right hand, in his pocket, closed on the knife handle.

CHAPTER

23

THE Baron moved to the window and closed the curtain. "We don't want the whole of Paris spying on us, do we, *Liebchen?*" In the three seconds his back was turned, Hugo took two steps forward. His adversary fixed him with a sad, shrewd smile. "Put it on the table," he said, his tone firm but kind. Then, when Hugo made no move to obey, "Don't think you have before you another Snagov, a potato-head who will let you slice him up any way you want. Do me the favor, save it for the kielbasa."

Lest there be any doubt, the Baron withdrew from his own pocket a small Luger. It occurred to Hugo that he had only to lunge at him to be shot dead, but tempting as this idea was, he decided against it. Anyone else, perhaps, but not the man standing in front of him right now. He put the knife on the table.

"Perhaps without your coat you would be more comfortable?"

Hugo was in no mood for further cooperation. He stared rigidly, trying to radiate contempt and defiance through every pore of his body.

"Then allow me to play the headwaiter, since here is my restaurant in a manner to speak." The Baron walked around the table and pulled out a chair. "Sit."

Hugo made no move to comply, even when the chair was obligingly shoved to a position directly behind him.

"So you fancy kielbasa, *hein?*" The Baron continued to be genial. In the next instant Hugo's knees seemed to give way and he sat down with a thump. Next thing he knew, his arms, which had come to rest naturally along the arms of the chair, had been swiftly strapped down with Velcro strips. Even in his outrage, Hugo had to concede that the man was deft, a deftness honed no doubt in countless "interviews" in the grisly torture chambers of totalitarian Europe. His legs too were bound together at the ankles.

The Baron unpacked his shopping bag at the sink: a couple of loaves of bread and a large bottle of schnapps. He lit the gas under the kielbasa. "It's too bad," he muttered, "really too damn bad." The cat appeared and rubbed against his leg. He tossed it a chunk of meat. Then Hugo heard him rummaging around in one of the cabins.

He emerged minus his overcoat carrying a small stack of newspapers. "It's really too bad," he reiterated, this time quite loudly, as he dropped the papers onto the table. One by one he picked them up, passing page after page of print before the eyes of his guest and reciting headline after headline. All, as far as Hugo could tell, were Polish language publications. One or two he'd heard of, but most not, perhaps émigré, perhaps from the motherland itself. All, in their own way, said the same thing. TRUST BETRAYED, TELL US THE TRUTH, REVERED PRIEST IN BOY SEX SCANDAL, THE PRIEST THE FLESH AND THE DEVIL, PRIEST LOOKS LESS SAINTLY NOW. Many papers had picked up the photo of Hugo on the stretcher.

"So *Liebchen,* you are famous. Your splendid features are being seen by Polish people all over the world. But no, you are right not to smile. I should apologize. Really, I must say, it's too bad." However apologetic the Baron may have tried to look, the puckered lines of his fleshy face arranged themselves by force of habit into the usual sneer. "Against you personally I have no quarrel at all, understand? But because to die is too good for *him,*" he brought a heavy foot down on the stack of papers now on the ground, "to make a short story, a substitute is sadly necessary." The sizzling of the kielbasa momentarily distracted him, and he turned the gas down, giving Hugo an idea. "But let us not spend our last hours in regrets." Brandishing the schnapps, the Baron returned to the table and filled both glasses. "To success."

Hugo looked on in disdain.

The Baron drained his glass and splashed himself another. "You came here perhaps hoping to meet your brother. Let me tell you frankly, instead of a brother you would find a stranger, unrecognizable from the good old days. This man has become—how to say—the holy ghost. Holy, holy, holy. He thinks he's on his way to life after death in heaven with the angels. If I kill him, he's happy.

"You know the first time I saw Viktor?" The Baron thrust his face close to Hugo's. "It was near the town of Kamenets-Podolski in the Ukraine. Reds, Blacks, Whites, Greens, all colors, blundering around the countryside shooting each other. He'd stopped an old hay cart. Inoffensively it was creaking along, a boy wielding the whip over a couple of skinny bullocks. Viktor beckoned to the boy to climb down. I tell you he put a rifle blast up those cows' arses so they took off as if Old Nick himself was after them, which maybe he was. The cart careened along scattering hay in all directions, and out of the hay, like so many maggots, crawled black-frocked priests clutching gold and silver icons. I never laughed so much in my life. That man's for me, I said. 'Warm heart, cool head, clean hands'—the complete Cheka man—that was Viktor then.

"So when the boss ordered me to serve up something hot in the Baltic, I made sure Viktor came with me. Dzerzhinsky met him and agreed. An excellent judge of men, to some extent, Felix Edmundovich. He taught me the lesson of leadership: 'No one ever killed his successor.'"

The Baron forked kielbasa from the pan onto two plates and set them and the bread on the table. "Even now I cannot believe how this so-called comrade betrayed me, me who brought him from a hay cart to, to . . ." Words failed him. He turned instead to the schnapps. "Ah, but fifteen years later, in Moscow, I learned a thing or two. For all those years, *he* was spying on *me*. Think of it. The dossier was this thick." He kicked the stack of newspapers at his feet. "Of course, I had him packed off to the Solovietsky Islands for his trouble. But for me he certainly would have been shot in thirty-seven along with the other scum. Yes," the Baron smiled, "you could say I saved his life."

Hugo watched the papers topple toward him under the table and decided that something useful might be done with them.

"Frankly, whether Dzerzhinsky himself put Viktor up to it, who knows? Sometimes, in Warsaw or even Moscow, when I pass his statue, I shake my head. 'Felix Edmundovich,' I say quite sadly, 'I forgive you. But, believe me, there are those I do not forgive.' On Policeman's Day, if I lay a wreath on his shoulders, I can't help thinking that, had I been his successor, as, by rights, I should have been, my shoulders should also feel the touch of the flowers now and then."

Hugo wondered if the Baron would go so far as to dab his eyes with a napkin. But he contented himself with tipping back another drink. Then, pushing away from the table, he stared inscrutably at his guest through tiny, deep-set eyes.

"It wasn't long after our first encounter that Viktor spoke about you. Perhaps, even at that stage, he had in mind to manipulate you for some scheme of his own, against me. Because of course he knew when the time came you would always be on his side. This was my big miscalculation, and my downfall.

"When, that night, he failed to get you to cross back over the Zbroutch to our side, he found you again at Gdynia and lured you patiently to Hamburg. And believe me, *Liebchen,* you were a star—of all my agents, one of the best. I was greedy for more of you." The Baron popped a chunk of kielbasa into his mouth and tore off a wad of bread. "So when our little outfit was assigned a very big fish to catch, I had the perfect role for you. If I delivered Wrangel alive and kicking to Moscow, my future, I had reason to believe, was assured. You see, I had already met Stalin at Lwow. We saw eye to eye." He went to the nearest window on the river side and brushed back the drape. Outside it was already dusk. "Every detail was in place, one piece fitting perfectly into the next. Wrangel was to be delivered by barge to a boat off Le Havre.

"I told Viktor not to interfere on pain of death. He'd jeopardized the Hamburg operation; this one could not go wrong. He disobeyed. Deliberately he sabotaged the plan. Following his instructions, instead of calling Wrangel to the telephone, you warned him of the danger." Hugo was on the verge of protesting, but the Baron thundered, "Don't lie to me. I had a man in the room watching you the entire evening."

If only, thought Hugo, it was true—what the Baron said. If only he could salvage the slightest little bit of heroism from all the tawdriness. If only Viktor *had* tipped him off. He wanted to throw back his head and laugh at the absurdity of what had happened. He wanted to taunt the Baron with the real way his plot backfired. There was no point. One look at the man across the table was enough to convince him of that. Reality, for the Baron, was what he decided it was. Had he ever believed in a cause bigger than himself?

Hugo finally spoke. "What about the German, the one they found in the river? Was that your doing?"

"Homosexual trash," the Baron blurted, "disposable junk. I am doing the human race a favor. He should be happy he did something useful." He filled his glass again. "No, my dear Hugo, you are the one I am afraid of. If you only knew how desperately certain people are hunting for you. But I cannot let them find you, because I have an obligation. If you borrow something, you must return it, *hein?* For these few weeks I borrowed you," he brought out his pistol and laid it by his plate. "I borrowed you from the grave. Now I must return you."

Hugo looked dispassionately at the gun. "Who's hunting for me?" The cat had jumped up on the table and was helping itself from his plate. "Elie?"

"Perhaps. That one has the nerve to call herself secret

police. So I'm an embarrassment to the new order? Is that it? So they go along with my little scheme thinking Uncle Max will hang himself if we give him enough rope, *hein?* So who is hanging?" Again he kicked the pile of papers, then set back his drink with a disgusted air. "Amateurs, baby-sitters, pussyfooters. See how long they last, pandering to that bunch of *Dummlings:* electricians, plumbers, central heating engineers, bad poets, peasants with bank accounts who think they're running a country. When this picnic is over, who's going to clean up the mess, *hein?"* He swept the cat to the floor.

Hugo measured with worried eye the amount of schnapps left in the bottle. It might work. If only the Baron would turn his back for a minute or two. "What are you waiting for?" Hugo nodded at the pistol.

"Patience, *Liebchen.* When it's dark enough outside, we have a little journey to make together. No bullet holes this time, my friend. No 'execution-style killing.' By the way," he leaned forward, "ah, the bruise hardly shows. I wouldn't forgive myself to return damaged goods."

Again the Baron moved aside a curtain and looked out. Apparently he liked what he saw, because he turned to Hugo, "Don't worry. I have one thing to do upstairs and then we are ready."

Hugo heard him moving around in the cockpit, then walking along the deck. Using his teeth, flushed and dizzy with the strain, he managed to double over and peel apart the Velcro strip that held his left wrist. Soon his right wrist and his legs were also free and, shakily, he stood up. He knew exactly what he would do. Sitting, staring at the Baron, he'd thought it out item by item. EN CAS D'INCENDIE, GARDEZ VOTRE SANG-FROID. Prophetic indeed, the words from the morning.

Grabbing up the newspapers, Hugo scattered them around the table and pushed the chairs together. Then he doused the entire pile with schnapps. Turning the gas full on, he held the roll of paper towels in the flame till they caught, then tossed the flaming brand onto the table. At the heady taste of alcohol, the fire jumped with greedy relish to the tablecloth, then to the papers, then to the table itself. Hugo meanwhile staggered from one of the cabins with an armful of bedding and the Baron's coat, which he dumped onto the still lit stove.

Smoke now filled the room, and tears streamed down Hugo's cheeks as he ran back for more bedding to fuel the flames. As he opened the door to the end cabin, the cat shot through ahead of him and made straight for the far wall. Hugo seized a load of pillows and blankets and was turning to leave when he saw the cat, up on its hind legs, scratching and clawing at the wall. As Hugo looked, the animal turned its face to him with an expression of reproach and desperation he couldn't ignore.

Cats are practical creatures. They have wonderfully focused minds. And this one, no doubt about it, was trying to tell him something. He dropped his load and stared at the wall and saw that, yes, there was a crack in it. Hugo kicked out with the flat of his foot, a door opened, the cat leaped through into blackness. Hugo followed. A healthy crackling noise from the main cabin told him his bonfire had caught.

Hugo slammed the door behind him. He found himself in utter darkness and guessed that he must be in the hold of the boat. His eyes smarted and he rubbed them constantly. Hardly had he got his thoughts together when the blast and rumble of an explosion shook the boards he was standing on and the door he'd just closed crashed open. It was all he could do to stay upright. In spite of the smoke that now billowed around him, he managed once again to close the door. Now to get off the boat.

As he inched forward in the darkness of the seemingly empty hold, another noise close by, like the rattle and bang of an engine starting up, filled him with fresh alarm. The sound grew fainter, and he dared hope that the Baron perhaps had a motor boat standing by and was making that little journey he'd mentioned, alone.

When Hugo managed to scramble up into the fresh air, neither Baron nor cat were anywhere to be seen. The flames on the barge were flickering merrily against the dark sky, their reflection reaching out across the water. A white launch of the river police bore down from one direction, while from the land the scream of converging fire trucks grew insistently. As Hugo escaped along the quai, one was nosing its way down the ramp.

CHAPTER

24

"MET un franc. Met un franc, s'il vous plaît."

Hugo could hardly believe it had come to this, but there he was, begging. A beggar on the Rue Saint-Denis, competing moreover for attention with every type of female prostitute. The brazen, the demure, the part-time, the first time, the pro, the young, the ageless. He had procured a paper cup, which he was unable even to rattle because it was empty. In the hour he'd stood there on the crowded street, not one person had seen fit to make a contribution. So much for the generosity of Parisians.

And why was he subjecting himself to this humiliation, a man who wanted nothing so much as to slip away and die? Quite simply, he owed it to his brother. His meeting with the Baron on the barge had opened his eyes and stiffened his resolve. The heroic impulse that deep down Hugo had hoped for but denied now clamored to be released. He must find Elie. As simple and as difficult as that. He and Elie were the only ones who could help Viktor now, neither one without the other. And stay out of the clutches of the man who, even now, might be treading the sidewalk toward him, sniffing him out, the old bloodhound that he was. He needed money. Enough to keep body and soul together a few more days.

"Met un franc. Met un franc, Monsieur."

A man was watching him, had been for some time. A

stately old graybeard with flowing white mane who might have stepped out of a production of *Le Roi Lear* at the Comédie-Française. Hugo put him down as a harmless eccentric, possibly because of his glasses. These had two sets of lenses hinged together, and as he stared from across the narrow street, the top pair, standing to attention, gave the impression of raised eyebrows. All the same, it was disconcerting to be looked at so intently by anyone, particularly when engaged in the shameful business of begging.

"Met un franc."

The old man was crossing the street, his eyes fixed on Hugo. The eyes, as it turned out, of a connoisseur. Hugo would have walked away, but something held him, perhaps the realization as the man approached that along with the two sets of lenses went two sets of eyes: the alert little face of a Chihuahua peeked out between the buttons of the man's greatcoat. It was the Chihuahua, in the end, who made the introductions. Sensing in Hugo a kindred spirit, it struggled partway out of the coat, a garment that might have weathered—complete with mud—the Battle of the Somme, and tried to lick his face.

"Ah, *mon vieux,* but he salutes you, the little Frédéric. He knows another Parnassian when he sees one, *un vieux de la vieille.* And I know a man who has never begged before in his life. Allow me to introduce myself. The Director of the Paris Institute of Panhandling, at your service." He bowed.

The Director quickly disabused the neophyte as to the charitable instincts of Parisians. "They will step over a dying man in the street not even bothering to pretend to consult their watches," he exclaimed. "But they will not step over a dying dog." This accompanied by a generous wink. A deal was struck. It was arranged that Hugo would have the loan of the little Frédéric for one hour at fifty percent of the take.

When at the appointed time the Director reappeared and counted out the money, Hugo was surprised to find he and Frédéric between them had pulled in thirty-two francs and five German marks. The marks the Director flung disgustedly into the gutter. Catching his new pupil's aggrieved look, he said, "One man's charity is *not* as good as another's. You will find we are not devoid of principles at the Institute."

After a filling meal at a cheap restaurant in which Frédéric participated with relish, the Director pushed back his chair, produced a tobacco pouch, and rolled a lumpy cigarette. He had listened sympathetically to Hugo's story and been particularly impressed by his United States passport, examining it minutely, even mentioning the possibility of opening a branch of the Institute in New York. Now, as he blew a smoke ring into the air and watched it melt away, he floated a second idea. A partnership. Himself and Hugo, with Frédéric as silent partner. It was usual in these circumstances, he explained, eyeing Hugo's watch, for each party to put up some sort of good faith collateral.

All of which gave Hugo an idea. He rummaged in his pockets, came up with the Franz Josef coin, and pushed it across the table to his new mentor. "What would this be worth?"

The Director picked up the piece and scrutinized it through both sets of lenses. Then he bit it in a professional looking way. "I'll tell you what we'll do," he said. "Tomorrow we'll take it to an expert." He was about to stash the coin in his pocket, no doubt for safekeeping, when Hugo held out a hand.

"At this moment—perhaps I mentioned—the Institute is housed in temporary quarters. As my student and prospective colleague, I trust you will not be inconvenienced." They were strolling down one of the boulevards enjoying a fine night at the end of a fine day, a day of emotional and physical gymnastics such as Hugo had never known. He found he could barely set one foot in front of another. The mere idea that he was going somewhere, that he was in someone's hands, that he would not have to freeze on some park bench filled him with gratitude.

After a while he noticed the abnormal quantity of policemen they were passing, sitting smoking in parked trucks and standing around outside buildings. The Director seemed unconcerned. "The Institute must be adequately protected," he declared. When Hugo realized they were passing the Élysée Palace, the White House of France, such faith as he had in the Director dwindled. He was therefore surprised when his companion came to a halt in the Avenue Gabriel and waved airily up at what must have been one of the primest bits of real estate in all of Paris. *"L'Institut, voilà."*

So awed was Hugo by the sight of the elegant cream and white building gleaming in the moonlight, with its balustraded windows and mansard roof, that he did not at first notice the hovel that attached itself to the railings on the right of the main entrance. When it did sink in that a cardboard shack was to be his home for the night, he was filled more with resignation than with horror. And there was a comic side, he discovered, as usual. The Director had gathered together the elements of a bedroom suite—brass bedstead to china chamber pot. Only a gilded ceiling and brocaded walls were lacking.

As he lay in bed fully clothed under a pile of probably lousy covers—the Director had insisted on sleeping in the chair—Hugo pondered his fate. If only—he found himself wishing—he could talk things over with Father Vince. Vince would come up with something. With his church connections he'd know his way around in that department. He might even get a lead on Elie, perhaps through one of the New York consulates. The idea of walking into the Russian or the Polish Embassy in Paris and asking for her had been quickly rejected. Too fraught with hazard. He smiled, imagining Vince's face if, by magic, he suddenly appeared before him; and on that comforting note, with the warm heart of the little Frédéric beating close to his, he drifted off.

To awake from one of the best sleeps he could ever remember to a Paris itself just waking up, to be serenaded by the sparrows in the trees, to be escorted by a solicitous host down imaginary corridors *"pour faire sa toilette,"* to be presented on his return with a steaming bowl of café au lait by a charming maidservant (actually a waitress from a nearby cafe), what more could a man of discrimination and sensibility want in his old age? Yet the sole pupil of the Paris Institute of Panhandling and would-be partner in its impending international outreach still knew he had to deal with the reality of the moment. He had arrived, so it seemed, at a dead end. Hugo looked up into the windless sky, which hung gray with the threat of rain over the roofs and parks of the capital. If anyone had told him he'd be up in that sky above those clouds before the day was done, he'd have put it down to a misplaced belief in the ascent of dead men's souls to Heaven.

"Enfin," the Director consulted his timepiece, an intricate maneuver involving hauling on a long chain at the end of which an old-fashioned alarm clock appeared complete with legs and, on top, a bell. He pinged the bell. "The Institute is now in session."

Across the road people were setting up small covered booths on a patch of bare ground. A market was held here two or three times a week, the Director explained, trading in everything from stamps to phone cards. He seemed to await someone, eyeing each new arrival. At last he beckoned to Hugo and they made their way through the encampment. Everyone seemed to have a word for the little Frédéric. Soon Hugo was showing his coin to a dealer with a magnifying glass jammed under a bushy black eyebrow.

"Nothing to get excited about," remarked the dealer. "I'll take it off your hands for the weight of the metal. Say, a thousand."

The Director smiled and held out a hand, and Hugo, in turn, held out his. They moved away. "Whatever *he* says, we can at least double it."

Doubling it, by Hugo's calculation, would raise about three hundred dollars. The thought depressed him. To accede would be an insult. He had carried the Emperor Franz Josef around for the best part of a lifetime. If he couldn't return it to Viktor, he intended to use it to help his brother.

Three hundred bucks! He'd rather toss the coin into the Seine. The Director had other ideas.

He steered Hugo to a bus that left them in the Rue Drouot and from there, he said, it was only a short walk. The domes of Sacré-Coeur, gleaming white above the housetops, had always struck Hugo as a sight more suited to Istanbul or the East. Now, through association, they brought painfully to his mind the Baron's accusation on the barge: *Instead of calling Wrangel to the telephone you warned him of danger.* How often as he walked to work at The Capitol Club or left early in the morning to return to his lodgings had the domes hovered above him, in sunshine and moonlight. How easy, too, had seemed his prospects. Was he really a coward, always running away? Was this what he'd fooled himself into calling freedom?

They had entered one of the covered passages that burrow left and right through the heart of Paris. The Director strode purposefully ahead and stopped in front of a glass-paneled door on which were painted in gold the words, NUMISMATIQUE. ACHAT VENTE ESTIMATION. MONNAIES ET MEDAILLES. He buzzed, and to Hugo's surprise—because the sight of the Director looming beyond the glass must have been startling—was admitted. A man bustled forward, a shrunken mustachioed figure wrapped in a tweed suit that once might have fitted. He indicated chairs for the visitors around a low table and sat down himself. Hugo detected a mutual respect in the atmosphere, and when the old gentleman asked after the little Frédéric—who obligingly flashed a beatific smile—and fed him a barley sugar from a tin, Hugo realized they were well acquainted. Which would only make it harder when the time came to say no and walk out.

Again, the coin was produced and examined and Hugo, prompted by the Director, found himself telling how it was that he came by it.

"A remarkable tale. And it looks to be in near mint condition. Do you mind if . . . ?" he indicated the back of the shop.

"By all means," said the Director, and the proprietor withdrew with Franz Josef to his office.

"You are friends?" Hugo enquired nervously, seeing himself the victim of a confidence trick.

"More than friends. In the days of the *Résistance*, ah the documents we forged together. They fooled even the French. Don't worry, Monsieur, we can trust this man. Indeed, I am thinking of asking him to be guest lecturer in Numismatics at the Institute. You never know what may turn up in a begging bowl."

A hushed silence greeted the return of the tweed suit. It bowed slightly in Hugo's direction and laid His Imperial Majesty on the table. "I'd be happy to offer you a thousand, Monsieur."

The Director struggled to his feet. "I do not believe my ears," he declared, fighting to maintain his composure.

The proprietor looked at a loss, so obviously had he anticipated an agreeable response to his offer. Then his face cleared. "Not francs, *mon ami*. Dollars."

Within minutes all was arranged. And not long after that Hugo and the Director of the Paris Institute of Panhandling were in an *Agence de Voyages* on the Place Kossuth buying a ticket to New York, for departure that same evening. It was a solemn moment, symbolizing for one man an end to running away, for the other the fulfillment of a dream, the establishment of a branch of the Institute in New York City, the panhandling capital of the world—no matter that the dream had occurred to him only the day before.

A haircut and shave, a new winter coat for the little Frédéric, a last meal for the three of them, a small donation to the Institute. In this way the afternoon passed and the time came to board the train for Charles de Gaulle Airport. If there was one thing that Hugo wished as he sat back in his seat, clutching the small bag he had purchased and trying not to close his eyes, it was to be traveling incognito. Under Smith, perhaps. Anything but Hugo T. By that name they had found him once. Wouldn't they find him again?

CHAPTER

25

TO few mortals is the chance given to be present at their own obsequies. Emperor Charles V, in 1556, went so far as to lie in the coffin at a dress rehearsal for *his* funeral. In 1831 a certain Edwin Rowbotham, a joiner, "woke up" at his viewing in Manchester, Vermont. No doubt there are others. So Hugo T must be numbered among a select handful of his fellow men.

Landing very late at night at Kennedy Airport, he decided to invest what little remained from the sale of the coin in a bed at the Holiday Inn, and next morning boarded a bus for Manhattan. Having lost track of time, Hugo was amazed to see in the papers that February wasn't quite over. So long did it seem he'd been away that he wondered, fleetingly, whether a whole year hadn't passed. But no, he reflected as the familiar cityscape hove into view, a life had passed. This was a second coming. Rubbing his hairless upper lip, he wondered whether to risk a crack along those lines with Father Vince.

Father Vince, Hugo was informed by the duty person at the rectory of St. Hildegard's, was tied up at a funeral mass in the church and wouldn't be available for a while. Would Hugo care to wait?

Hugo did not care to wait. He set off to walk the few blocks to his apartment. Since it was still February, and he'd paid February's rent, he reckoned that it still *was* his place even if his things were gone and he had no key. To avoid a scene if Herself or her minions should be lurking nearby, he rearranged his scarf over his mouth and nose, which left only a pair of eyes peeking out anonymously from under his cap. A perfectly natural precaution, he told himself, considering the nip that was in the air.

Nothing about the block seemed to have changed. Hugo climbed the familiar steps and pushed open the front door. There was the notice he'd seen every day for at least the past twelve years: REMUVE BYSIKELS FROM HALLS AND KIP AUT FROM HALLS GARBICH ROBISH OCONT VIOLATIONS. Signed, LANDLORD. For the inside door, he needed a key. Hugo stared at the little row of buttons and at his own name corresponding with one of them. He hadn't come to visit himself, but what the hell, he pressed it. In the silence he imagined hearing the harsh buzz and running through to the kitchen from the front room where perhaps he'd been reading. The silence stretched out. He pressed the second floor rear. This, after all, was why he'd come. He pressed again. You never knew your luck. But either the buzzer was kaput or no one was home. It was a long shot anyway. He'd hardly expected Elie herself to be there, perhaps just someone who could take a message.

The ever-vigilant Mrs. Foley had opened her door a crack. Now she poked her face out into the hall. Hugo tapped on the glass. After all, she might know something, was bound to in fact. Mrs. Foley stayed put. He couldn't blame her. In his scarf and hat he must look like some kind of bandit. He pulled off his disguise and tried a "let bygones be bygones" sort of smile. Mrs. Foley shuffled closer and closer. She looked unwell, he thought, with a weird, staring expression about her as if she'd seen a ghost. With her face just inches from his own through the glass, he watched as she raised a hand to her forehead, made the sign of the cross and crumpled out of sight.

Alarmed, Hugo rattled the door. Sometimes it opened that way, but not today. He buzzed all the buzzers up and down the board. Nothing. He was about to run across the road and get the doorman in the building opposite to call the police when the mail lady appeared. With her passkey she opened the door, and they both squeezed through. In no time she had scooped up the recumbent form of Mrs. Foley and deposited it unceremoniously on the couch in the front room. All in a day's work, apparently. Then she left him to it.

Hugo stood as close to the body as he dared and was relieved to see signs of life. Two words kept blinking on and off in his mind: smelling salts. He cast about the cluttered room wondering if Mrs. Foley had a bottle and if so where she kept it when a screech behind him made him jump. "It's on the sideboard." A bottle did indeed stand on the sideboard. Its label said whiskey.

After a glass or two of restorative, a sprinkling of the Water of Noch from a container marked as such, and a judicious application of the Oil of St. Jude, Mrs. Foley felt sufficiently revived to come to the point. "You could have knocked me down with a feather," she declared. "Is it indeed yourself?" She kept shaking her head and fixing him with suspicious little glances as if trying to catch Hugo not being himself. When she pointed to a card the size of a baseball card stuck in the frame of a mirror, and told him to read it, he realized why. Under a colorful depiction of the Virgin holding the Baby Jesus were the words, in heavy Gothic type, PRAY FOR THE SOUL OF HUGO T, followed by the date—some three weeks earlier—of his presumed demise.

"Well, you can stop praying," said Hugo, trying to dispel the gloom.

Mrs. Foley again crossed herself. "They cleared everything out," she volunteered. "Father Vince came—from St. Hildegard's." Dabbing her eyes she looked accusingly at Hugo. "Said you'd passed on, he did."

"He was right, in a manner of speaking."

Mrs. Foley appeared unconvinced. "Funeral's this morning."

It was Hugo's turn to be shocked. "How can it be? I'm here, I'm not dead."

"I was all set to go myself," Mrs. Foley was undeterred, "when I had one of my nasty turns." She leaned toward Hugo and hissed conspiratorially, *"She* went."

"To St. Hildegard's?" No mistaking who *she* was.

Mrs. Foley nodded dramatically. "Going on now, it is." She was beginning to feel herself again and to appreciate the spot the man was in. Here he was supposed to be at his funeral and he was standing in her front room. She wondered aloud if it was an open coffin, and was annoyed when Hugo changed the subject.

"That new couple in two rear, would you know if they were still around?" Too late it had occurred to him to question the mail lady.

"Them," she sniffed. "Up to no good, as I'm an honest woman." She added darkly, "Paid her cash, twice the proper rent, no questions. Comings and goings at all hours. Good riddance."

"So they left?"

"Gives a building a bad name, doesn't it, that sort of thing."

All the same Hugo had to make sure before leaving. He climbed the stairs to the second floor, listened, knocked, and listened some more. On the way back down, he checked the gap under the door. No telltale shadow this time.

On the way to St. Hildegard's, Hugo passed the restaurant where his friend Cassidy worked. On an impulse, he went in. The early lunchtime business was brisk, but he managed to get the bartender's attention. "Cassidy around?"

"At a funeral. Unfortunately not his own."

He turned and was halfway out the door when he heard a shout behind him. "Hey, Hugo, what the . . . ?" He kept going.

Poor Father Vince, how would he get out of this one? Hugo felt bad for his friend. All he could hope for was that Vince would see the humor in it and exercise some Christian forebearance.

St. Hildegard's is a noble edifice. It takes up half a city block and resembles—so Hugo always thought—an enormous mausoleum, something imported from Woodlawn and inflated by Superman. It had fat, round columns, puffy-cheeked stone cherubs and a cupola. And an intimidating number of steps up which Hugo had never walked. He did so now with a mixture of trepidation, foreboding, and curiosity.

The vast door swung to behind him, and he stood for a while in the warm, gray gloom getting his bearings. A faint, sweet whiff of incense tickled his nose. Someone was talking. He couldn't see who. He couldn't see anyone. The body of the church was screened off by clusters of pillars. Hugo moved forward and peeped between them. Father Vince was standing a long way off in front of the altar. Here and there in the intervening pews his listeners sat like rocks, dark, hunched, and still. That even a handful of people should turn out in his memory amazed Hugo. Moving down a dark side aisle, he slipped into a pew, noting with relief that a good half of the congregation looked to be homeless, like himself, and were snoozing. The whistle of one nearby snorer sounded like a kettle on the simmer.

Now the words were getting through. He heard his name. What in tarnation was Father Vince saying? ". . . and it seems to me that Hugo's personality can be summed up in words that one of you expressed to me this morning as we were gathering here. 'He'd have never offered you a glass of cloudy water.' Seems like a small thing, you say. But what is friendship but love in little things? Hugo loved life. Not in the abstract sense of the word—he hadn't much time for the abstract—but life in all its tiny detail. As we all know, he loved to walk. He didn't have to get on a jet plane and take off for the wonders of the East or the splendors of the West. He'd walk out the front door of his building and notice things. A flower in a tree pit. A child in a stroller. A bird singing. Little things. They all add up. Friendship.

" 'Lord, who may dwell in your sanctuary? Who may live on your holy hill? He whose walk is blameless and who does what is righteous, who speaks the truth from his heart and has no slander on his tongue, who does his neighbor no wrong and casts no slur on his fellow man. Who does these things will never be shaken. . . .' "

The words flowed. The kettle simmered. Hugo blushed. If

he hadn't actually heard his name, he'd have wondered who Father Vince was going on about. Some candidate for Saint, perhaps. This round definitely was going to the priest. So let him take it. The next round would be his: the knockout. All the same, Hugo was uneasy and a bit annoyed. Here was his friend taking unfair advantage. Like the time in the hospital after his stroke. They had him in a wheelchair, and one Sunday morning Father Vince, without so much as a by-your-leave, grabbed the chair and wheeled him down to the chapel. He left him for a minute to prepare for mass. As soon as Vince's back was turned, Hugo got up out of the chair and walked back to his room. Vince said mass for a wheelchair. Suddenly, Hugo didn't feel so guilty about still being alive.

They were standing now, shuffling toward the center aisle. Hugo, kneeling as in prayer, watched through his fingers. What he saw he could scarcely believe. First up the aisle was Herself. Swathed in black lace, the impersonation of grief, she leaned heavily on the gigolo whose suit of crushed velvet seemed several sizes too small. Following unsteadily in her wake, holding the Yorkshire terrier that boasted a large black bow, came Frank the Handyman, tipsy as usual. If her outfit had had a train, thought Hugo, he'd be holding that too, or treading on it. Cassidy came next, still limping a little from his run-in with Snagov, then a couple of doormen and a security guard Hugo had worked with over the years. He was happy to see one of the old German waitresses from Eighty-sixth Street who he'd always suspected had a crush on him. Last of all came Sydney, chewing on a dead cigar, and Hugo instinctively ducked down in the pew until he was safely past.

What, Hugo wondered, had become of Father Vince? Perhaps he'd slipped back into the rectory. He edged to the end of his pew and peered into the side aisle. In the shadows someone was walking swiftly towards him.

"Hugo, you old reprobate, you're looking great," exclaimed Father Vince. He added, "for a corpse."

CHAPTER

26

"NO, seriously," Father Vince protested, "you're looking tip-top." They were in a small reception room at the rectory right behind the church.

"The rest cure did me good."

"When I saw you come in I said to myself, 'Hold on, that's no apparition. That's the real thing.' Couple of minutes sooner I'd have changed the text. 'But the Lord provided a great fish to swallow Jonah, and Jonah was inside the fish for three weeks.' What on earth happened to you, Hugo?"

"I guess you could say I had a date with Jaws, but Jaws stood me up, or the other way round," said Hugo ruefully. Then, having been assured by Vince that he had all the time in the world, Hugo told him more or less everything.

As the story unfolded, Vince could only shake his head in horror and amazement. Normally a man who managed to keep a turbulent emotional undercurrent from making waves, at times he had trouble holding in the tears. Once, to cover an explosive moment, he had to get up, plug in the kettle, and make instant coffee. "Am I putting you to sleep?" Hugo enquired anxiously.

"The first thing to do," said Father Vince, "is see if you can stay here for a bit. I'll have a word with Father Joseph, and perhaps we can bend the rules. I don't want you wandering about the streets. Not with this gangster baron on the loose.'' Truth to tell, he was more afraid of what Hugo would do to himself than anything this larger-than-life Frankenstein clone might come up with, if indeed he existed. It had occurred to Vince that his friend was hallucinating, though the airline ticket, the stamped passport and the press clippings argued for at least a basis in reality.

While Vince went off to buttonhole Father Joseph, Hugo sat and waited. Bend the rules, eh? Alone with his thoughts he was struck by the futility of what he was doing and the sheer presumption of barging in on his friend's life and dumping his troubles on him. As if he hadn't caused enough problems already. He felt as though he'd been on some sort of twenty-four-hour high since walking out of the coin shop in Paris and had now suddenly crashed. Impulsively, he stood up and was struggling into his coat when a timid knock at the door made him pause. It opened to reveal a slender Latino carrying a tray. The youth set the tray on the table and, thinking Hugo was getting *out* of his coat, tried to assist him. After a brief struggle, Hugo capitulated and was wordlessly ushered to a chair. Just my luck, he thought, lifting the cover on a plate of food.

Father Vince, when he returned, looked pleased with himself. Justifiably so. Father Joseph, far from giving him the skeptical squint he was famous for, exhibited a surprising enthusiasm. Just the night before, inspired by an item on the eleven o'clock news, he'd been on his knees asking how the Order could best help the brothers and sisters of the Faith in Eastern Europe at this crucial time. Though hazy on the details of Hugo's story, it sounded enough like an answer to his prayer that he dare not disregard it. He gave Father Vince his blessing. One of the brothers was on retreat, and Hugo could have his room. Father Joseph looked forward to welcoming the stranger to their midst at early communion.

Father Vince had no such illusion. He didn't disbelieve in miracles, but he didn't exactly believe, either. Years ago, to protect his sanity, he had managed to reconcile himself to the bifurcation of language and belief with which his calling seemed fraught. Now, his hammock slung between the poles, he basked fairly comfortably in the rationalism of late middle age.

Hugo retired early and dozed awhile. As he came to and his mind limbered up, one part of it explored an eclectic array of saints, martyrs, ex-presidents of the United States, cartoon characters, astronauts, and sports heroes stuck on the ceiling, perhaps for inspirational purposes by the brother whose room he occupied. The other portion dwelt on a less exalted but more immediate concern: Father Vince's promised efforts to find Elie. Already that afternoon he'd called both the Soviet and Polish Consulates *and* their missions to the United Nations, and from all the response he'd gotten—as he said to Hugo—glasnost and Solidarity and the retailing of the Berlin Wall on Fifth Avenue might never have happened. Painstakingly, they'd taken his name and address and promised to look into it, but Vince could sniff a runaround as well as the next man. Though he had to admit that a first name and a two-word description weren't much to go on. "Imagine calling up the CIA and asking for a short, fat guy named Joe."

Intended to cheer Hugo up, this only depressed him. What a fool he'd been to come back. Vince had even called Herself on the chance Elie had left a name and address there. But word of Hugo's reincarnation had been spread by Mrs. Foley, and all he got was a threatened lawsuit for misrepresentation of fact and the name and address of her lawyer. Meanwhile, attempts to discover the protocol for contacting a priest in Poland were stalled while he waited for someone in the Archdiocesan Office to call him back. From Hugo's point of view, things looked bleak.

Next morning they looked even bleaker. "I've been thinking," said Father Vince, closing the door of Hugo's room carefully behind him, "that it mightn't be a bad idea for you to spend a couple of days in bed. Complete R and R. You're a lot more stressed out than you think, and sooner or later it's going to hit you, wump." He had come from early communion and his first white lie of the day. When Father

Joseph peered about for "our brother from the East," Vince had described Hugo as suffering from exhaustion and suggested he take it easy for a day or two, to which his superior had assented. It was when Father Joseph asked to be reminded which Polish Order Hugo was with that Vince knew he was in trouble. And by not immediately clarifying matters, the trouble doubled.

Hugo's sensitive antennae picked up that all was not hunky-dory at the heart of St. Hildegard's, at least as far as he was concerned. As soon as Father Vince left the room, he started planning his escape. Unfortunately Vince—who also had antennae—had scooped up all his clothes for the cleaners, leaving him with a pair of borrowed paisley pajamas. The third floor window gave onto a dingy backyard from where, even if he could reach it, there was no visible exit. At least his door wasn't locked. Hugo peeked into the hall. Just as he'd feared. The Latino youth was mopping the floor. It was all too reminiscent of the safehouse in Paris, with Snagov lurking in the next room and hidden cameras in every corner. Not the physical aspect so much as the feeling of powerlessness, of extinguished hope.

It was after lunch, after the youth had cleared away his tray, that Hugo had the flash of inspiration that changed everything. Almost as if St. Hildegard had intervened. Looking listlessly through a pile of books Father Vince had left by the bed, he turned up one that normally he'd not have touched. But his mind, busy with the pros and cons of convincing Vince to let him go out to a pharmacy to fill a heart pill prescription, was less vigilant than usual. The book's title, *Steps to Faith: the Catechumen's Handbook*, said nothing to him. But in flicking through it some spark must have jumped out to ignite his imagination. The plan was devilish in its cunning.

Vince had been worrying about the evening visit to his friend. No more news, no leads to follow. The Archdiocesan Office had decided it was a matter for the cardinal. The Cardinal's Office had yet to call him back. Father Joseph, moreover, had come up with the idea of himself celebrating the Sacrament of the Eucharist with "our Polish stowaway" at the bedside. Vince guessed Hugo's state of mind and fretted that the only way he could help him was negatively—by trying to protect him from himself. The miracle was that the guy was here at all, alive and well, but Hugo would never see it that way. Perhaps the Almighty had something up His sleeve, something Vince couldn't imagine. Never say never, he reminded himself, as he tapped on the third floor door.

He was surprised to find a much more upbeat Hugo than he'd expected. "I thought you people ate boiled beef and cabbage." Hugo pushed aside his empty plate. "You guys live like princes. Perhaps Leona Helmsley'll buy you out, and you can retire to Florida."

For Vince it was almost like the old days again. And Hugo seemed to take his lack of progress philosophically. "So what are you doing with yourself tonight?" he asked as Vince made to leave. "Is she pretty?"

If Father Vince hadn't been naturally ruddy he'd have blushed. "Going over some educational films. And that's the truth."

"Oo la la. Naughty movies. So that's what the Fathers get up to at night."

"If you call devotional videos of the lives of the saints naughty. I have to review them for the schools." A trace of exasperation had crept into his voice.

"You expect me to believe that. How about if I tag along. I'm bored stiff here."

Father Vince was taken aback. "Sure. I didn't think you'd be interested."

He was right. They'd disposed of Mother Cabrini and were well into Thomas Aquinas, and it was all Hugo could do to keep his eyes open. He'd borrowed Vince's bathrobe, and they'd taken over one of the small downstairs reception rooms.

Suddenly, the door opened and Father Joseph's head appeared round it. "Ah, Father Hugo, I was told I'd find you here." He shook Hugo warmly by the hand. "Fully restored, eh? Well, don't let me interrupt. I look forward to seeing you at early communion and saying a few welcoming words."

"I'll be there," Hugo responded as the door closed.

Thomas Aquinas stuttered to an unscheduled halt. "What did you say?" asked Father Vince.

"Early communion. Is it okay to go like this?"

"Jeez, in pajamas? I'll see what I can come up with." Vince could hardly believe his ears.

Next morning he went a few minutes early to Hugo's room and was relieved to find him dressed and waiting. The clothes fitted pretty well. The pants were a bit on the long side, but the polo shirt looked great and the windbreaker, an old one he never wore, would serve the purpose. "There'll be a few people in the congregation. Just follow along with the others. I'll be assisting Father Joseph, so I'll see you right after it's over." At the connecting door to the church, he gave Hugo's arm a squeeze and left him.

Hugo sat up front and waited. When the time came he was among the first at the altar rail. The moment was an emotional one for all concerned. Father Vince, fighting back tears, said thanks be to God under his breath. Father Joseph, dipping the wafer in the wine, prayed not to forget the names of Saints Cyril and Methodius who'd brought the light of the gospel to the Slavic nations. He planned to mention them in his welcome.

Whether Father Joseph's memory served him or not Hugo never knew. He walked back to his pew and kept on walking, and the mumbling voices at the altar slowly died in his ears. Soon he found himself on the street. Snow was falling, traffic at a muffled crawl. He hardly registered. Snow clung to his head and shoulders like a soft white shawl. And there was something else he didn't notice. As he walked through the dim body of the church, a figure unbent itself from a rear pew and followed him.

CHAPTER

27

BEYOND his escape from sanctuary Hugo had no plan, other of course than the main business of the day. Instinct told him to remove himself quickly from the vicinity of St. Hildegard's. A cab was out of the question—he hadn't more than a couple of dollars to his name—so he took off down the avenue as fast as the slippery sidewalk would allow. After a few blocks, he eased his pace and glanced nervously around. As far as he could see, no pursuing priests pushed toward him through the throngs of umbrella-wielding commuters herding into the subway.

The subway. It wasn't his favorite place to be in New York, but beggars can't be choosers. Hugo let himself be carried along in the crowd, down the steps into the dank interior. Only waiting on line to buy a token did he realize how wet and cold he was. Yes, a good decision, to go underground so to speak. He'd be warm, have time to plan, and be well away from his old neighborhood. He found himself on the downtown platform and when the train came managed to squeeze into the front car. Twenty minutes later the train pulled into the Brooklyn Bridge station and the conductor announced that it was the last stop. "Everybody out!"

The Brooklyn Bridge. Was this where fate was leading him? Hugo had checked out this option a month ago and rejected it. While in the annals of jumping, the bridge loomed large, a site inspection showed it up as less than ideal. For one thing the walkway was in the middle, between the traffic lanes; for another, the chances of surviving seemed high with the comparatively low drop and short span and the sheer number of watching eyes.

Across the platform a train was waiting that would take him to the southern tip of Manhattan. What to do? Just as the doors began to close he hopped aboard. "Stand clear of the doors!" the conductor yelled. They opened and again chomped shut. The train jerked out of the station, slowly gathering speed.

It was still snowing when Hugo came up out of the subway. He walked straight ahead toward the harbor and the terminal of the Staten Island Ferry. Inside the terminal he took the escalator to the upper level, shoved his quarter into the turnstile, and walked on through. A smallish crowd was waiting. A clock showed ten minutes till the next ferry. For a moment he considered using his last quarter to phone Father Vince, just so he wouldn't worry, so he'd know all was well. But why stir things up? He decided against it.

With a great hoot that lost itself in the folds of the white curtain falling everywhere, the boat announced its departure. Hugo stood in the stern and watched as men in yellow slickers hauled up the ramp and fastened a chain across to prevent the cars and trucks from rolling back out. With a mighty roiling of water the boat began to move. "Last one of the day, if this keeps up," he heard a man shout. As far as Hugo was concerned, conditions were perfect. No last look for him at one of his favorite views in all the world, the skyscrapers of Manhattan. He didn't care. Nor would Ms. Liberty show herself, nor Ellis Island where, too long ago, he'd knitted the sleeve of a sweater. Soon he heard the ding-ding-ding of a bell buoy and the roaring of blind vessels challenging each other like rival beasts. It seemed the world had closed down around him and was no place anymore to be. He felt no fear, no dread, just a kind of tired longing to get it over with. He knew exactly what he was going to do. It was just a question of when. Ten minutes into the trip, or fifteen, should do it, as near to the middle as possible. Passengers and crew congregated inside, in the warm. Hugo had New York Harbor to himself.

Or did he? In the shadows behind him, in the narrow passage beside the parked vehicles, someone was standing, a stocky figure in a dark greatcoat, homburg pulled down over his eyes. It seemed to Hugo that the man was looking at him, or why had he turned as a person does—involuntarily—who feels the focus of another's gaze?

As Hugo watched, the man stepped out of the shadows and lifted his hat. "My dear Hugo, what an unexpected pleasure. But please pay no attention. In this case I am merely the objective observer, to see—in a manner to speak—the fair play."

Ironic perhaps for a man who'd devoted a long lifetime to treachery that these should be his last two recorded words. For Hugo, at that moment, the urge to avenge his brother superceded his longing to die. He rushed at the fiend who had come to taunt and gloat and God knows what he would or could have done to him had not the Baron fired. The shot brought Hugo down, but it also brought two burly Staten Islanders leaping from the cab of their truck from where they'd observed, in the rear view mirror, this strange interplay of two old men. One of them wrestled the Baron to the ground. The other rushed to help Hugo.

The second shot was not as loud as the first, but it was deadly. In the struggle to wrench the Baron's pistol from his clenched hand, the gun went off. A clean shot through the heart. Death was instantaneous. Suddenly, the decks resounded with the clamor of voices and the clatter of running feet. A few minutes later, with a shuddering, frothing roar, the great ferryboat reversed its engines.

PRIEST IN GANGLAND-STYLE SHOOTING, DEATH IN FERRY DUEL, TRUCK DRIVER THWARTS S.I. FERRY SHOOT-OUT. The papers, naturally, had it all wrong.

Next morning Father Vince was surprised by a call from the Archdiocesan Office asking how he was. "I'm fine," he replied, bewildered but touched, and they hung up. On turning it over in his mind he called back to find out what, if anything, was going on. Was it the transfer to Wayzata, Minnesota, he'd heard rumored. In which case he was not fine, he had all sorts of complaints.

It turned out to be an identification problem. A hospital had called about a patient admitted to emergency who was concussed. They were trying to find out who he was so they could bill him, and the only clue was a health club membership in one of the man's pockets. The card had Father Vince's name on it.

Vince's health club membership had lapsed ten years ago, not that he'd ever gone near the place. A birthday present from a sister who believed in the triumph of hope over obesity. But wait a minute. *In one of his pockets.* "I may be able to help," he said, and took down the name of the hospital.

When Hugo opened his eyes, he knew that his mother had been right after all. There was a Heaven, and he had gone to it. The vision hovering above him was the face of an angel. Then the angel blurred and the familiar features of Father Vince loomed up before him. "So they let you in, too," Hugo remarked.

"What's he saying?" asked a voice.

Father Vince shook his head. "He's not making any sense." This was his second visit to the hospital that day. In the morning Hugo had been out cold. "Hugo," he shouted, "do you know who I am?"

"Why are you shouting, Vince? I'm not deaf."

Vince could hardly keep from laughing out loud, "He says he's not deaf."

"Hello American dreamer," the angel was back in focus. "It's me, your neighbor, Elie. Do you remember?"

"You came," Hugo tried to sit up, but something was pinning him down.

"Take it easy," she said, laying a hand on his shoulder. "Now everything will be fine."

"Is he . . . ? Is he . . . ?" But somehow the words wouldn't come out properly. Hugo closed his eyes. Everything was fading away.

"He's lucky to be alive," the nurse said. "An inch to the left, the bullet would have shattered his spine."

Father Vince had found Elie waiting for him at the rectory on returning from his first visit to the hospital. After his calls to the consulates, she'd been contacted in Paris and had flown in on Concorde. He told her all he'd managed to glean from the police about the incident on the ferry, though he'd not yet succeeded in getting through to the truck driver for an eyewitness account. That gentleman was tied up with lawyers, agents, and relatives he never knew he had. It was obvious enough to Elie who the man the press had dubbed "the Ferry Godfather" was. He still had his people—loyal out of fear or foolishness—inside the Department, as she called it. And just as word had filtered through to her, so it must have to him—somewhat faster. She'd heard that the Baron had been in New York already a day or two.

It was Vince—fresh from his saints on celluloid—whose idea it was to put Hugo on video. A vindication of his brother—and incidentally the Church—that the whole Polish nation could share in. No way would Hugo be able to travel anytime soon, not to the rectory, certainly not to Warsaw, where, according to Elie, Viktor was safe and in seclusion. Pneumonia had set in. "With that plus his heart, to operate would be ninety-nine percent fatal," as the doctor put it. Hugo had days, perhaps hours, to live.

Elie was delighted at the video idea. "Typically American," she called it. This would be precisely the ammunition they needed to break the grip of the old-guard Stalinist tendency at the Department, the Baron's cronies, the unrepentant Party hacks still slavishly reporting to their Moscow counterparts. She herself was prepared to prompt off camera in the hopes that Hugo might say a few words in Polish.

Father Vince sat up with Hugo until a nurse came and

administered a sleeping draft. In the old man's conscious moments, the priest tried to explain about the video and how it would be a way of talking brother to brother and would, as he put it, get Viktor off the hook. He wasn't sure how much was registering until Hugo, with a mischievous glance, said, "So you want me in one of your dirty movies?"

"You said it, pal," Vince responded. He snatched a few hours' sleep at the rectory and was back downtown at the bedside at first light.

Hugo seemed stronger. He motioned Vince to lean over and whispered, "Am I on the way out? They won't tell me."

"Yes, you old son of a gun, you're on your way."

The smile was all the reassurance Vince needed.

When Elie arrived they went over together the few sentences Hugo would say. Somehow the Cardinal's Office had got in on the act and had induced one of the networks to do the taping, for broadcast that evening on the news. By ten o'clock Hugo's room resembled the set of "St. Elsewhere" and the camera was rolling.

The words came slowly, but Hugo's delivery was strong, and Vince, watching, knew that sentence by sentence it was costing him his life. At last, after a longer pause, Hugo switched from English to Polish. "Viktor," he said, "if you want your hundred crown piece back—the one you left in my cot—you're out of luck. I sold it in Paris last week." Another pause, and he launched shakily into the patriotic hymn, "Rota," sung to him by his mother night after night when he was a child,

We shall not yield our forebear's land
Nor see our language muted.
Poles we are, our nation Polish
By Piasts constituted . . .

After a couple of lines, Hugo's voice faltered then petered out. There came a smattering of applause. Elie, her eyes streaming, bent down and kissed him on the forehead, at which he smiled serenely. There was a stir at the door, and someone announced that the cardinal and the mayor were in the elevator.

"Jesus, Hugo, you're famous," exclaimed Father Vince, bending to pinch his friend's cheek. But something stayed his hand, and he ended up closing Hugo's eyes.

Some weeks later the midnight ferry churned out into New York Harbor bound for Staten Island with a smattering of people aboard. The night was clear and chill with a fierce wind blowing in from the ocean. Two hardy passengers stood braced against the railing on the starboard foredeck. One, a stoutish man in a parka with the hood up, was clutching a plastic bag emblazoned with the name of his local supermarket. Weighing down the bag was something resembling one of those black, waxed cheddar cheeses from Vermont. It had arrived Express Mail from a cemetery in the Bronx the day before. The second passenger was a woman, tall in knee boots and a dark coat, her head swathed in a black shawl.

As the boat approached the Statue of Liberty, the man became visibly nervous, glancing around to convince himself that no one was watching. For what he was about to do was against the law, and he knew it. Quickly, he pulled the box out of the bag and tossed it overboard, muttering a prayer of committal. That's that, he thought, that's what he wanted.

"Look!" the woman pointed, leaning over the rail. Bobbing alongside in the froth of the vessel was the black box, white label uppermost.

"It's supposed to sink." Hydrodynamics was not the man's strong point. He watched the box till it was out of sight. "Well, I guess it goes to show, you can't keep a good man down."

"I wonder if he knows what he did for our country."

"Sure, he's up there now, having the last laugh. He always said he would."

217

Elie looked up at the sky full of stars. "Do you believe that?"

Father Vince sighed, but the sigh was lost to Elie on the breeze. "I guess we all find out."

Ding-ding-ding chimed the buoy bells all around.